Uncorked

LaChappelle/Whittier Vineyards - Book 3

Kelly Kay

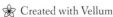 Created with Vellum

A note for the readers

This is the third book in the LaChappelle/Whittier Vineyard trilogy, if you've not read Crushing and Rootstock, this one might not make sense. And it's such a ride to get to this point you don't want to miss out. They're just one click away.

End of Rootstock

Josh

Asher Bernard is Darren Marcus. A man with a lifelong revenge chip on his shoulder. Everyone I hold dear just walked into a trap twenty years in the making. His lifelong vendetta against my grandfather and four other vineyard families has led us all to sacrificing our wineries. We had no idea what this asshole was capable of. We have to warn them. We have to stop the deal from happening. I've just realized that my life is in our grapes, and with Elle finally at my side, I have to save the life I want, at all costs.

Elle

I have to get in touch with Josh's mom and dad or all of the wineries will be destroyed. He can't take ownership. I start calling Sarah and then Tommi, and he called his dad. No one is picking up. I madly group text The Five. Only Sam tells us it's a trap, and it's too late for Langerford Cellars. We have to salvage LaChappelle/Whittier from this deal. I've only just discovered what my life is going to be: Josh, this tight community of friends and family, and this winery. I can't have that taken away. I won't let that happen.

Also by Kelly Kay

FIVE FAMILIES VINEYARD ROMANCES

LaChappelle/Whittier Vineyard Trilogy

Crushing, Rootstock & Uncorked

Stafýlia Cellars Duet

Over A Barrel & Under The Bus

Gelbert Family Winery

Meritage: An Unexpected Blend

Residual Sugar

Yet to come- 2024

Pietro Family (Pre-Order is live)

It's time to tell the whole story of a different kind of family.

Langerford Cellars - 2024

* * *

BOSTON BROTHERS: a second chance series

Keep Paris

Keep Philly - a newsletter exclusive novella

Keep Vegas

* * *

CHI TOWN ROMANCES

A Lyrical Romance Duet

Shock Mount & Crossfade

A Lyrical Spinoff Standalone

Present Tense

* * *

CARRIAGE HOUSE CHRONICLES

Funny, steamy, smart Chitown Romance spin off novellas for when you don't know what to read next. Released randomly throughout the year!

Follow Me - Now available

Sound Off

Something Good appears in Twisted Tropes anthology

For the Rest of Us Holiday M/M

* * *

STANDALONE

Side Piece: A workaholic romance

* * *

EVIE & KELLY'S HOLIDAY DISASTERS

ROMCOM Holiday Novellas with Evie Alexander featuring Tabi Aganos from the 5 families Vineyard Romances

VOLUME ONE

Cupid Calamity

Cookout Carnage

Christmas Chaos

Reading orders, playlists and book info can all be found at www.
kellykayromance.com

Family Trees for the 5 Families

LaChappelle/Whittier Vineyard

Will
Whittier ········· Sarah
LaChappelle
Whittier

Josh
Lucien LaChappelle
Whittier

Schroeder Estate Winery & Vineyards

Adrian
Schroeder ●━●━●━●━● Bellamy
Schroeder (d.)

Baxter   Tommi   Ingrid
Schroeder   Schroeder   Schroeder

Stafýlia Winery & Ranch

Costas
Aganos ········· Goldie
Aganos

Tabitha
Aganos

Langerford Cellars

James
Langerford ········· Theresa
Langerford

Sam   Jims
Langerford   Langerford

Gelbert Family Winery

Tina
Gelbert ⟩━━━⟨ Arthur
Gelbert ········· Jana
Gelbert

Poppy
Gelbert

David   Becca
Gelbert   Gelbert

Definition

Uncorked

Definition: / ˌənˈkôrk/
Verb
past tense: uncorked; past participle: uncorked
Uncorked simply means to pull the cork. In other words, to open a bottle of wine. The interesting part for the wine industry, when you uncork a bottle of wine, is you're often not sure exactly what you're getting.

For the Alpha Readers and Beta Testers. My friends and confidants. Those who know my soul best.

Elle

Josh parks illegally, and we bolt into the offices. Sarah is shaking hands with them, and my heart sinks. Josh is pulling me down the hallway when Asher emerges from the conference room.

"Hail, hail, the gang's all here."

Josh bellows down the hallway. "Mom! Did you sign it?"

"Yes, dear. It's all done."

Josh lunges at Asher. "You fucker. You son of a thieving asshole fucker."

Will quickly blocks Josh from landing a punch on Asher and pulls him away. Asher straightens his tie and pocket square, and his voice drips with self-satisfaction.

He says, looking right at Josh, "Looks like someone figured out my secret. Here's what you don't know, Joshie: I own your ass. Finally, some restitution for my family. You and all the cretins who cast out my family will now be nothing. Your legacy and labels will be systematically destroyed, but if you ever miss it, feel free to look on the bottom shelf where they keep the wine that has spigots."

Will's face goes slack, and his eyes look wild. "What is he talking about? Elle?"

Asher's head spins around in my direction, seeing me for the first time. His lips curl into an insidious smile. I begin to unravel all of this.

There's a small crowd gathered, and they all acknowledge me. I've been dealing with most of them over the course of the wooing and selling process. I speak distinctly and without emotion. "We should probably go sit back down, without the Vino Groupies. Gentlemen. You've done your deed already, but I'm pretty sure you had no knowledge of how much these vineyards meant to the people selling them. Or who this man actually is."

There's an impressive and sexy man I've never met. In fact, I only know two of the group of people exiting the meeting. A gorgeous, gruff, muscular, towering, tattooed man speaks to me with a lip curl. The tattoos are peeking out of his sleeves and adorning his wrists. His face is chiseled like granite and his grey eyes are cold until he turns to me. They warm instantly as if he can turn on and off his emotions. He's formidable and intimidating. But the way he moves is elegant; not what you'd expect from someone who looks like they could be one of Sal's muscled bodyguards.

His voice is strong and commanding. "We wanted grapes and land, and he got us grapes and the land. We're good." He winks at me.

Josh screams, "At what cost to the Valley? The five wineries you're about to dismantle will only influence the rest of the Valley. The Valley will go to shit."

Sarah steps forward. "Please, Josh. Explain it to us. What have we done?"

Asher is quick to answer, "You, dear Sarah, didn't stand up for me. But that's it. You were always kind. It was your father, and you share his blood. And it's quite evident that it runs through the veins of your thug of a son. But Lucien's the reason I now get to burn down the fucking Valley that shunned us."

Josh speaks directly to his parents, "Mom, Dad, allow me to introduce Darren Marcus. I believe you knew his father, Barry."

There are audible gasps that only fuel Asher's revenge. This is the day he must have dreamed of since he was thirteen years old.

Josh got a text from Sam just as we arrived that it was too late to stop any of their other deals. Josh told him that there was a lot for them all to discuss. Sam's collecting the rest of The Five to meet up at Creekside Cafe on the far end of Sonoma in Boyes Hot Springs. It's where the grandparents' generation used to take their coffee together every Thursday and Monday mornings. Usually of the Irish variety. We'll fill them in when we get there. But we need more information.

Asher turns to me. "Come, Noelle, we should go."

"I'm not going anywhere with you until you explain the real conditions of the contract." I stand rooted.

Josh roars from behind his dad, "And she sure as hell isn't going anywhere with you."

"We'll see," he says slyly.

I need Josh to be quiet and let me work this problem. Get him to tell me everything.

I say as coldly as I can to Sarah, "Please remove your son. Get him out of here." Josh's eyes flare at me.

Sarah still looks befuddled and betrayed. She speaks directly to Asher, "Darren, how could you do this to us? We had nothing to do with your father's crimes or my father's treatment of him. We always treated you and your mother

3

decently." Sarah pleads and then does as I asked. "Dear, I'm a bit shaky. Will you help me down the hall?"

Josh growls and wants to go nowhere. Will stays behind with me, his hand on my back. They exit down the hallway before anyone speaks again.

"Bye, Joshie." Asher needs to stop baiting him. He sits back down smugly, and it's just Will and me in this legal conference room.

He speaks directly to Will. I back away from him to distance myself. If he thinks I'm on Will's side, he won't fuck up and reveal too much. He'll stay guarded. I sit near Asher and on the opposite side of the table from Will. Will shifts his weight and looks nervous. I hope he trusts me.

Asher adjusts his overly creased pants and flicks some lint off his lapel. "We wore that stigma my whole life. My darling Noelle, I'm not sure anyone has shared my plight with you."

"No. But I'm sorry if there was a stigma."

"Not after today there won't be. Lucien and my father were best friends. They were partners in the winery."

Will steps up. "Barry was never a partner. He worked for Lucien."

Asher turns to Will and screams, "THEY WERE PARTNERS." I nod to Will.

I approach Asher to calm him down. "It's okay. Ignore him. Tell me your story."

Asher fixes his hair and pulls his suit jacket into place again. Then he turns to me and summarizes his family history that I already know. He remarks how he was cast out by Lucien and that he's the rightful heir to LaChappelle/Whitter. I cringe inside, but I don't show it. I need him to explain what Will and Sarah actually just signed.

Asher sits and finishes his story. "After my father killed

himself, we were still persona non grata everywhere. My mother died picking almonds outside of Sacramento. That was the only job she could get, and it's all LaChappelle's fault. I heard rumblings of a group wanting Sonoma grapes, reputation labels, and land. Mostly they wanted land. I heard they were aggressive and had mountains of cash. And I knew that Will and Sarah needed to sell. I needed all of the despicable five on board. They all shunned us." Will crosses his arms and I can see him bite his cheek to keep from speaking. Asher sees him and then turns back to me. He continues his delusional story.

"My casual suggestion to David Gelbert at one of your dinners, dear Noelle, got the ball rolling that Vino Groupies might be looking for more wineries. The Gelberts have a small cash flow problem. So, if the offer were sweet enough, the others would fall in line for cheaper distribution and wider audience. They didn't know that the Vino Groupies don't give a shit about legacy or quality. The land and juice. That's where your value lies. Not in your fucking family fairytale histories. No one gives a shit how long a building has stood. LaChappelle/Whittier will be no more in a year."

Will inquires, "Why in a year?"

I offer up something that I'm not sure Will has grasped yet. "That's your term limit of custodianship, right?"

"Oh, don't you worry, you'll get half your sale check as soon as possible. Sit here, my pet."

I still my nerves and revulsion, and Will looks like he's going to stab him with a ballpoint pen. I shake my head at Will and move one seat closer next to Asher.

He speaks again. "The turnover of the wineries to Vino Groupies won't happen until next harvest. They have to get all their ducks in a row for their next phase. So, here's the clause that I, the custodian of your properties, am invoking, the one that you all overlooked. You must all continue to work the land, under me, for one year. The only thing standing in your way is a downturn of profit. All wineries must remain as profitable as they were in this calendar year."

Will spits out, "Then we let the grapes rot."

"Nice thought, but your contract also states that you must continue production in good faith, or you'll all be subjected to a breach of contract suit and not only lose the money but pay penalties, and we still get the fucking land. I get to watch you all like a hawk over the next year. Dance puppets. Dance. And after that, you can all go to hell for all I care. I own your asses for one year."

Josh and Sarah hear the end of his little speech. I stand.

Asher turns to me and says, "Now, Noelle dear, let us continue our dalliance."

I can't move. "I think I've been used by you long enough. Go to hell, Asher. Or should I call you Darren now?"

"My real name from your lips is golden. Look, you got a plum contract out of it and a quick roll in the vines with this idiot alpha male."

Sarah gasps and says, "You're disgusting." Sarah is physically restraining Josh. But Josh is letting me handle this piece, and that's when I know he does trust me completely.

"After what you said to me today, I'm a little curious as to why you think you're not coming with me?" Asher asks.

Josh steps forward, calmly. "Mom, Dad, I'd advise you to cover your ears."

I flash my eyes at Josh. I got this. "Are you referring to my texts from earlier?"

Josh

"Did she share them with you, Neanderthal Joshie? Are you into erotica?" His grin is so smug. We might lose the winery, but we'll take a tiny piece of his dignity with us. And there will be no mistaking where Elle belongs.

"Asher, dear," Elle says as Asher puts his hands on her face. "I wrote them while Josh ate me out and made me come harder than you could ever dream of doing. Oh, wait, you don't do that, do you? You force women to have to service themselves in the bathroom after you get off in record time, with your big old blobby tongue and needle dick. I think it's time to go home. Bye, Bye, Dasher."

Will reacts, "Oh shit. You got served. Sorry about the tiny dick, there, Darren. Tough break." He doesn't respond, but his face gets red. He sits back in his seat.

I turn back as we exit. "And mark my words: when we get the winery back, you will fucking go down for this, Darren. And LaChappelle/Whittier will thrive without you anywhere near it. My grandfather knew what kind of man you were. He saw it. He knew you couldn't handle the work. He saw your character when all of us overlooked it. Somehow he saw that you were a weasel at eight years old, just like your father. Choke on your contract for now, but we are far from done."

"You forget one thing, Joshie. I own your ass too. If you've worked at the winery in management, in the past year, you're required to continue employment or the deal is null and void. Not only will your parents get nothing, but the winery will be ours anyway. I hear Parkinson's meds are expensive."

From out of nowhere a giant fist connects with Asher/Darren's chin, and he goes down. After we watch him fall, we look up and see Will holding his own hand and smiling at Asher on the ground.

"Shut the fuck up, little Darren Marcus. You're a punk-ass piece of shit just like your father."

* * *

We arrive at Creekside, and we've taken over the entire place. All generations are here. Everyone looks pissed, depressed, or just shocked. I texted Sam and Becca all the specifics so they could relay them to everybody.

The Schroeders: Adrian Schroeder and his daughter Tommi and son, Baxter. The Aganos family: Costas, Goldie, and their daughter, Tabi. Gelberts: Poppy and her mom Tina. The other Gelberts, Tina's brother Arthur, his wife Jana, and their children, Becca and David. We join the Langerford table with James, Theresa, and their sons, Sam and Jims. I need to sit with my best friend, my brother, right now.

Theresa Langerford stands and holds my mom. We look

around the room. Dad picks up a bottle of whiskey from behind the bar and nods to the owners. He takes a long pull directly from the bottle and hands it to Costas, who does the same. After the bottle has made its rounds, we begin to speak to each other.

Arthur looks at Elle. "You brought this here. You flaunted that man around, and now we have nothing."

Arthur Gelbert has always been a dick. I glare at him. "No. Lucien did this. And my grandfather was justified in his actions. Maybe he could have found some compassion, but the man stole a lot from our winery and family. Elle was used just like the rest of us. Hell, you used his services a year ago. She didn't bring him into the mix, he brought her. He could have been collecting intel on your financial situation. You didn't have to overextend on that plot in Anderson Valley that never produced and then sell it for half it's worth. And you didn't have to sign." Becca takes her dad's hand. And then the volume of the room ramps up to a fevered pitch. Elle takes my hand in hers and I settle down. I nod to Mr. Gelbert. I shouldn't have gotten that heated.

My dad looks at the faces of the people that mean the most to him in the world. He drags my mom close to him and puts a hand on Artie Gelbert's other shoulder. And the room settles a bit. My father has a quiet and commanding power. People are calmer in his presence.

Adrian Schroeder asks in his forceful voice, "What the fuck do we do now?"

And before the anger can rise again, Dad does what Dad does. He disperses the negative energy and replaces it with hope.

"We do what we've always done. We put our heads down, ride out the bad harvest, and plan for a better one, together. There is nothing in the world that can't be undone, except death. And we're healthy," he nods to Mom, who waves her new cane in the air, "we're loved, we're fed, we're incredibly wealthy for the moment, and we're family. And in the wine country, when life hands you noble rot, what do we do?" Everyone looks around, and there's a moment where no one says anything.

It's Goldie Aganos who answers loudly in her bubbly Americanized Greek accent, "We cut it out and then we make a feast."

"Exactly! What else?" My father eggs the crowd on.

Mr. Langerford slaps my dad on his back and addresses our sad collective, "We lift our chins and pop a cork."

Mom smiles. "There's supposed to be a party at our place tonight."

Elle offers up, "Let's make it a celebration of The Five instead of just the end of LC/W's harvest, if you guys can help potluck it. Let's invite all of your winery workers. Everyone who sacrificed for all of us."

Tommi yells from the back, "Hells yeah. Let's drown our fucking sorrow then saddle up tomorrow."

I laugh and joke, "Or we could just burn it all to the ground."

Becca Gelbert says in her best lawyer voice, "Then we'd all be in breach of contract and facing massive penalties. Let's just drink instead. I'll start really looking into undoing this deal tomorrow. Josh, can your team help?"

"I'll call my assistant. He's very good at digging up motives and dirt for company profiles."

And just like that, The Five start again. I worry that there will be nothing left for them to rebuild. I know Elle feels guilty. She got played hard, for her abilities and drive. By being good at what she does, that asshole exploited her. I want to bury that fucker in the ground, but I have to remember Lucien set all of this in motion. Because he shunned Barry Marcus, Elle exists in my life. Fucking Lucien, controlling the outcome of my life whether I wanted it or not. Fuck you, old man. Fuck you. And thank you.

Elle

Before everyone arrives, Will and Sarah sit down with the staff. I hang in the background setting the courtyard up for our epic pity party.

Mrs. Dotson is stunned. "I swear I did not recognize that terrible boy. He was always trouble. And lazy as hell. He's one of those shortcut boys. Always looking for the fucking easy way. And if he has Barry's blood in him, he's no good. Barry tried funny stuff with me, and I cut him. I literally cut him with a wine opener. And look, Lucien was a hard man. A hard man to love, but I did my best. But he was never duplicitous. He was a straight arrow, too blunt and rigid, but honest. Tell me, Joshie, tell me we can take down this little fucker?"

All of us let our jaws drop that a) she just admitted to loving Lucien and b) Barry tried to rape her and c) she's a badass. Josh gives her a giant hug.

I call in a couple of favors to help me pull this off and give Wade Howell, who works at the *San Francisco Chronicle*, the exclusive on what went down. Becca Gelbert and her law partner, Francesca, who is also Wade's wife, are here decorating and arranging tables. And Meg Hannah, who runs the local film festival, is here with Brian and Sondra from the girl & the fig restaurant. They brought food and are helping put together silly table-toppers.

Meg tapped a bunch of resources for me to get this whole night expanded. A lighting guy is coming, and she got a projector and screen to show a movie in the amphitheater for the kids. Even the local owner of the Sebastiani Theater, Roger, is going to come and do magic for them. Other than Meg knocking over a large bottle display, and ripping her skirt, she's been insanely helpful. She gets shit done. I like that woman.

Josh

Originally there was a planned catered dinner and bubbles to celebrate the sale and the end of harvest. But now, in an afternoon, somehow Elle has turned it into a community spectacle. One that will raise all our spirits but also celebrate our colossal failure.

Poppy immediately left Creekside, went to her café's kitchen, and began cooking everything she could find. The town is small, and word travels fast. Elle spent her afternoon accepting offerings from all of Sonoma Valley. Pans of lasagna from Della Santina, a shit ton of cheese from Vella, bread from the Basque, boxes of booze from Starling, and cured meats and homemade terrines from the girl and the fig restaurant. Juanita Juanita is bringing rice and burritos. Pizza and those insane pesto breadsticks arrive from Mary's. Glen Ellen Star dropped off a ton of tarts. She invited them all to return for the party, and most stayed to help set up. The whole freaking town will be here. It will be better than the annual City Party.

Eight and ten-foot tables arrive from the Community Center, and chairs from the Veterans hall show up, courtesy of that film festival woman. Sonoma Market sent over paper products, plates, and napkins and cutlery. Hopmonk kicked in kegs of beer, wings and grilled artichoke. Sushi was donated by Shinge along with steamed dumplings. Broadway Market kicked in nonalcoholic drinks and more paper goods. The families began arriving with dishes and glassware in hand. Bottles are opened, and Goldie's feast begins.

Sam and his ad hoc band set up on the far end of the cave, where Elle's created a lounge and dining area. Our tasting room manager's San Fran boy toy sets up his sound system in the courtyard for dancing. Elle's invited everyone she's ever met here. No one says no to her. And although people keep trying to rearrange what she's done, she quietly puts it back to perfect. She's never wrong either.

I've been so myopic. This is my town and someone how I forgot to be a part of it for so long.

The wine flows freely. My mom keeps filling everyone's glasses, and my dad sits very quietly with Elle in the corner, the two of them chatting away. I wanted nothing more than to get rid of this anger. I wanted to go running or punch things. I wanted to take her up to the Farmhouse for the afternoon to make myself feel better. Malbec isn't cutting it either. I'm holding onto and don't know how to get rid of this rage. I finally saunter over to my father.

"Josh. My son. I don't want to be Lucien. I won't force you to stay. I'm so sorry. I don't want to hold you here." My parents thought they were free once the sale happened.

Elle feels as if it's all her fault. I see it in her eyes. She needs to let that go. There were multiple lawyers. I am no slouch at a contract, and neither is she. None of us saw this coming. Asher spent a lifetime working towards this moment; we barely had six months to catch up. She's tearing up and keeping her distance from me.

Will wraps his arm around her. "Honey. Your boyfriend screwed us."

He attempts to make a joke, but it doesn't land, and she tears up. "I'm so sorry. I'm so, so sorry."

Dad is horrified. "No. Oh, goodness no. No. Sweetie, stop. You were a pawn. No more responsible for all of this than we are." I approach them to listen. He's holding her as she sobs. My mom joins us after handing off her pouring duties and sits down next to Elle, rubbing her back and stroking her hair. "But what he gave us far outweighs what we lost." He looks at me, and as always, my father will find the good in any situation.

Elle spits out, "Trouble, that's all I gave you." She misses my dad's point entirely. And my mom is in her ear.

"He gave us back a family. The one thing he set out to destroy, and he gifted it right to us. You. Josh. Our connection with all of The Five Families has never been stronger. Family. Dirt and money can come and go, but it's this, my dear, that matters."

She turns to my mom and falls into her arms, sobbing. She lets the last of her walls crumble, releasing a lifetime of loneliness into my mom. Giving away her guilt. My parents did for her what I could not. Opening her up perfectly to the idea that we are family. I love her so much at this moment I can barely stand it. I love them all. And I love this fucking winery, and I don't lose. I won't lose any of this, not one fucking grape, employee, or moment. There has to be a way. And finally, my anger gets redirected into determination.

My mom sits down next to my dad, taking his hand. I smile widely at Elle, seeing everything the way it should be. The way I want it to be, not the way I need to manipulate it to be. I'm done pretending that Joshua was a good idea. She saved me from a life I thought I wanted and gave me the life I'm lucky to have.

Elle's eyes pierce my self-reflection as she says, "Oh, Will, Sarah, you're all more than I let myself dream I could have. I'm in love with your son and I could never leave any of you."

My mom squeals as I pull Elle into my lap and hold her tightly. Then I set about explaining what my lawyers and my assistant John in Santa Barbara have discovered. "You still get half the money in the next few weeks. Surely it's enough for the year."

"It's actually more than enough for our lifetime, but if they're still willing to pay us for the rest, we'll take it. But do we need to return the money if we get the wineries back?"

My dad speaks the truth. No one truly needs thirty-five million dollars and certainly not my unassuming hippie parents who were planning on staying in hostels for their European vacation. I have more than that in the bank just sitting there or getting reinvested in things I barely care about it any longer. My mom will never have to worry about a medical bill or vacation. And until we unravel what we've done and how to get the fuck out from under it, we probably shouldn't spend a penny of it. I'll park it somewhere and see if I can turn a profit with it.

"Don't spend any of it yet. If it undoes all of this, then we can absolutely give it back. I have more than you could ever need. Take it. I'll set up a fund, and you can draw down on it. I can't legally gift you thirty-five million, but I can give you access to an account that will be just for you.

Mom, I want to set up a separate account for you to give away."

"What do you mean, sweetie?"

"I want to give back. Elle's kind of forcing me, but that's your thing, not mine. I would just dump it into a tax shelter at the end of the year. But figure out where it will do the most good. Especially locally and for Parkinson's. Where's the best research coming out of and give them a shit ton of money. As much as you want."

"Son. That's kind, but..."

"It's done, Dad. No lectures or false humility. I have it. I'm not using it. Buy a Lamborghini if you want."

"Really?" His eyes light up.

Sarah hits him. And I wink at him. I'm totally buying him a Lamborghini for Christmas. I mean, I've spent it on toys and an image, but I had no idea my mother needed it. I suck. I've sucked for a long time. Elle is my salvation.

"We'll just have to figure out how to stop the dismantling of our lives. But we do have a year to do it. There has to be some wiggle room in those contract terms that they must have overlooked. And if Dasher is actually the architect of the deal, then I can certainly figure out a way to stop all of this. He's not that clever. We have a year to heal and figure it out."

My mom says, "That's sweet of you to say 'heal,' but today's the best I'm ever going to feel, honey. At least they tell me the decline is slow." Will wraps his arms around her, and I feel Elle's shoulders tense at the thought. "We need to hire people, and you can just pretend to be here. That way you can get back to your life, and our mess stays our mess. You don't have to clean it up."

My dad nods. "The problem is finding valuable, trustworthy people to run it immediately. We have to maintain a profit in the next year, so it maintains its value."

Elle blurts out, "We'll stay and run it. We'll take it."

I kiss her hand and say, "Yes. We will."

"Josh, honey, I don't want you to do this out of obligation. We are fine if you want a different life."

"I do want a different life. My other one wasn't working."

I can honestly say I don't remember smiling for months on end in Santa Barbara. Since being home, I can't stop. I want a robust life of vines and noble rot and crush. It's who I am. It's my roots, and Elle is my rootstock, grafted on the original to make it stronger and flourish. "There's no amount of money or flash that can take away the fact that the dirt under my nails is also in my DNA."

"Elle?"

"Yes, Will?"

"A toast to you, for bringing us back together as a family."

I stand on a picnic table and address everyone in the courtyard. "Hey! LaChappelle people! If you'll have me, I'm willing to stay on and guide us through this clusterfuck. But only if you'll guide me. You are all the backbone of the winery. I'm going to make a shit ton of mistakes. And as my parents set out on adventures of fun and hopefully miraculous medical miracles, I'll be here. But I do come with baggage now."

Elle hits my hip, and everyone laughs. I turn to her, and she's looking up at me so adoringly. Her green eyes are full of hope and forever. I'm compelled to toast her too.

"I don't know what the future will bring any of us. It's time to stop trying to fit a round peg into a square hole. I'm where I'm supposed to be, and that finally feels right."

Sam screams as he joins the party, "About fucking time, you pussy! Welcome home, Josh! Welcome back to a winery you don't own! Everybody, drink!"

I yell back at him, "Dude, you lost your winery today too. Not sure what you're so happy about!"

Everyone laughs again at my exchange with my best friend, Sam. His brother, Jims, is standing behind him sipping a beer. He's followed by the entire Langerford vineyard crew carrying cases. Then the Gelberts appear with their wine and some DJ turntables. Tommi Schroeder and her dad, Adrian, appear right behind them, and this parade of winemaker heritage warms my heart. There are still people in the tasting room, and they're welcome to join our impromptu winery wake for our vineyards that we all sold to the devil this week.

Theresa Langerford is now pushing me off my picnic table. She's like my second mom, so I give her the floor. "To the Valley. My friends and yours that are here, and to family. To those who can't be here." She nods to the Schroeders, and we all think of Bax, Ingrid, and Tommi's mom, Bellamy, who died of cancer long ago.

Theresa continues, "I'm not sure what the next year brings, but I have a hunch it's going to be a wild ride. Thank fucking god we're on this path together. And let's get fucking lit tonight."

Cheers erupt, bottles are opened, and I don't yield the floor just yet. I jump back up. "One more thing."

Sam throws a cork at me, and everyone else holding one does the same.

"Fine. Let me just get to the most important part of this toast. To the newest hire who's now officially an employee of the LaChappelle-Whittier Vineyards and the love of my life."

Elle

My breath catches, and my heart stops as I look at his eyes twinkle in the dusk. The courtyard fairy lights are our only source of light except for the full moon. I am sort of having an out of body experience as he speaks. This is happening to someone else. This is happening to someone from a book or movie, not real life. And certainly not to the cold bitch from New York. I jump on the picnic table and kiss him.

"I love you more than I thought was possible in the world."

Music blares from the turntables, and people begin celebrating. We're left to whisper in each other's ears. "You are my world. I was just too much of a jackass to see it sooner."

"I'll give you that you're a jackass, but you'll always be my first real crush."

* * *

We drink, dance, and eat and laugh. Everyone is having the best time. This community is not unlike the farmers I grew up with. The communal spirit, gentle competition, and rivalries. I only wish this life was going to be for more than a year. We still have bottling for this season, and crush for next but this year will be all about closing shop if we can't figure this out.

I see Josh get on his phone from across the courtyard. I wonder how long it will take for our other lives to intrude upon this. They'll have to be dealt with, but I'm hoping to keep Joshua at bay a little longer. I see him frantically looking around the party. I hope he's looking for me, but he stops when he sees Sam. He waves him over, and the two of them huddle over his phone.

Within moments they're joined by David, Poppy, Becca Gelbert, Bax and Tommi Schroeder, Tabi Aganos, and Jims Langerford. Will peers into the crowd. He clicks his heels together.

I turn to Sarah and see her beautiful but tired face. She speaks clearly to me. "You do see that, right?"

"The boys?"John

"The boys club. I was unable to break it completely apart, but I did crack it open a bit in my day. You're going to bust right through it."

Grasping her hand, I squeeze it. That I can do. Will leaps up on a picnic table, and the music stops again. "Hey, everyone here. Are you all committed to us over the next year? It seems as if the Vino Groupies aren't who we thought they were. Josh's assistant might have found some-thing. So, will all of you hang in there with us?"

The crowd affirms.

"You're all going to drink our booze until dawn, right?"

The crowd cheers again.

Every family member, every worker, every employee, friend, and Sonoma city council member cheers in unison.

My eyes dart to Josh's, and he rushes to me. He takes me in his arms.

"I'm going to need your help to pull this off. Becca's looking for a crack in the contract. John might have found something. You might be the smartest of all of us, my love. We need you. Crafty and smart. But I'm formulating a plan."

"What are you planning for next year, my One Perfect Thing? What's next?"

"Total destruction, degradation, humiliation, and vindication. And getting my legacy back."

Elle

It's four in the morning, and the party/wake for lost wineries rages on. There's no stopping it. Our party has morphed into a city-wide gathering. The Sheriff is here and with a designated driver. I called in a fleet of trolleys to run people home and have Wine Country Limo buses lined up the driveway. No one drives tonight. I'm grateful my trip home is across the parking lot. Although now that Sarah and Will are home, our era of noisy sex has come to a halt.

LaChappelle/Whittier Winery has become the nexus of the Sonoma wine universe for the evening. As much as I've consumed tonight, I'm still fixated on how Dasher, as we've taken to calling him tonight, found a way to wipe out five family winery legacies because of Sarah's father, Josh's grandfather, Lucien LaChappelle. He threw Dasher's father in jail for embezzlement years ago. Lucien was a hard man and didn't take betrayal easily. He made sure that the Marcus family was never welcome in California wine country again. Dasher's vengeance made sure he thought he could eradicate everything these people hold dear.

And yet, we're all hopeful tonight that we can stop him. We maintain partial ownership of the vineyards for one year. Until the last grape is harvested from the last of the five wineries. They will be under his stewardship to maintain profits. But right now, we're all joyous in each other's company. I feel like it's the end of *How the Grinch Stole Christmas* and the Whos are still celebrating Christmas even though it came without ribbons, tags, packages, boxes, or bags.

Every time I think the celebration is winding down, it amps back up. Will and Sarah went to bed at ten. But then they reappeared with a ton of popcorn, bottled water, and an insane number of hot dogs at three a.m. Everyone is chowing. We've all made speech after speech. As Josh hops back up onto the picnic table, everyone groans, including me. My sexy as hell and drunk man needs to shut up already.

Will stands in front of him, yelling over the music, "Josh, get down. Everyone's tired of hearing you. Eat a hot dog." The music stops as Josh waves his arms. He kneels on the table and looks at his father very pointedly.

"Dad. This is my last speech of the night." Then he hops back up and starts screaming, "Where's Elle? ELLE!" He's screeching my name, and my heart warms as well as my panties. "Where's my woman? WOMAN. COME TO ME."

I'm sitting on the hill above the courtyard with a bunch of people from Gelbert. Becca's friends, Wade and Meg. Meg accidentally rolled backward down the hill earlier. It was hilarious. She's quite the klutz.

We're all sipping Gelbert's Pinot Rosé, and it kicks ass, and I am so hooked. Although no one really has a palate right now. We blew that shit out hours ago when we did

25

Fireball shots. I'm lost in my thoughts, and then I hear him again.

"Answer me, Hellcat! Where you at?"

I yell down to him, "Here!"

"Get your cute, perfect ass down here."

"No."

Everyone woos at us. I laugh as I stand up and make my way down the hill towards the courtyard. "What?" I put my hands on my hips and glare.

"Dammit. Patience, Cosmo!"

He looks to his mother and nods. "Hey, Mom. Can I have it now?"

Her lips pull to the sweetest smile, and she nods at him. She says, "Are you sure? You're very drunk."

"Mother. I am far from drunk."

Sam yells, "True. He's been drinking water most of the night."

"Even though most of the town is currently drunk. Asher is Darren. Mrs. Dotson used to fuck Lucien. You've got Parkinson's. Dad hasn't slept in six months from worry. The Merlot doesn't smell so good in the tanks. We lost all the wineries today, and I'm not in Santa Barbara working. I'm sure of nothing but this."

Everyone laughs very hard.

"Yes," Sarah says, "but you're shakier than me right now.

"Mom, this is the only thing I've ever been sure of in my entire fucking life. Despite popular opinion, I haven't had a drop to drink tonight. I had other plans for the night, but of course we had to go and lose the wineries. But I want to reclaim the day. I want to carry out my fucking plans." The crowd cheers.

"Don't swear while you do this," Sarah scolds.

My body freezes while Sarah removes a ring from her right hand and slides it across the table he's standing on. He turns to me, and my sleepy eyes get super wide. I need to wake up. I need to be awake for this moment. I need to be woke AF. My synapses are firing in a million directions with adrenaline dumping into my system. My cheeks get super pink. He gestures widely to me.

"I don't even care that this is fast. You've been mine from the moment I saw you with that letch at Steiner's."

Dr. Jones pipes in, "That's me!" I did not realize he was here.

The doctor is dancing on the fringes of the crowd without music. Everyone laughs, boisterously again. Then Josh bellows over the din for them to shut up. He turns to me. "I have no doubt that you were made for me and I for you. You flipped every fucking thing in my life. Upside down and inside out."

"Language, Josh!" Everyone laughs again as Sarah scolds her son. But I need everyone to shut up so he can continue.

"Brittany Noelle Parker Doyle, powerfully strong, pain in my ass, worldly beauty, brilliant mind, cunning opponent, love of my life, and my One Perfect Thing. Elle, marry me. Will you marry the winery and me? Let me have your back forever." I jump onto the table, and he catches me in his large and gorgeous arms. I'm instantly sobbing.

As everyone erupts into hooting and hollering, Will and Sarah surround me. My heart is bursting out of my chest, and my body is warmed by everyone around us.

Josh screams. "Everybody shut the fuck up! She didn't answer me. Shut the hell up so I can hear her!"

"Josh. Joshua Lucien LaChappelle Whittier, of course,

I'll marry you. I'm yours. And as for your winery, I do have some notes on your merchandise. It's all out of date and..."

"Always with a new criticism. And correction, it's *our* out-of-date merch now, baby, not just mine." He holds me close and whispers in my ear. "You know you can't escape me now."

I turn it on him. "And you can't leave."

He puts the simple gold band with a series of diamonds on my finger. "We can get you any ring you want, but this was Emma's. It's the only piece of jewelry she kept when she came to America. She sold the rest for seed money."

My breath is gone. My tears stop in their tracks as I look to Sarah. I hold my hand to my heart and cover it with the other and mouth 'thank you' to her. Tears stream down her face as Will holds her from behind. She blows a kiss to me, and then the two of them turn to go back to the Farmhouse. I look up at Josh. I swim in his deep ocean blue eyes that are glimmering in the moonlight.

"I love you so fucking much, Cosmo."

I go up on my tiptoes to his ear and nip it suggestively. Just having his body close to me has me heating up. I need to have him right now. "Show me."

He winks. "Lead the way."

Everyone tries to congratulate us, but the music of the Commodores blasts and thankfully the dancing starts again. I take his hand and weave through the crowd quickly to the barrel room towards the far end of the cave. I need him hard, fast, and right now.

He grabs the hem of his shirt and tosses it off quickly. I lick, nip, and kiss his perfect chest then down to his V and back to his neck. It's not a new view but one I can't get enough of. His abs and the divine trail of coppery blonde hair leading down to his insanely large and stunning rootstock. Scooping me up, his hands feel commanding on my ass. He thrusts my back against the cave wall. I'm clawing at his shoulders and biting his bottom lip.

"I'm not capable of sweet and seductive right now," Josh grunts.

"Not looking for it. We have a lifetime for that. Right now, I need to be fucked hard by my fiancé."

He rips into my mouth as I put my feet back down on the ground, unbuckling his pants. But the kiss changes from one of insane passion, and I settle my hands on his hips as he cups my face. The kiss softens and lightens. It's sweet with a hint of forever in it. As much as I wanted this time to be just sex, with us, I guess it never was. He pulls back and puts his forehead to mine.

I whisper, "I guess you were capable of sweet." He brushes his lips over mine and pulls me closer to him. We stand there holding each other for longer than I would have expected, but it seems time has stopped for us. Just for a moment, we get to be us, engaged. No family or raging party, friends or details to tend to, just us holding each other.

Then I back up just enough to go up on my tiptoes to kiss him again. I nip at his bottom lip and his eyebrow hooks up. "Future Mrs. Whittier what are you doing?"

I gasp as he says that and then shrug and roll my eyes to the side. We're in a barrel room, and there's nowhere to lay down. I slowly unbutton my shirt and his eyes get hooded and filled with lust.

His jeans slide down, freeing his steel-hard cock as it juts towards me. I give it a quick tug as he reaches into my jeans and swipes my lips below. I moan, and we quickly remove my pants.

"How the hell are you this wet right now?"

"You."

With my thong off, he hitches me back up on the wall. My legs are wrapped around him like that day in the parking lot that we never got to finish. With his hands firmly holding my ass up I lower myself onto him as he thrusts upward suddenly. It tugs for just a moment as he enters so quickly, but I flow for him and smooth out the ride. He's thrusting madly, and I'm grinding into him, up and down, holding onto two different barrel racks. My rack bounces in his face. Each time I come down on his cock harder and faster. He's madly bucking into me. This is rough, raw, and fucking amazing. I love his bare cock pumping into me.

"You're mine." He claims me over and over.

"Forever." I can't stop wanting more of him. I need him to fill every part of me.

"Yes. Yes. Yes." He affirms that he will.

And just when I don't think I can take it anymore, I clamp down around his dick and ride the orgasm that captures me. I gasp with wave after wave while he relentlessly pounds away. Driving me over the ledge again. He's so hard and mine. "Oh, god. Oh fuck. Yes." I moan loudly as I come again. His eyes wild on mine and I say, "Do it again. I need more."

"Fuck, yes, you do."

Our hips realign with our bodies tightly fitting into each other. He's deeper than I think he's ever been and it's still not enough. I crave him everywhere. He pulls me from the wall and leans me back slightly, placing his large hand between my shoulder blades.

"Lay back. Trust me."

"Circus act. Oh, Jesus." He's even deeper and hitting some unknown spot inside of me that just fired up my entire body. I roll my abs to grab all that I can. I'm clutching his biceps as he continues to pump into me. "Your pussy is perfect. It's fucking perfect. I fit perfectly. It's so tight. I'm going to fill you. Come with me again. Elle. Come with me. My dick needs to feel you come again. Let me feel it."

And he lets himself spill into me, tearing any resolve I have, and he unleashes another orgasm. It's so intense and deep that I feel it in my toes. I contract around him. It won't stop. We're moaning together and then both crumple onto the floor of the cold cave. I collapse into his warm, strong arms as we catch our breath. I felt his knees get weak for just a second as he came.

I look into his intense face and say, "What the fuck was that? How are we getting better at that?"

He grins. "Practice makes perfect."

"So happy that nothing is ever perfect so we can keep practicing."

"Elle, baby, that was fucking amazing."

With my head on his shoulder, I lift my left hand for us both to admire. "So is this."

His forehead is touching mine, and he says, "Promise me we'll always be able to make each other scream like that."

"Till death do us part."

Josh

I'm on my laptop at the kitchen counter. It's been a few weeks since the wake for our wineries. We're in a holding pattern. But I do need to figure out how to get out of my parents' house before they come back. We have a couple weeks. Mom begins her controlled study clinical trial today, and they found Dad an extra bed. Because of course he won't leave her side. I get that now.

The love of my life glides down and picks up my empty cereal bowl and deposits into the sink. She kisses me on the cheek, and I try to catch her, but she twists away.

"What?"

She gets a cup of coffee and talks to me without turning around. "What what?"

"What's on your mind? I can see the furrowed brow."

She exhales and turns around. "Okay. Do not freak."

"If you're leaving me, I don't have time for that today. It's a crazy day, and then you have that stupid-ass cocktail thing you promised we'd go to tonight."

"Do you remember I told you about this locket that was my mother's?"

"The one you can't find but think is in New York. Spill it, Parker."

"Well, turns out I left it somewhere with my mom's earrings. Not the good emerald ones, I have those, but these crystal ones that she loved and wore all the time." She shifts her weight and backs away from me and bites her lower lip.

"No." I know exactly where the fuck she left them.

"Hear me out."

"No. You're not fucking going over there. He can mail them."

"I told him that, but he's traveling or something. So he's not there."

I stand up and get in her face. I don't want her to breathe the same air as Asher. Dasher. Darren. Whatever the fuck he's called. No. No. There's no way. "No."

"I didn't have to tell you before I went, but I'm giving you this courtesy. I have a crazy busy day too. I'm going to pop over to his house, use the key—"

I interrupt her, "You still have his key!"

"I do but listen." She places her open hand on my heart. "My love. He's not there. I know exactly where they would be. I walk in, grab my stuff, and then I leave the key when I leave. Five minutes tops."

I ball my fists. "I don't like it. But I know these things are important to you. Let me wrap up this email and I'll go with you."

"You can't. You have to meet with the tax lawyers and your parents' accountant. You have to do that today so it's all sorted."

"Shit. You call me the moment you are out of there. And if he's there, you get the hell out of there."

"Look, Josh. I know you believe he's horrible, but he's never been horrible to me. He's innocuous. I mean, not

33

totally. He did pull off that revenge thing of getting all of our wineries. Nothing is going to happen. And he's not there. Trust me."

I pull her into my arms. "It's not you I don't trust." I kiss her on the top of her head. I need to calm down with this shit. "Babe. I'll buy you any locket in the world. Don't go."

"You know you can't buy that one, right?"

"I don't like this."

"Noted, my overprotective man. I'll be back before you know it."

I kiss her and let her go. I don't like to be without her, but she is a grown adult and I have to trust her. But I don't trust him.

Asher/Darren=Dasher

"You're not supposed to be here. You said you'd be gone. I'm just going to get my things and go." Her voice is fiery as she enters my house and I surprise her. She's a feisty bitch. It's been three weeks since the sale, and it's about time she comes to me.

"And where's your winery posse? Your Brut squad, if you will. Those pathetic idiots who surround you in Sonoma."

"They don't surround me."

"I haven't been able to find a moment to approach you alone."

"Were you stalking me?"

"No. I was in the area and wanted to clear the air between us. Get some things straight, that way we can move forward from this. But you're constantly with one of those losers."

I walk past him, trying to get my stuff and get out. "I thought you just hated Josh. But you really hate all of them, don't you?"

"They're garbage, my angel, you should know that by

now. You should hear Poppy and David talk about me. You'd hate them too. This garbage dates back to Lucien and Helmut. And then there's that fucking useless cuddly-looking Sam. He's a joke. And don't get me started on that mouthy bitch Tabi."

Elle speaks up, "Please don't call her a bitch."

But she *is* a mouthy fucking bitch. Elle walks right by me in my foyer, so I follow her and speak louder. "They chatter on and on about what they'll do to get the wineries back. I'm in control. I'm untouchable. They're so smug. I see their flaws. I hear and see everything. Don't forget that."

"Okay. Is this a witty repartee or do you have a point to trashing my friends?"

I am witty. Why didn't this bitch ever see that? She will. Whatever is Joshua Whittier's will be mine. Turns out ruining his winery isn't enough. I need more. I'm thinking of bankrupting him and throwing him into a scandal. It seems he has some mob dealings that I can spin in my favor. I have the backing to get this shit done. I will destroy his name, his winery, his legacy, and now that he loves this little pawn, it's time to take her back too. I'll ruin her as well.

Lucien replaced me with Josh. All of that was supposed to be mine. It's no secret that Sarah and Will never wanted the winery. He told me that I was being groomed for it until the day he decided to believe that inconsequential spineless asshole Helmut Schroeder instead of my father. There was never an investigation into his embezzling, just conviction. That's what I remember. And now that's why all their children and grandchildren will suffer too. Sins of the fathers will be rectified. The Schroeders will suffer right along with the Whittiers.

Lucien trashed his trusted friend, his brother in arms. Hell, they were more than brothers, it seemed as though they were the same person sharing a brain. I didn't set all of this in motion, their fucking families did. I turn to Noelle, damping down my well-honed and familiar rage. I put on my Asher mask again.

"You look lovely, Noelle."

"Stop, Asher."

"Complimenting you? Never. When was it you jumped into Josh's bed? Was it while we were still together in our relationship or when you realized that he had the power at that winery? Is that why there is a new adornment at the end of your ring finger? I heard something about that."

"Stop. You and I were over. And whatever we shared was not a relationship. We dated."

"You lived with me."

"In separate rooms, for one week." She's not as compliant as I'd like her right now. Time to turn the screw a bit.

"I wanted to talk about that. Why the saint act while we lived together when we all know you're actually a whore?" She's grabbing a couple of jackets in the hall closet. She pulls a small jewelry bag out of one of the coat pockets and places it in the pocket of her jeans. Then hoists up the duffle onto her shoulder and stares at me, a bit in shock of my language. Time for us all to stop pretending. Fuck the Asher mask. I'm tired of pretending to be something else.

She turns to me and puts her hands on her hips. "Really? You're going to call me cruel names now? Didn't know you were capable of any of this, to be honest. You are so not who I thought you were. I'm going to grab my things and get out of here. My whoreness won't be a bother any longer."

She has no idea what I'm capable of, but she's about to fucking learn a lesson. Bitch. "You'll answer my question.

Why the act?" She pushes right past me to get down the hallway. I grab her arm, yanking her back to my side. "Acknowledge me."

She tries to pull her arm loose, but I tighten my grip. "What the hell? That hurts. Stop it. Let go. That hurts. I'm not going to dignify that with an answer, Asher."

"Call me Darren in private." She looks at me with anger and disgust flashing in her green eyes. It's a turn on.

She says, "Since this is the last time we're going to be in private, Asher is fine." Noelle tugs her arm away from mine. I release her. I turn and follow close behind down the hall-way. I lean against the open bedroom door frame where she's packing her left behind items and searching a drawer.

"I can do this on my own and quickly. I'll be out of here in a moment, and you'll never have to see me again." She picks up a pair of earrings and puts them into her pocket with the locket I conveniently hid so she'd have to return to me at some point.

I smirk at her and say, "But that's not what I want at all. I want to see all of you right now. And I *will* keep seeing you whenever I say. And today you can even leave his ring on, but nothing else."

"Oh, good god. Come on. No way that's happening."

I move swiftly to her and roughly pin her against the wall. My left hand at her throat. Her eyes instantly fill up with confusion and a touch of fear. My member is getting hard at the thought of taking back what's mine. I adore the sudden panic in her eyes, and her quick sharp breathing. I want to ruin her for Josh or any other man she tries to trap with her chaste, innocent act.

"Asher, stop it you're hurting me. Please," she squeaks out.

The begging only makes me harder. "DARREN. You

call me Darren in private. Now listen to me, my little lamb. I won't stop. First, I took back LaChappelle and now you. I will never stop taking what belongs to me. And you won't and can't stop me either. Well, not today at least. Not until I jizz all the way down this pretty little throat of yours."

She's tearing up. That only makes this better. I stroke her cheek while still holding firmly to her throat. "I'd sooner bite off your dick, Asher." She spits out while I'm slightly cutting off her air supply. I release my hand, and she attempts to move away from me, gasping for a full breath. I instinctively backhand her and bruise her lip. She looks at me shocked, horrified, and with all the intensity of hate she can. Her chest and face bloom red. And my dick grows harder.

"Don't talk back to me, bitch. You don't get a say here. I'm not going to playfully punish you like Josh, smacking your ass in the tasting room. Or denying your orgasms in the wine cave. I can and will punish you better than he can, now that I know you like that sort of thing. Now that I know you were a slut all along. A slut I should have conquered. Instead, you played this chaste little girl with two rooms and rules about when to suck me off and when I got to plow you. You wanted it rough the whole time."

"No, I didn't. That is not true. Asher, you're not this person. Why are you doing this?" I tighten my grip on her upper arms and push her back against the wall. "No. Stop. Stop it. Stop it."

She smacks at my arms and tries to wriggle out of my grip. I hit her again twice in rapid succession. Once on her cheek and the other on that lush and now swollen lip of hers. Her head bounces off the wall. And she yelps in pain. It's the sexiest thing I've ever done. My ring caught her lip and made a little cut on her cheek. I lick the drop of blood that's formed.

"Today, you're going to suck me off, or Sarah and Will don't get the second half of the money. And you'll keep coming back here to do what I tell you when I tell you or I'll ruin them. I'll take everything they have." She says nothing but cries silently. "You're getting the hang of this. You may now speak."

"Okay. Darren."

"Good little lamb." That shows me she can listen. She just need a firm hand. She's trembling when she speaks again, her voice demure and defeated. Perfect.

"May I please clean the blood of my lips first?" She's shaking a bit.

Her trembling submissive tone is all I want to hear in life. I affect her on a level I'm sure Josh never has. The fear in her voice is because of me, and I could not be more turned on. I may have to tape it and send it to Josh fucking Whittier for a new ringtone.

Elle

The pain is so intense in my arms where he's been pinning me with his grip. It's radiating down to my fingers. I can feel the blood dripping from the side of my lip and cheek. I don't tongue it off. I don't want him to see my tongue. My head's foggy from cracking against the wall. I choke back the vomit that has risen into my mouth. I breathe in and out. Breathe in and out. What the fuck is happening? How am I in this situation? Asher is certifiable. He hid all of this. He hid it. I am not this person who ends up in a situation like this. Oh, my god. Josh is going to kill him. I mean, bare hands kill him, and I'm going to have conjugal visits with my fiancé for the rest of our lives.

The last smack smashed my head against the wall a bit again. Fuck. I don't know what to do. Oh god. Oh god. The pain is shooting through my cheek and head, and I try to focus. To clear the fuzziness. I must calm down and figure out how to get away from this monster.

He's still close enough to my face that I can smell the foul stink of his cologne and feel his breath on my face. The taste of copper in my mouth, the feel of his touch as he cups me below and then rubs himself on my stomach are forming into the most horrible moment of my life. How is he aroused from beating me? I don't understand. I can't react again if he hits me. It's what he wants. I need to shut down my emotions. Shut down. Shut it all down. I need to go full on zombie, like I did after my parents died. Feel nothing. Be in control of my emotions and get control of this situation.

Sarah and Will wouldn't want me to trade myself for the money they'd lose in the deal. Josh would be furious for me even considering it. I'll make it up to them, but Asher's going to really hurt me if I stay. I'll make it up to Sarah and Will. I'll fix it. I'll fix it. But I can't stay here. I must get out. His attempted guilt trip over my love for Sarah and Will won't work. But I can pretend. I can use it.

My keys are in my back pocket, digging into my ass, but he doesn't know I have them. My phone is in the car. I'm stupid. I can't think clearly. Breathe. Think of Josh. Think of the next step. Why didn't I bring my phone in here? I could have called for help. I never thought this would happen. I only needed my mother's necklace, which I don't remember leaving here. Could I have fallen into yet another fucking trap? It's the only real reason I came here today. This locket. I just need to get out of here. I have to get out of here. Jesus.

His slimy voice oozes all over me as he caresses the red and angry welts on my cheek like he's proud of the swelling he created. I attempt not to wince but stare straight at him.

"I'll allow you to clean yourself up for me."

He licks the side of my face. I'm now allowed to go and assess the damage he did to me. He takes one step back but holds my upper arm in a death grip. My arm feels as if it's in a vice. He pulls me to the bathroom and pushes me in there while he fills the door again. His five-foot-ten-inch frame always seemed like a slight build before now. He's not very muscular and would be considered lanky, but right now he looks like an impenetrable wall. I see his shit brown eyes narrow and a sickening grin grows on his face as he watches me realize what he did to my face. It's red and puffy already. There's blood pooling in my cheek and dripping from my lip.

"If you do what I say, then they'll get the money. It's a shame about the land, though. They were such pretty wineries. At least they'll have time to say goodbye to them over the next year, that's much more time than I was given to say goodbye to the life I had. Poor Davey, Poppy, and that cunt Becca Gelbert. Their winery will be the first to go. Fucking level that bullshit. I even asked if I could push the buttons for implosion."

He is talking manically. I have to get out of here, and he's babbling nonsense.

"The Gelberts?"

"Yes, and their fucking parents. Fuck them all for calling me poor trash. Arthur actually spit on the ground once when I came to him and his father for a job. I went to them, when Lucien cast us out, he spat at me. They'll suffer for siding with fucking Lucien LaChappelle. Fuck Becca too for describing me like a leech, a no-talent hanger-on. She doesn't know shit about me. That lawyer cunt will weep for what we're going to do to her property. And she can't fucking stop it."

He's babbling, and I realize that this revenge is deeper than Josh. He's just the crown jewel. Dasher is like a terrible supervillain telling the hero his plan while he has them trapped. I just need to be James Bond and get the fuck out of here. I mean David's a sexist. His dad, Arthur, is an asshole but not cruel. And Becca's a lawyer in Napa and has nothing really to do with the winery. How does he know things she's said? Not sure what that has to do with his vendetta. I want to find out more before I get the fuck out of here.

"David's an asshole."

"They all are, darling, even the seemingly nice Langerfords. Sam's a piece of shit who talks behind my back. At least piece-of-shit Josh says it to my face. I brought you into their den, and I'll get you out of there. They'll all pay and watch their legacies burn to ash. And I'll be the one standing in the middle of the rubble with you triumphantly at my side."

Again, the vomit rises. Why fixate on me? Fuck. If I play his game, will he let down his guard? Flattery has always worked with him in the past. "I always knew you were smarter than them."

He smiles and then reaches down, unzips, pulls out his penis, and strokes himself. I paste on a gruesome smile and try not to react. He's a monster. I used to think his voice was this angelic tenor, but now it has this high-pitched, menacingly haunting cadence. I'm terrified, but I need to hold it together. I need to get out of here. I need a weapon. Standing in the bathroom, I can only remember two things I left here. Cuticle nippers or a hairdryer. I'd replaced those items so I didn't have to come back here. It seemed easier that way. Now I know that was the right call. Jesus, I need to get out of here. Those are the only things I know for sure are in the drawers. I guess it's escape by cuticle nippers. I look in the mirror at him looking at me, and I feel violated already.

My lip isn't bad, but my cheek is going to hurt for days. I won't be able to hide it. Josh is going to kill him. *If* I get back to Josh. What if Asher kills me? Is that even a possibility? Would he do that? I need Josh. I need to get back to him. I can. I can do this. I can do anything. Okay, Elle, you can do this.

I take a washcloth from the counter and open the drawer. I pretend to be looking for soap and palm the nippers. Then wet the washcloth and dab at the blood. I put the nippers in the sink under the wet washcloth and pray he doesn't hear the slight sound of metal on porcelain. My nerves are frayed as I hold my breath waiting and listening to see if he heard the noise. The clink of the nippers hitting the sink was so loud to me. It sounded as loud as a television set thrown off a rooftop crashing to the ground. He's going to rage if he finds them.

"All done?"

Breathe. He didn't hear it. I don't know how. Now I need to hide them. Next step. "I have to go to the bathroom."

"Go ahead."

Maybe if I play nice, he'll give me my out. My stomach is twisting and shredded. I amble towards him. I pull my swelling lips into a contorted version of a smile without breaking stride. I hold my breath and kiss him. It's a sick, wrong, and slow kiss that will haunt me forever. Then I pull back before his horrible blobby tongue can invade my mouth.

"It's my time of the month, and I don't want you to see something that might turn you off."

"That is a fair point. That would be disgusting. Good thing you're just here today to let me into your mouth. Or I could always bury my cock elsewhere."

I try not reacting to the threat of ass rape and ponder how deeply disturbed and how good of an actor he is. I run my finger down his cheek to try and play off the fact that I'm literally horrified and terrified by all of what he's saying.

His whole life he's played two roles. I've always seen through people. Even Josh. I saw the good when he wasn't displaying any of it. I just missed the full evil in this man. I wonder about other women he's assaulted. Where are they? Why didn't they press charges? He's not threatening me on a whim. He's too good at hitting women for this to be his first time. There's no hesitation or remorse. My face is throbbing already, and I need to push down the pain.

I close the door slowly and put the nippers in my bra. They're sharp and cut me a little. I am going to have to endure the scraping for a while. I hope I don't bleed through my shirt and signal to him. I need to position him so he can't immediately run after me, but I can pivot and get out quickly.

I also need to be sure that the place that I stab him matters. His stomach won't work because his arms will most certainly be directing my head onto his member. Or smash my face again. I'd like to stab his dick, but he'll still be able to grab me. I pray I don't have to go through with this in order to get out.

I can do this. No matter how long it takes, I'll get out. Getting out is all that matters. Asher will still be able to chase me if I stab his leg. I'm getting way ahead of myself. I'm flustered and overwhelmed. I have to play the part to get out of here. Focus on escape. Don't focus on the why or how. Just use instinct. One step at a time. Right now, just get out of the bathroom. Each step gets me closer to safety. One step closer to Josh.

I emerge, and his creepy grin overtakes his face. "Shall we?"

He grabs my upper arm roughly and drags me out of the

bathroom. He whips me around towards him. I whimper. He stops and backhands me once more across my cheek. It flairs with pain, and I don't say a thing.

"Good, my angel, no complaining."

I think I nod. My head is not as clear. Get out. Chair. I need him in a chair. One that's too puffy to get out of easily. I need to maneuver him. I can get anyone to do anything. I can do this if my head clears a little. Things are not connecting. Next step, just get him where I need him. I put on a pout that I think he'll find sexy but is truly sickening me.

"If you stand, I won't be able to get all of you in my mouth."

I need his back to the door. I need to be able to get out of here without him grabbing me. There's an armchair. Hopefully, the blood is already away from his head, and he won't realize that standing is actually the best way for me to take all of him in my mouth. Or that I don't need him to stand, it's not all that impressive. Or that I don't plan to put that thing anywhere near my mouth.

And then there's another smack to my mouth and then a hard crack across my face. That sends me to the ground. His ring connects with the top of the same cheek he's already smashed. The pain burns through my brain, and I struggle to keep composure. I see flashes of red and black spots. I can't focus. I'm trying to shake off the blackness and nausea. My lip's bleeding again. I lay there for a moment. I just want to rest a second. Just close my eyes.

I don't know how long I laid there, but he drags me to my feet again. I'm like a rag doll. The pain of where he's holding me pales in comparison to my face. My vision is still blurred, and my head is rattled. I struggle to get clear from the pain. I have to get clear. I struggle but work myself through it. I wipe my lip and smile through the tears leaking from my eyes from the pain.

"Dirty whore. I didn't say speak. You like pain and pleasure. Don't you?"

If I do, it's that I experience both, not my pain for his pleasure. If I get out of here, I'll kill him. I won't need Josh. I regroup, and my vision returns, albeit a bit blurry.

"Where do you want me? You do know that you never should have sent those naughty texts to me. Taunting me. Letting me know how much you care. But you never should have told everyone that I was less than adequate. But I know that was for their benefit. You are trapped in their world and would say anything to appease them. But that's behind us now, my angel. The sound of that last smack got my member so ready for you. I need you to give me an orgasm right now."

His words mangle my insides, and it feels like glass raking down my stomach. I reach out and touch him through his pants, and he grunts. Gross. I guide him to the chair. My adrenaline is the only thing controlling me right now. My face is swelling, and my eyes won't stop watering. I don't know if it's from pain or crying. My left eyelid is starting to droop and obscure my vision a bit. He must want to mark me. That must be why he's hitting my face. So Josh knows he did this. God. Josh. I just want to get to Josh. But I'm so embarrassed that I'm in this position. How stupid can I be?

He's sitting, and I undo his buckle and pull down his pants and briefs, leaving them wrapped around his ankles without him realizing. I squat, never going down on my knees so I can pop up. So grateful for the number of burpees I do in a day.

I let one hand rub up against his inner thigh while the

other one redoes the buckle of his belt around his ankles. That may buy me a second. If I can outrun most of the bored farm boys in Kansas, I can do this. I will not be further violated today.

He closes his eyes. Thank god. Keep them closed, asshole. He's grunting like a pig rooting around in slop, and then he throws his head back. I move the nippers into my hand. His one hand is in his mouth as he sucks his own fingers. It's disgusting. It's like he wants to suck himself. His other hand is on the back of my head gripping a handful of my hair too tightly, urging me to make contact. I massage his inner thigh again, and he grunts. I'm squatting. My pulse is racing. My adrenaline is pumping so hard that I may throw up on him. Next step.

"Suckle me, Noelle. *NOW*. Get your whore lips on me. Suck my magnificent member."

He tosses his head back again, and with one swift motion, I reach up and stab his hand that's gripping my hair. I've never done anything with more force in my life, and I'll always remember the feel of the two sharp points slicing into the soft tissue of his hand. He drops my hair and shrieks as blood spurts out of his hand. I pop up and bolt for the door. Down the corridor and to the front door, never stopping for a second. As the door closes behind me, I see him coming at me, screaming, bleeding with his dick out. He's screeching then falling on the tile floor because his belt is pulled tight around his ankles.

Josh

I fucking hate when she doesn't answer. I need to know if she got the email about the missing orders. This is already a shit morning knowing she had to run to Dasher's for her mom's jewelry. I should have gone, but there's so much going on here.

There's a glitch in the website, and that's so much more her thing than mine. I need to get to my own freaking work. I'm in Dad's office and trying to finalize some details on a contract with Magnus. Dissolving my partnership with my firm is a long and arduous business. I don't have time to do Elle's job too. Where the hell did she go?

I call Sammy, and there's no answer there either. I call the fig, EDK, and Poppy's. She has no reservations for lunch, and no one has seen her. She did mention a surprise for me. Maybe it's the wedding planner she's been thinking about. Okay. Whatever. But she was supposed to call me when she left Dasher's. I call again. I'm sent to voicemail. She knew I called. I text.

JOSH: Elle. There's so much shit for you to do here.

Please come save me from your paperwork. I have to jump on a series of calls soon. Save me, Cosmo, you're my only hope.

* * *

I get off my latest annoying call and she still hasn't come home. It's been hours. I'm incredibly irked at her.

JOSH: Babe. Where are you?

No answer. I call and then text again twenty minutes later.

JOSH: Cosmo? Answer me. You know I don't like this. I know you sent me to voicemail. Come on, Cosmo...

JOSH: Hellcat, are you just trying to get punished? I will redden your ass the color of that nail polish you love so much if you don't answer me.

Well, at least I know how our evening is going to play out.

I text again in fifteen minutes.

JOSH: Babe. Where are you? Answer me, please.

Elle

Once in the car, I fumble with the keys. It feels like an eternity before I can turn the car on, but I do it. I slam the car in reverse and gun it backward out of his driveway, taking out his mailbox in the process. As I'm speeding away, I try to maintain my breathing. I don't want to pass out or hyperventilate until I know I'm far enough away.

The pain is coming in waves. I pull over, throw up, and then peel out again. I need to keep driving until I know I'm hidden from him. I just keep driving, but I'm going in the wrong direction, away from Sonoma. Josh can't see me like this. I'm so ashamed I let this happen. Josh can't see this. Josh knew he was garbage, but I didn't believe him. I didn't stay away from him. I need to be on the highway around lots of people. Dasher might think I'm going back to Sonoma. He might come to find me. I need him not to go looking for Josh or me. I can't lure him to Sonoma. I need him not to go near Josh.

I pull over to the side of the road to vomit again. I'm a good half hour from his place when I take a series of pictures. My eyes won't stop watering. I take pictures of my arms and neck with the handprint bruises that will only get worse in the coming days. Then my face. I didn't look in the rearview mirror but now staring at the pictures of my swollen eye, scarlet-colored cheek, and busted and engorged lip, I sob. I can only see out of one eye. The tears stinging the open parts of me. My phone rings and I let Josh's call go to voicemail. I can't. I shut it off.

I wish Sarah were in town. Josh will try to kill him. He almost killed one of his best friends for calling me a bitch. I can't have him going vigilante on this piece of human garbage. One thing at a time. First, I need to be safe. I need to feel safe. And to lay down. Safety. I went there willingly. The police won't listen. I have a key to his house. What happens to the winery if I go to the police? I need to think. My brain isn't working right. I need to slow it down. I need to breathe. That's my next step. And ice. Lots of ice.

Elle

There's a knock at my hotel door. I left Dasher's house three hours ago. My face is a fucking mess. I slept a bit. Or I passed out. I don't know which one. I did call for help. There's another knock. I suck in a big breath and open the door. I let Sam and Sammy into my hotel room. They gasp at the sight of me and Sam panics.

Sam inquires, "Are you okay? Holy shit. What the hell happened? What do you need? Where's Josh?" He moves to me and takes me in his bear hug arms, and I cry again. Samantha's at my back rubbing and caressing my hair.

Sammy states, "Ice. You need ice. Advil. Epsom salts and weed. And probably a hospital."

"No hospital. They'll call the police. But I'll take you up on the ice. And no Josh right now."

I do need ice. I've just been sitting here as it gets worse. I was afraid someone would see me in the hallway if I tried to get it and I didn't want in-room dining spreading rumors. I don't want someone to call the police. I'd been putting cold beer and wine from the mini-fridge on my face and eyes. I rend myself away from Sam and sit down. Sammy

54

runs for ice. I've eaten all the Advil in the room. I've also googled concussion about ten times. Pretty sure I've got one of those.

"Talk to me. I'm here. I got you. Who did this?" Josh's best friend guides me to the couch.

I can't stop crying, and I know how bad this looks, but I can't stop myself. Sam just keeps his arm around me as I sob into his chest. He keeps trying to say sweet things.

"It's okay. You're okay. Are you dizzy at all? You're okay, aren't you? No internal bleeding or anything? Are there other injuries? Was it a car accident? Do you need a doctor?"

"No, doctor. I'm not as dizzy anymore. It's just my face and arms. Not a car. And I'm so tired."

"No. That is a really bad idea. I think. Shit. I don't know. But my best guest is no. You can't sleep. Let me see your eyes. Well, your eye." Sam sparks up the flashlight on his phone and checks my eyes. Apparently and miraculously, they're dilating and not blown out.

I have on a tank top and shorts that I bought at the tennis shop downstairs. I'm also in the giant hotel robe. I let the robe slide down my shoulder to reveal the hand imprints on my arm, neck and the one I know is on my back.

"Holy shit. We need to call someone. Police, a doctor."

"I bruise easily, and I'm fair-skinned, so it looks so much worse than it is. I promise you." The bruises have bloomed in the hours since contact. The handprints are more pronounced, and I need more pictures. "Sam. I need you to take photos of all of this. Please don't show them to me, just take them."

"Where's Josh?"

"I can't."

"You know he's going to kill whoever did this. And then

55

he'll kill me for not taking you to the hospital. And I won't be able to stop either of those things."

"I do. I'll stop him from killing you. Thank you for coming. I can't tell him yet. I need a minute to collect, but I was afraid to be alone." Sam can't hide his wincing as he takes pictures of my injuries. I sit still for the macabre photoshoot. When he's done, I tell him, "I need to go lie down."

Sammy's back with ice packs and helps me with the robe. They guide me to the bed in the back of the suite. Sammy props up a ton of pillows, so I'm kind of sitting up lying down. She insists that I drink two bottles of water before she leaves me alone.

Sammy tells me, "I'm going to wake you up in an hour. Every hour. But sleep for now. Rest, and then we'll talk." They make me sip more water. I don't know why. I do it. I'm actually very thirsty. Then she kisses me on my fore-head, and Sammy says, "You're safe. You're strong. You're safe, and you need sleep. We won't leave you." Sam covers me with the blankets. As I drift into darkness, I hear Sammy begin to cry. And Sam comforts her. I welcome the deep darkness with ice on my face.

I rouse, and my head lolls back a bit. I wince at the pain as I try to turn over on the pillow. I just want to stay sleeping. But Sam is on the bed with his arms around me, pulling me up to sitting. I blink a bit, and my one eye is useless. Sammy puts more ice on my face and sits next to me. She gently massages my face with some kind of gel. Then puts Gatorade—blue, I think—to my lips and drink I greedily. Blue is a flavor, right? Sam talks to me for a while, and I think I answer while I take a handful of Advil and two Turmeric supplements. She also has me hold CBD oil under my tongue for a minute then swallow. It's minty and herby, and Sammy says it will help with the swelling and pain. Then Sam eases me back to the propped-up pillows, and the darkness surrounds me again.

* * *

I feel Sam scoop me up again and, in my haze, I react as if it's Josh and snuggle into him. Then I feel the beard.

"Hey, Elle. Come with me. You need to get up and walk around. It's been like four hours."

Sammy helps me get up. I feel better. There's more ice and more Advil, more gel, which I now know is arnica. Then there's another check of my pupils. The swelling seems to have gone down, and I can open both eyes. Sammy had me sleeping propped up. If I do have a concussion, it's not a full-blown one. She puts warm Epsom salt compresses on my face and then insists I eat pineapple. I chew and swallow a CBD gummy. There's also ginko, zinc, vitamin C drinks, and vitamin D. But I'm not allowed to take vitamin D until I have some avocado. She's like a strange holistic bruising expert.

Once I'm seated on the couch with my legs tucked under me, Sammy walks to the kitchen yelling at me as she goes. "You're scaring the fuck out of me with this deep ass sleeping. We literally took turns putting a mirror under your nose for the last four and a half hours. I don't need that shit."

I toss back to her, "It's adrenaline depletion, not a concussion." And suddenly my mind is sharper than it's been all day. Sammy hands me a banana, more pineapple, and Gatorade. It's afternoon now, and I feel a little more equipped to deal with what the fuck happened to me this morning. I turn to Sam.

"I'm so grateful you guys are here. Thank you." Sam puts his arm gingerly around me again.

"Sammy didn't tell me where we were going, just that we had to pick something up. It's the first time she's ever lied to me. I adore you, Elle, but don't do that again. Don't make my girl lie to me again."

"I'm so sorry. I won't. I won't ever. I wasn't thinking clearly. I couldn't risk you calling Josh," I say.

"Like I'm going to do right now. Do you know what happened? Or where this all went down?

"Please. Just give me a second to catch my breath. Then I'll call him. I promise I'll call him. Just not yet. And yes. I know who did this."

I walk to the other side of the room and look out the window over the city. It's a gorgeous view all the way to the bay. It's four-thirty in the afternoon, and I have a cocktail reception tonight for the Boys and Girls Club of Sonoma. I don't think I'm going to make it.

"Did they do anything else?"

I turn to Sam, and his face is worried and hard. As if he's steeling himself to find out that I was raped. Thank god I give him the answer he wants to hear. "No."

"Are you sure?"

"I am. He hit me, and there's more to the story that I owe to Josh or the police, but just know I wasn't raped."

Sam approaches me and looks at my chest. "Elle. Did he have a knife or something? Your left breast area looks all cut up and scratched. Not that I looked. I mean, you know."

I grin at him. Well, I pull my lips up as much as I can. "I do. But I did that."

"What?" Sam leaps up and crosses the room to me. "I'm done fucking around, Elle. You have to tell us what happened."

I begin to cry again and whisper, "Please lower your voice. I've had enough demands and screaming for the day."

He takes me back into his arms. "I'm sorry. I'm so sorry. I don't know what to do in this situation. Tell me what to do. Can't imagine what you've been through. I just don't know what to do. You have to call him. Where does he think you are? You can't stay here."

"Just a minute to regroup, please."

"Where's your phone?"

I turned it off after I took pictures of my face. I nod to it just as Sammy comes in the door with more ice. She gives me more CBD oil then makes the ice packs, and I sit at the little bistro table in the suite. She also doctors up the scrapes on my breast.

"Later I want you to smoke up some weed so you can sleep. Alcohol will enhance the swelling; pot will reduce it."

Sam's on the other side of the room. I listen and really look at Sammy. I make sure Sam can't hear what I want to say to her. I take her hands. "Someday, Sammy, if you need to, you can tell me why you know how to do all of this. How to take care of me in this way."

"Thanks, Elle. I'll never need to tell you. It's safer for everyone. But thank you for being a true friend, I don't have a lot of them. And you're probably my best. I don't make many."

"Same." I grin at her. I'm so glad she's here.

"And if I were going to tell someone, it would be you. But know that right now none of that matters. I'm good." She looks at Sam. I wonder if he knows that he's healing some past we don't know anything about for her.

I hug Sammy, and we stay in hold until we hear Sam's phone spring to life. I look at him and shake my head. He sends it to voicemail.

"I'm only doing that one more time."

Sammy breaks the tension by saying, "You should know that Josh is calling everyone looking for you. He texted me like six times. I lied to him and said I hadn't seen you. And Poppy, Tabi, and Jims covered for you as well, but they have no idea why. How did you get such a fat hideout anyway?"

"Thank you for doing that. As for my surroundings, I hid behind sunglasses when I checked in, so I'm not sure how much the room is going to cost me. I'm sure it's crazy expensive. I just needed to get somewhere where I felt safe."

"You've blown a month's salary on a hideout." Sammy is trying to lighten my mood by telling me about the room. "You know there are two bedrooms? And a grand piano."

"I didn't know there was another bedroom. I really haven't left this area. And I wasn't thinking too clearly."

Sam offers up, "I ordered you a club sandwich and some tea. I didn't know what else to do for you right now. But you need to eat."

"Fries?" I ask.

"Of course. And asked for malt vinegar as well."

Sammy hugs me and walks away. I can tell her eyes are a bit swollen from crying. I can't imagine how gruesome I look. I'm sure it looks worse than it hurts. But it does fucking hurt. I wouldn't mind an actual painkiller now. Perhaps some wine will help. Maybe later. I don't know if I can smoke what she wants me to. I always get a terrible headache, and that seems counterproductive in this situation.

Sam's holding my phone in front of the terrace doors. It

comes to life and goes apeshit. "You have forty-seven texts, twenty-seven from him. And your voice mailbox is full. Call him."

"Shit," Sammy exclaims.

Sam commands, and I agree. "You have to tell him."

"Let me eat first and then I'll call him."

"Don't fuck around, Elle. Call Josh. You have to. This isn't fair to him or us. He deserves to be here for you. But first, tell me where you were when this happened."

It comes out as a pointed whisper, "Asher's."

Josh

S he's never flighty. She never misses an appointment. Never. She's too anal retentive to be late for anything. She's too Noelle Parker for this. Something's off. Her calendar is never wrong. She updates it even if she's the only one who needs to know. She misses nothing. She's never without her charger. I'm holding her cord in my hand and pacing back and forth. I'm going out of my fucking mind. My parents haven't heard from her either. No one has heard from her. I've texted everyone I could think of. I left a message for Evan at the office. I don't have his cell number.

What the hell is she doing? We need to be at a reception in like a half-hour. Each message I leave I'm getting more pissed off and worried. I'm dressed for the event she seems to be blowing off. This isn't normal.

I contemplated calling Dasher and seeing if she was still there but didn't want to give him the satisfaction that I didn't know where she was. And if she is there like eight hours later, I'd be pretty pissed off about it. She went over there at like eight this morning.

John, my Santa Barbara assistant, usually texts her about some insane reality show around noon every day, and he hasn't heard from her. Sam's not answering. Sammy's phone goes to voicemail as well, but her text said she didn't know where she was. Poppy hasn't heard from her. She blew off their Rosé Tuesdays with Poppy, Tabi, Becca, and Becca's law partner, Francesca, and their friend Meg. Another thing she holds sacred and wouldn't miss. Especially without calling one of them.

Now I'm getting suspicious and a little panicky. She's left me no choice. I'm going to do something I swore I would only do in the case of an emergency. I use her 'find my iPhone.' Knowing her code makes it easy, and it's linked to mine. Melissa linked all the people I love to my phone during the Sal shit, and I never told them.

It pings in the city. It pings at the Ritz Carlton. My hands instantly ball into fists, and my palms get sweaty as the vein in my neck rages. I scream in the kitchen, "She's at a hotel? What the hell is happening?" I instantly call the Ritz, and they tell me that there's a 'Do Not Disturb' on her room. Are you fucking kidding me?

Now I need fucking Sam. I need him to talk me down before I fucking break a bunch of shit. No one can find Sam at our winery or his. Rage is rearing its ugly head. Fuck. I'll kill Dasher if he's there with her. I'm so fucking confused. She wouldn't do this. How could she do this to me? No. She can't. Then who is at this hotel room with her?

My head is playing with me, and I can't make it stop. Jealousy is thundering through me. She wouldn't. Goddamned Sam isn't answering. I ring again and this time he sends me to voicemail. I don't know what else to do. I jump in the Porsche and take off for the city. I will find her.

Blowing through stop signs and running lights. I get

jammed up on the 101 through Tiburon, getting angrier by the second. I try her phone again. This time it rings but her voicemail is full. At least her phone is on, and I know she's actively avoiding me. Sam doesn't answer again. Fuck it. I ping his phone too.

My heart drops to my stomach, and my breath goes shallow when 'find my iPhone' reveals Sam's location. The Ritz Carlton.

Are they together? What is happening? I am so confused. A little less pissed because I really find it incredibly hard to believe that Sam and Elle are screwing. But he's clearly in on something that I'm not. My birthday isn't soon, so they're not planning something. They're hiding something. They're hiding something big. That's not how any of this works. This is not how Elle and I operate. Maybe it was when I didn't tell her about Sal but not anymore. And it sure as hell isn't how Sam and I operate.

I can't get there fast enough. I have no idea how I'm going to get up to the room, but I've charmed people out of billions of dollars, surely I can get a fucking hotel key. The element of surprise is all I have that will get me answers the quickest.

I look at the valet and say, "Put it on my wife's room. Shit. I don't know the number. I was supposed to be here hours ago, a first-anniversary surprise. She's going to kill me, and now I can't remember the damn room number. I'm the worst. Just put it on Noelle Parker. I'll call her and don't you dare fucking laugh as she bitches me out." I wink at the valet.

My bluff works as the valet winks back at me. "Yes, sir. She's waiting in the Presidential Suite. 909."

I hand him a hundred. A suite. Why the hell does she need a suite? "Thanks, you saved my ass."

I bolt to elevators and realize I need a key card to access her floor. I stroll to the front desk. "Hi. I hope you can help me. My wife checked in hours ago and was putting together an anniversary surprise for me, and I need a key to room 909."

The man looks at me and says, "Hmm. Let me see what I can do."

I add for clarification, "Noelle Parker."

"Mr. Parker, is it?"

"No. My feminist wife wouldn't take my name."

I smile at this man who's clearly into me. I remove my jacket, revealing my tight custom shirt underneath. I throw the jacket over my shoulder, so the dress shirt pulls on my pecs a bit. It's Elle's favorite because of the way it highlights my chest. I'm dressed for the event we were supposed to attend tonight. Hopefully, this can help me get to the bottom of whatever duplicitous shit she's doing. I loosen the tie and stuff it in the pocket of my jacket. Then I unbutton the top three buttons revealing a bit of my chest. I wipe my lips slowly like there's an invisible film on them, knowing he's watching the show from his peripheral. Flirting always works.

"It seems she left access for other guests to be given a key. But explicit instructions that it is only them. What's your name?"

I don't hesitate, "Sam Langerford."

"Well, Sam. Seems you're on her list."

Jack-fucking-pot. My best friend and my fiancé are upstairs in the Presidential suite, and I'm going to bust them wide the fuck open.

"Ms. Breazel is already up there."

Sammy? Why the fuck is Sammy here? Jesus. Something is seriously wrong. And this guy thinks I'm about to have an Anniversary threesome. I wink. As long as it gets me the fucking key card, I don't care if he thinks I'm attending an orgy.

He hands me a key and winks back at me and says, "Is there anything else I can do for you? I mean anything."

He's a good-looking man. I lean in taking the key, getting closer to his face. "Not tonight, thank you. Sadly, I'm hopelessly in love with my wife. But if I were so inclined, you'd be just my type."

"Why are the good ones always straight?"

I bolt to the elevators.

The utter shock on Sammy's face at my appearance tells me I did, in fact, interrupt something no one's willing to share with me yet. Sammy makes an awkward gesture of ushering me into a deluxe two-bedroom apartment. The place is insane. I frantically scan the room and run into the bedrooms. She's nowhere. Then I see Sam enter from the terrace.

"Josh. Oh. Shit. Josh."

"Yeah. Oh. Shit. Sam." I say a little too forcefully. My teeth are clenched. My hands are balled in fists at my side.

"What the fuck are you doing here?"

"Hell no, Sam. You fucking tell me what is going on. Right muthafucking now. Where is Elle? Is she with some-one? Why are *you* here? Is she okay? What is happening? Who do I need to fucking kill? Her? You?"

Sam walks over to me and puts his hand on my shoul-der. Anger and frustration are radiating off of me. I want to slap his hand off my body and deck him. He hands me a glass with a large pull of brown liquor in it.

"Drink this. You'll need it. Take a breath. It's not anything you've thought of. Your woman is insanely in love with you."

My entire demeanor changes. The jealousy is subsiding, but the rage about the hiding is firmly in place.

Sam continues to talk while I finish the drink. "Calm down. Be gentle. Be Josh, not Joshua. She's on the terrace. Be there for her first and then we'll sort the rest out. I'll be right here inside with Sammy."

I shoot the drink and then move quickly to the terrace door. Elle's wrapped in what appears to be an extra blanket staring at a fire pit. My chest eases, and my breath returns in full. She is safe. She's my oxygen. And she's not leaving me. And she's not with someone else. And she's not missing. She's fine. She's here right in front of me.

I close the door behind me. I start walking towards her. Her blonde hair, scraggly and falling down the back of the chair. She slumps deeper into the chair. Then I see her shoulders tense a bit as she sits back up. She knows it's me.

She gasps but doesn't turn around. "Josh. I'd know your scent anywhere. I can feel you." Her speech is slightly impaired, but I ignore it.

"Yes, it's me, my love."

In a more alarmed tone, she halts me. "Stop. Please stop walking. Stay where you are." She won't look at me. I hear her voice crack. But I freeze in the position even though all I want to do is rush to her.

She continues, "I have to show you something. Then I need you just to hold me. Hold me until it goes away. No questions. Not yet. Promise me, my One Perfect Thing, no questions. I need to be in your arms. I need to feel safe." Her voice is full-on shattered. Thank god she called me my love. I draw in a big breath and steel myself.

"I promise."

She stands to turn around slowly, and my deep breath is gone. Rage fills me again. I can't keep it at bay as I take in all of her face. My fists are balled up again as I look at the most beautiful woman in the world.

"I'm okay."

"Bullshit."

She crosses the terrace in an instant to me, and I wrap her in my useless arms. Arms that should have protected her from whatever horror she's endured.

Elle

His arms around me begin to heal my soul instantly. He's the sun warming me from inside and pushing out all the gloom. I'm safe. He found me. I don't know how, but I know he always will. He'll always come for me. He's on my side. He's part of me, and I'm part of him. I am his. I should have called him, but I didn't know how to start this conversation. I'm so thankful he found a way for me to start this dialogue.

I'm so embarrassed. I'm angry and frustrated that this happened. I feel stupid and childish that I couldn't handle it. Sammy is furious at me that I seem to be blaming myself for this. That I'm victim-blaming myself, but I never should have gone there alone. I never should have sent those texts. And now I have to tell Josh precisely what happened. I have to say the words.

We stay entwined for a long time. He keeps kissing the top of my head and smoothing my hair. Then when my sobbing relents, I look up at him. He moves his hand to my face and tries to place it on my cheek, but I wince.

"I didn't want you to be mad. I didn't want you to think I was stupid." I'm sobbing.

"You don't have to tell me anything right now. But you do have to come with me." I nod. He speaks again, "I got you. I'm not leaving your side. I'm going to take care of you right now. Do you understand? Just sink into it and let me take care of all of you. No objections. You're safe now. I'm not leaving your side."

He guides me into the room, and Sam and Sammy stand at attention. He gives them orders. He's in control now. Thank god.

"I'm taking Elle to the hospital. We'll come back here. I'd like it if you could stay. I'd like to get a timeline on what happened. And we'll need pictures of her face."

Sam says, "We took them, and of her arms, back, and chest." Josh looks as if the wind has been knocked out of him.

Josh

I'm fucking torn in half. The one person on the entire fucking planet I can't live without was afraid to call me because of my temper. My Lucien side fucking me up again. I will spend the rest of my life struggling with burying that, but I will never ever let her be in danger again. She will never doubt a single moment or reaction from me again. Apparently, I still have things to show her. I would never have been those things, but she didn't know that yet.

I take her to the bedroom and gently but quickly disrobe her. I see the deep bruises on her arms where someone grabbed her. There's a large bruise between her shoulder blades and deep scratches on her left breast. There's clearly handprints on her neck. Someone marked her. They marked what's mine. They tried to take what's mine, and I'm fucking nauseated at how useless I feel. I will burn this city the fuck down to find the people who did this. I can fix anything. I can make the impossible happen, but I can't fucking take this away from her. I will put those fuckers in the ground. I will find the assholes and make them fucking pay.

Sammy's at the door and offers up what Elle cannot, "He didn't rape her. Just hit her."

"He?! Not they? This was one person. What the fuck are you talking about? Did he take your money? Your mom's jewelry or the car?" She shakes her head.

Sammy speaks as Elle gets her clothes on, "No. That's not what he wanted. But he didn't get the thing he wanted."

"Oh, Christ. You know this person?" I spin around in a frenzy. She nods and begins to cry. Tears sting the back of my eyes as the pieces of this puzzle fall into an enraging and grotesque place. "Please don't say his name until we talk to the police."

"No police."

"That's not your choice anymore." I see her shoulders relax as I take the burden of control away from her.

We grab an Uber to the hospital, not wanting to deal with the valet. Her sunglasses are in place, and it's dark. I don't want anyone to think it was me. We quietly enter the emergency room.

I place her in a chair in the waiting room. Sammy put her hair up in a ponytail, but she looks a mess in her jeans, Birkenstocks, her blood-stained blouse, Gucci sunglasses, and my suit jacket. She insisted on wearing what she wore there. I couldn't love her more at this moment. My sassy girl's spirit seems to be tarnished, and I need to get her back. I need her to fight with me. I need her to fight this. He can't own even a small piece of her. Not her dignity or her mind.

Whoever the fuck this asshole is, he will regret the day he tried to fuck with Elle Parker. I can't go to the place I think we're going. I can't think it's him right now. Because then it's my fault. I'm the reason. She'll bounce back and take his balls. She has to. She must come back to me.

"Hello. My fiancée was assaulted this morning, and aside from physically, I believe there was an attempted rape. She needs medical attention, but I don't know the protocol for getting the police involved." I hand them her insurance card and ID from her purse. I get a text from Sam.

SAM: Instagram. He's going to make it a he said/she said thing

JOSH: Can't look right now. Screenshot everything. Document everything! Including when you and Sammy got to the hotel. Write everything down now. Did you FasTrak on the Golden Gate? Get those records. Call Becca. And if she doesn't answer, get her partner Francesca on it. I need a lawyer on this shit tonight.

SAM: On it.

JOSH: Thanks, man. Thanks for taking care of my everything.

SAM: You'd do the same for me.

JOSH: Damn straight.

His name burns at the edge of my mind. His hatred of me put her here. "Sir. We'll take her back here, and we'll get the authorities, but you'll have to wait here."

"No. I'm not leaving her."

The nurse gets a firm and furrowed brow. "I'm afraid that's not possible."

"WAIT. *You think I did this?*" I unleash the full volume of my voice at this woman.

"We need to be sure, sir. It's protocol."

I look over. A stocky orderly and a young, energetic nurse are helping Elle to her feet. She shuffles with them looking at me, confused.

I regain my composure. "Elle. I need to fill out paperwork. I'll be right here. And as soon as I can get back there, I will. Go with them. Tell them everything. You can do this, my love, I know you can. Tell them every single detail you remember. It's okay. Tell them everything. I love you, my One Perfect Thing."

"My phone. I need my phone."

I pull it from my pocket and move towards her, but I'm intercepted by the orderly. I surrender the phone and my girl.

I mutter an apology to the woman behind the desk.

"It's okay, baby. She's in good hands. We're just protecting her."

"Thank you for that." I nod to the orderly.

Elle

I'm exhausted. That's the only thought I have right now. I feel completely depleted and limp. I'm behind a curtain when a doctor and nurse enter to help me onto the table.

"Wow. That's a fantastic shiner. I don't mean to make light of it. But that is some impressive work."

The doctor disarms me with his humor. It's exactly what I need. Someone to not take this too seriously but while knowing I'm in capable hands. He snaps me back into a version of myself that can begin to deal with this.

"He certainly was proud."

The room erupts in a strained laugh, and my mood lightens even more. The nurses help me disrobe and bag my clothes as I remove them. The doctor examines as this happens. They put a gown over me and point out some folded scrubs for me to put on when this is all over.

He's listening to my lungs and lifting my arms. He pushes on my ribs, and I don't feel pain at all. "Do you know this genius?" He continues to explore around on my face, and although I wince, I don't pull away.

"I do know him."

"Well, you're lucky. It seems he's not done anything that won't heal. I'll do my best to even mask any scar from that cut on your cheek and lip. Now. Do you want a rape kit done?"

"He didn't rape me. But could you scrape under my fingernails?"

"You've seen one too many episodes of *Special Victims Unit*. Yes. We can, but it will be part of a rape kit."

"If he was trying to force me to give him head, is that attempted rape?"

"If it was against your will, yup that's sexual assault."

"Then, yes. A rape kit. And some of he blood on my clothes might be his. I stabbed him with cuticle nippers." A nurse steps to me. She has kind eyes and is carrying the scrubs.

"Damn, that's a new one. We'll take note that there might be two sources of blood."

"Thanks." The nurse turns to me and places a hand on my shoulder.

"You can put these on after the doctor examines your torso." I nod. "I need to hear your consent."

"You're the only one who wanted it today." The doctor laughs again. The doctor examines my chest and ribs again. He has me breathe in and out, and it feels like the first time I've done that today.

"Okay. You can put your shirt on in a second. We need to clean out those scrapes. We'll take a look at that face."

I straighten up as everyone in the room's eyes turn to the two people walking in. "This is Officer Daniels and Detective Ginnetti. We can all leave if you want privacy as you speak with them. Or you don't have to."

"No. I want to speak to the police. And please stay,

you've already heard the worst of it. I know the man's name, but it's not my fiancé. Can he be here too?"

The tall, serious female officer speaks to me. "First we need to know if you feel in danger with your fiancé around. Or if you feel coerced in any way to protect him."

"It wasn't him. His name is Darren Marcus, or his alias is Asher Bernard. Do you need his address?"

Josh

I'm pacing like a wild man, and I can't calm down. And then the large orderly comes to fetch me. I approach the room, and she's behind a curtain just beginning her story. She's in a secluded area so no one else can hear her. But I listen from here. I know it will be harder for her to tell if she sees me, so I stay out of sight.

"Ma'am, how well do you know this Asher, or is it Darren?"

Even though I knew it was him, the confirmation is unbearable. I want to leave here and begin hitting him and only stop when his skull cracks open. White skull, red blood spilling from this fucking asshole. I will eviscerate that man. I will be consumed by ruining his entire existence. My guilt is crushing, and I only want to take it out on him. Fuck.

"His real name is Darren Marcus, but he does business and has a life under the name Asher Bernard. That was the name I knew when we met. We dated briefly but remained business colleagues."

"When did you break up?"

"We only dated a few weeks, but I broke up with him in March of this year."

The doctor chimes in. "Seems like a wise choice."

"I thought so."

The detective says, "How did he take the breakup?"

"He seemed fine with it. He was dating other people. He didn't care until I began dating my fiancé. He has a life-long vendetta against his family."

"What's his name and did you know this when you began dating?"

"Joshua Whittier. No. I didn't know of Asher's anger towards the family. He changed his name, so no one really knew who he was because he knew them when he was younger. I knew none of this."

"You know him as Asher Bernard, but he used to be this Darren Marcus?"

"Yes."

"What were the circumstances of you seeing him today?"

"I stayed at his house for a couple of days back in March and left some clothes and my deceased mother's jewelry there by accident. I've asked him to return the items during our business dinners, but he never did. I texted him two days ago so I could go and get them. He may have hidden the jewelry to lure me back, but I can't be certain. Shit. He probably did that. I don't know. I lived in New York and was temporarily relocating to California. I stayed with him for a week or so in a separate room. And yes, we'd had sex before that but never at his home. We only had sex twice before I broke up with him. He wasn't very good at it. I know that's not relevant, but I feel as if I can't stop the words spilling out of my mouth. I'm sorry."

"No apologies. Just keep spilling." The doctor puts a reassuring hand on her back and nods for her to continue.

"The last time he attempted to have sex with me was on March 13. But I refused him and then had a talk with him several days later about how we weren't dating. It's also the night I met my fiancé."

I had no idea she saw him earlier that evening. I picture her pure sweet face in the lights of Steiner's. No makeup, Sunflower Caffe t-shirt, so unlike any woman I'd ever dated. She's like no other woman I've ever known. My dear, dear sweet, strong Elle. Her voice isn't wavering or cowering. I need her to stay stable.

"And when was the last time you had sexual relations with him, or any kind of genitals contact."

"Today. Sort of."

"What!" I can't help myself. I leap up and pull the curtain back. She looks shocked. It's like an out-of-body experience I'm so fucking angry. She said he didn't rape her. Just beat her.

She stares at me with tears in her flat emerald eyes. They look like dulled beach glass instead of the gems they should be. I know I need to somehow tamp down the rage and let her talk. I need to get that sparkle back into those eyes. If that's the last fucking thing I do in my life. They will sparkle again. I need to give her all my strength right now. I step into the area and sit behind her on the bed. I don't touch her. But I'm there.

"Go ahead, Elle. You can tell the story. I won't say another word. It's all okay."

"Please start at the beginning," says one of the police officers. A nurse, still holding her hand, wipes her eyes, and she continues.

The horror that burns inside of me as she tells us of how

he pinned her and hit her will never be matched. He denigrated her by calling her a whore. No one speaks to her that way. Or any woman. He told her she could leave the ring on. I want to pull his spine from his body.

Then my heart breaks as she tells me of his threat to my parents. I know her, she probably had a moment of doubt. And then she begins speaking about her escape plan, and I see a spark of my girl fire up. There's my Hellcat. She stabbed him, tripped him, and escaped. But he tried to make her touch his dick. He will die for that alone.

"Ma'am, did you willingly go to his home?"

"Yes."

"And this happened today?"

"Yes, at eight forty-five in the morning."

"Today, November eighteenth?"

"Yes, ma'am."

The officer pulls his phone up and shows the detective. "I know you're probably eager to press charges, but I'd like to save you some time. He has an alibi."

"What the fuck are you talking about? My fiancé is battered. And he somehow has convinced you without question he didn't do it."

They show us the phone. It's time-stamped 12:00 p.m. It's a picture of him sitting at a judge's table. "He was on a plane headed to Indianapolis at the time of the alleged assault."

"Alleged, my ass. Does this look alleged?"

"There's more."

They pull up an Instagram photo of Elle sleeping in his bed. It says, 'Sleep well, my angel, be home soon.' Then he hashtagged the shit out of it about getting on a plane to Indianapolis.

Elle's tears stream down her face, and there's a storm in

her voice. "But that's not what happened. He made this up. And so fucking gross. He has a photo of me sleeping in the other bedroom, where I stayed alone. And look. I have bangs in that picture. I've grown them out since. That's an old picture."

"Be that as it may. If you want to file a report, we will look into this, but I can't press charges today. But we will examine your items and get an investigation sanctioned and send your items to the lab for processing. And I would suggest you get some guidance on how to proceed. Perhaps a restraining order."

I speak, "She has a lawyer already working on one and she's on her way here now."

Elle's head whips around to me as she whispers, "Becca." I put my hand on her arm and nod.

Her body should collapse. It should crumble before me, but she puts her head up. "Can I still have DNA evidence on me if it happened earlier today?"

"Yes."

"Well, scrape me, comb me, do whatever you need. And is there a ring print on my face? He wears a signet ring with a dragon on it. I know, cheesy, but he does. Can you see anything like that?"

The doctor steps to me with a flashlight and looks. "There's an impression of something, but the swelling is so severe. I will try to make a plaster impression of it, but you should keep taking pictures of it. And come see me in two days, and we'll look again. I'll measure the wound, it might help. It's possible that as the swelling decreases, there might be a bruise impression of the ring. And I'll swab it to see there's any
transfer into the wound."

"Thank you for believing me."

The police nod at her. "For what it's worth, we believe you, but somehow the evidence is pointing in a different direction."

I speak up, "It's circumstantial until we can prove he was on a plane today. There has to be records of him at an airport. Can't his phone be traced to his location?"

"These are all things that can be done, but for now we'll file the report. If you remember anything else or have any other evidence, please reach out. I am sorry that this happened to you, ma'am."

"Thank you."

Dammit, she sounds defeated again. We have to nail this fucker.

The doctor is examining her cheek again. "Now. I don't want to give you a cat scan. The radiation will be far more damaging to you than whatever slight brain bruise you might have. You're lucid and have no other signs of head trauma. You're fortunate. You do have a mild concussion. You need rest. And lots of it. Tylenol, and avoid alcohol while you recover. It appears he slapped or backhanded you rather than using the full force of a fist. I am going to give you a quick x-ray for your face to make sure there's not a crack in that cheek.

I wince at this, and the doctor puts his hand on my shoulder. "She needs food, water, sleep, and more sleep. Her body, your body needs to heal, and it needs plenty of sleep to do so. And you're also dealing with the aftereffects of shock and trauma. I believe your vomiting was a reaction to the shock. That will sap your system pretty damn quickly. Rest. Support her and force her to rest."

"That I can do."

The doctor takes her chin in his hand. "These will all heal. I heard the tone of your voice. I've heard it before. I need you both to listen. The fault only belongs in one place. Guilt and what-ifs won't do you any good." Her eyes fill. "And tears will only swell you further. So, for tonight, knock it off. I'll be back after the x-ray."

Elle

We're back at the suite. Josh just held me as we rode in silence back to the hotel. I'm wrapping my head around all of this, and I remember there's something else. I continue, "There's more to all of this." I'm more lucid than I've been all day.

Josh leaps up and is instantly red-faced. And then Sam says, "Jesus, Elle. What more can there be to this human piece of fucking garbage? You said he just hit you."

"No, you misunderstand. Yes. Just beat the shit out of me, but I mean there's more to this than just hating LaChappelle/Whittier. It's like he's not just angry at Josh, Sarah, and Will but with all of you. He despises all of your fathers and mothers too. He's wrapped you all up into one massive revenge stew plot. He was saying horrible things he'd like to do to David Gelbert and his dad. He talked about you, Sam, as the ultimate poser prick. He went off on how sanctimonious Tommi and Bax were when they were discussing him. Also, how they didn't even know anything about their winery. He hates you all. And damn does he hate Becca. Then he called Tabi a mouthy bitch."

Sam and Josh kind of shrug and nod at each other.

"Maybe not a bitch but..." Josh jokes as he sits down next to me and hands me a glass of blue Gatorade in a wine glass. Becca is going to come to see me tomorrow afternoon with her law partner Francesca. She does criminal work.

We're all sitting around the fire pit. My fuzzy head keeps trying to pick out details from this morning.

Sam asks, "Like the next-gen crew is in some kind of revenge soup in his warped head? Like we're responsible for his shitty life?"

"Yes, Sam." Then I turn to Josh. "But baby, he really fucking hates you."

Josh nods. "I'm getting that."

"It's more, though. He let loose with information like we should say goodbye to the wineries themselves. That they're pretty and it's a shame that they have to be destroyed. Apparently, Gelberts' will go first, and he said something about imploding buildings. But I don't know what the hell he's talking about. He made it sound like the vines themselves were getting destroyed or something. He quoted things Becca had said about him. How does he know what people say about him?"

Josh takes my hand and then says, "You need to rest your brain. But what we need is information. And between you and me, no one is better at fucking research and recon. Tomorrow. Tonight, you rest like the doctor said."

Sammy pulls her feet onto her chair, "I know this is all horrible, but I kind of want to live here forever."

We all laugh again, and it's so welcome. I get it. I quickly answer, "Only Josh can really afford this."

"It's on your credit card, baby. And there's no wedding ring on this finger yet."

"Shit. I guess I didn't marry you fast enough for your fortune."

It feels good to joke with these people. Proving once again, I don't have to face things alone. A foreign feeling. I'm so grateful they're here. I do feel a bit muted, though. I feel as if I make one wrong move, it could all happen again. Those texts. I keep torturing myself about the texts. Are those the reason he snapped? Or was he like this all along? I feel a bit paralyzed. I start to feel like Dasher's around every corner waiting. He said I could never be too far from him.

Work will make me feel better. Focus on something clinical, not emotional. Time to compartmentalize. Get to the business of unraveling whatever Dasher has done and how to stop him from ever hitting another woman. I have an idea. We need the wineries back and him in prison. I need clear objectives right now. A plan I can control and adapt to, not emotions and failure.

I speak up, "I think I know someone who might be able to help at least get some information and clarification."

Sam says as he gets up to get us all more wine, "Of course you do."

"I have a guy for all occasions." I grin.

Josh gets my drift and says, "I don't have the burner."

Sammy and Sam say at the same time, "Burner?" I relay a brief history to the room. And hope she's not in jail.

"I think I know a way. I'll use email." I grin.

"You're going to email her?" Sammy asks.

"No. I'm going to email me. Kind of. I'll wager this shiner and busted ass lip that she still hacks my email on the reg." Josh runs into the room and comes back with my laptop.

Sam scoffs, "Well, we certainly can't trust anyone

around here. We have no idea who works for Dasher or who he's paid off for information. Or how he knew things."

I continue remembering things. "He said that he can see and hear everything. I thought he said that just to freak me out. But what if he can? I thought you had all that shit swept when Sal was our biggest worry?"

Sam remarks, "Dasher knew our tanks broke and that our Sav Blanc production is going to be limited this year. It was added into our contract. There were only three people with that knowledge, and he brought it up at the closing."

"Or holy shit, that Josh..." I struggle for a moment to put this into a PG place, "may have swatted my butt, playfully, in the tasting room the night of the Member's party. He knew that. He referenced it to make sure I felt like a broken-down whore." Josh winces and then holds me. I put my hand on his heart.

Sam smiles. "Playful?"

"At least it was consensual." Josh winks at me. "And you have seen her ass, right? I cannot be held accountable for what had to happen."

I smile widely at him, remembering that night.

Sammy asks, "Did that pig say anything else?"

"He did. He said that he knew Josh had denied me certain, um, releases, in the barrel room."

"Please let me fucking kill him. No. NO. I want him in fucking jail and getting his ass reamed by a long line of giant hairy felons."

"How did he know that?" Sammy knew the story but was shocked he did.

Josh gives Sam a directive. "Text Dave, Tabi, Bax, and Tommi to see if he said anything he shouldn't have known in their meetings. No. Ask them in person. Can you hit Wednesday night at Starling bar tomorrow? Don't text.

That was the big thing I learned from Mel with the Sal thing."

Sammy smiles. "I don't know who Mel is, but I'm trusting you. We need to figure out what the fuck he's up to and how he has this information."

I turn to Josh and say, "Do you think he knew your Mom was sick and that's why he knew they'd sell? That he manipulated them into meeting me to get all of this done?"

"I do *now*. But we've gotta be smarter at this game than he is. I didn't do too badly in cutthroat corporate politics. I just didn't think it would come in handy in Sonoma."

"This is all my fault." I breathe in and try not to cry.

Josh leaps across the room and scoops me into his arms. "Don't ever think that. He's clearly a monster. He used you, it's not your fault. Elle. Stop that. You can't blame yourself for any of this. I could make a case for how it's my fault. I've been doing it all day but let's not do that."

"No. It's not you."

Sam pipes up, "Let's just blame Lucien."

I remember something else. "And someone named Helmut. He really hates that guy too. Sees him on par with Lucien. Who is he?"

Josh says, "Really? Helmut?"

Sam explains, "Helmut Schroeder. Bax, Tommi, and Ingrid's grandfather, Adrian's dad. But he was kind of a quiet, shrewd businessman. Not really flashy if memory serves."

Josh nods. "Yeah. I know he and Lucien did a bunch of deals together, but I don't remember hearing much about him. We knew him. But he died before Bax's mom."

Sammy moves to Sam's lap. He takes her happily, enveloping her in his arms.

Josh kisses the top of my head, and I sit back down at his computer.

"I want him to go down before he does to other women what he did to me. There. Now we wait." Sammy, Sam, and Josh crowd around the computer to read what I wrote.

"And that's going to work?"

"Yes. Occasionally she puts notes in my email to say hello or fucked-up cat videos in my draft box. She's in and out of my email all the time."

Sam asks, "Josh, is your server secure in Santa Barbara?"

"Fuck. Not even she can get in that thing, and yes, I'm aware of her awe-worthy skills. She aided me in the Sal thing. She freaking stunned Mark."

"Our friend at the FBI," Sam adds for Sammy's benefit

"I'm going to direct her there so we can communicate. If Asher knows things, he might have access to my email or texts. I'll write one that appears that I'm simply recommending someone to you And she'll read it." Everyone looks alarmed, but I simply shrug. I've come to terms with the fact that she reads everything I write. I'm not all that exciting.

TO: JLLCW@magnuspartner.com

CC: NParker@parkerandco.com, EParker@lcww.com

SUBJ: Melissa's unique skills and employment URGENT

Josh,

I'd like you to revisit the idea of hiring Melissa Grandy for that position you have open at Magnus. I believe her extraordinary skills are a perfect fit, unlike her design toolbox, her other talents will be in high demand. I'll have her get in touch with you when I hear from her. It should be in the next day or two. I recom-

*mend a face-to-face meeting as soon as it's convenient for
all parties.*
   -Noelle

"You can't sign it Noelle. That would be a red flag to
Dasher." Sam points it out, and I agree. I change it and push
send.

Excitedly, I ask Josh, "Can I have your phone? I want to
pull up your Magnus email."

"Why?" Sammy looks totally confused.

"If she's as good as I think she is, she'll probably pull the
email from your server before anyone notices."

"I told you. That shit is locked down."

"She's hacked the SEC and Nasdaq for fun. Trust me.
She told me this when I fired her. Such a long story."

And it appears in his email box. It's one in the morning
after an insanely long day, and I pour a huge glass of
Gatorade. Sam and Sammy call down for food. The advan-
tage of renting this baller suite is that they're at our beck
and call. Sammy was right about the arnica gel. My arms
seem less red and swollen and moving towards bruising.
The swelling has gone down around my eye as well, and the
pain is subsiding a bit. We keep icing. It has to be worse for
them since I'm not looking at it. I'm snuggled into Josh with
the worst of my bruises facing him, Sammy's magical anti-
inflammatory concoction working as my face begins to look
more like my face.

"Holy shit. You can see the dragon."

I pose for a photoshoot that might get the job done but
who knows. He's slippery, and I need to nail his ass some
other way. I'll go see the doctor tomorrow, but I send the
pictures to the police detectives immediately, asking if
there's anything else I need to document. We email all the

photos and police reports to Francesca from Josh's work email instead of mine.

I've also discovered that Asher was a judge last year at the Vintage Indiana Wine Festival in Indianapolis. He never posted any pictures from it. Maybe if the picture of me is from March then perhaps the picture of him at the festival is a year old. Sammy emailed them under the guise of the winery getting involved and asked about the judging panel for the past five years. Then we can check the other names in the picture. She also asked for a broad spectrum of images from the event for the past two years. They're putting all the information together to send to Sammy tomorrow.

"We need to get to him in a way he doesn't know is coming. I need information, and it's killing me. I've reread all the winery sales contracts, and there's no strange language I can pick up. Other than the fucked-up clause about us having to maintain a profit, I can't come up with anything strange."

Sam offers up, "Becca is still scouring all the contracts. I only hope she figures something out."

"I need her to figure out what's similar and what's different in each one. We were all under the impression that we'd maintain control of the vineyard activities, and so far, we are. Well, except LaChappelle."

I helped design the deal. I start running the contracts through my head as I understand them. The deals were all complicated in their own way. LaChappelles' land, name, juice, and vines were sold, since Sarah and Will were completely stepping away from the business.

The others were supposed to maintain management, and winemaking while the Vino Groupies take on the pricier and riskier tasks of marketing, distribution, and property taxes. The families will continue to live on the land and work it for generations to come in a partnership with the Vino Groupies. As long as the vineyards produce wine, the families remain in their homes and work the land as usual.

They essentially sold the labels and land but will maintain a piece of the profits in the future. I believe they mostly ended up with a thirty-seventy split of the profits after operating costs. All the five Sonoma wineries will be bundled as a collection and distributed widely. The influx of capital to widen distribution will make sure the wineries remain operating and will be more profitable in the long run. It's a good deal for the smaller wineries like Langerford and Stafýli to be bundled in with the larger production wineries like LC/W, Schroeder, and Gelbert. It's actually good for all of them.

I get up and walk around a bit, stretching. They all settle onto the couch, and I sit back down at the dining table and check Josh's phone. The email is still sitting on his server. Come on, this has to work.

Sam says from the lush comfy blue velvet couch, "How long are we going to make this command central? I might need some pajamas."

Sammy tackles him. "Since when do you wear pajamas?"

"Since we're holed up in luxury with roommates."

"That's up to Elle."

"I'd like to stay at least another day or so. I'd like the bruising to go down, so there aren't so many alarm bells at home."

Josh crosses to me and pulls me onto his lap. He rubs my ass a bit. I moan lightly. He kisses my head. "Don't start, Cosmo. You're bruised."

I turn to him and whisper in his ear something I need, "I

93

need you to make me yours again. I need your hands on me to erase his." I do think I actually need that. I have yet to process, and I know that.

"Soon, Cosmo. Soon." He growls at me, and it feels more like us. The connection both emotional and sexual finally bubbling back up. I don't know if it will stay.

He kisses my forehead and is looking down at the phone. "We can stay as long as you want." Then he snatches it up and madly scrolls. "It's gone. Disappeared. Not opened or read. Just gone."

My phone rings and I pick it up on the first ring. "Melissa!"

"You called, you mad, beautiful perfectionist?"

"Yes, I did, my favorite creeper. I need..."

She interrupts me quickly. "No. No. No. May I ping?"

"Of course. Thanks for asking."

"I already did. I was asking to be polite. I'll see you around eleven. I usually sleep later, but I'll get up early for you."

"You're here? You're close?"

"Perhaps. Don't bother emailing Reggie anymore, I'll handle it. Order me pancakes with chocolate chips and a shit ton of whip cream. And everybody goes to the airport."

"Done." And she hangs up. I turn to my weary compatriots. "Okay. We're on. But first, nobody emails anyone and put your phones on airplane mode."

"Why?" Sam asks.

"I don't know, but she told us not to bother with emailing Reggie. He's a guy that Evan and I fired for stealing. And we discovered it when he hacked into our email. I'm guessing it was code for don't do it. Evan and I really do have shitty cybersecurity. Now we sleep."

Sam picks up his phone. "Should I call the others? Are they part of this?"

Josh speaks up, "No cellphones till Mel. We're all part of this but first, let's figure out what *this* is. She might be paranoid and crazy but give her the benefit of the doubt. You guys enjoy the food and fire. We'll take the back bedroom."

Josh drags my hand and pulls me to the bedroom. I lay down, depleted of everything and sore all over. Even in parts of my body that had nothing to do with the attack. Josh strips to his boxers and wraps himself around me in our now familiar way.

He kisses my head and whispers, "How are you doing?"

"I don't know."

"I get that. We'll find a way through this. It's not your fault. I love you so much. Baby. I'm so sorry this fucking happened."

"My brain understands that, but it's going to take a minute for me to believe it. I love you too. But this isn't your fault either."

"Don't ever fucking hide from me again. Don't hide a thing. There is nothing on this earth that would ever make me change my feelings. You are always my priority, know that."

"I'm sorry. I didn't know what to do."

"The words he spat at you mean nothing. You know, that, right? He's broken and bitter. He wants power any way he can get it. He tried to make you feel less than. Don't give him the satisfaction."

"Promise me we'll get him."

"I swear to you, he'll never get near you again. You go nowhere without one of us with you right now. Soon, you're going to meet Lou."

"Who's Lou?"

"Ask Sam in the morning."

"Was he your Sal protection guy at Langerfords?"

"See, you're so smart. How can we not fucking nail this piece of shit? You're safe now, and you'll stay that way. He'll never get close enough to touch you again. Or I'll fucking kill him. And that's not a euphemism. I will kill him."

"I know you would. And now you know why I hid. I didn't want you to get yourself into trouble defending me. I love you so desperately."

"You're mine."

"And you're mine."

A year ago, I went to sleep alone every night. I prayed to be heard and seen. I wanted a life that made me happy. I thought it would be my business that would bring me joy and a fulfilled life. I prayed for something to happen that would turn my business into my ultimate dream. And now a year later, I don't ever want another client meeting. Asher may have tried to take my pride and dignity today, but no matter what he tries to take from me, it will never equal what he inadvertently gave to me. The scales will always tip towards happiness because of him. He gave me a family, friends, community, love, purpose, and direction. He showed me a path where I could surrender being such a control freak and submit. Asher is ultimately responsible for my blissful happiness. And there's nothing he can do to diminish that. I know all of this intellectually.

I hate that all these things are linked. But I also can't stop remembering his contorted face when I touched him. I hear the sound of his hand making contact with my face. I still taste the blood hitting my tongue despite the Gatorade and brushing my teeth. I can't get his powdery smell out of my nose. Even Josh's smell has diminished in its haunting wake. I need Dasher to fade. I need all of this to fade.

"Settle your head, Cosmo. There's plenty of time for your worries tomorrow. Sleep." He knows me so well. "I can feel it coming off you in waves. Let it go. Or I'll go get those pills the doctor gave to us."

"I'll sleep." I turn over to Josh, and he kisses me as lightly and sweetly as possible. "Please just hold me."

"Always. Goodnight. Until tomorrow, Cosmo." I drift off before he finishes taking me into his arms.

Josh

I force Sam to get up and go to the gym with me. He walks casually on the treadmill while I pound out ten miles. Then I do several rounds with the heavy bag followed by as many sit-ups and pull-ups as I can fucking do until I'm able to handle my rage. Rage and sexual frustration. I will be chaste for her as long as she needs. I will never push her or rush her back into my bed, but I don't have to like it. I blame fucking Dasher. I feel a little better after smacking the shit out of something. My knuckles are wrecked.

When we get back upstairs, the girls are up and sipping coffee. An insane amount of food is laid out on the table. They present it like they cooked it instead of paying a fucking fortune for it. I'm going to say our vacation plans for the year are shot since we're blowing it all on this makeshift room service buffet. Elle's face looks better and worse. She's more colorful, the swelling is down, and she's starting to look a little more like her again. But only a little. She's sporting a bit of blood spot in her right eye. It rips me up inside.

I head to the shower, and she follows. I'm standing in front of her, and despite her battered face, I find myself hard as hell. She comes into the shower. I grab her to me, but she turns towards the water and backs into me. And now my erection is jamming into her back.

"I can't. I'm sorry. I just wanted to be close to you." She tears up, and the rage returns.

I say as she turns towards me, "Baby. No. Oh my god, no. I can't help my rootstock. Isn't that what you secretly call my dick? I can't help that it still finds you desirable no matter what. You're still you. I don't want to do anything about it. I don't want anything from you, Cosmo. Shh. No." I hold her close and kiss her head. And now my hard dick is pushing into her stomach. I try and think about anything else, and the thought of killing Dasher helps, and it begins to go down.

"I don't know when," she ekes out.

"We have forever. I'm not going anywhere. There's no timeline on this. I don't expect anything. Take that out of your head and off your plate. You have enough to deal with. We will work through all of this, but for now, do not think I'm expecting anything. Do not think you have to do anything about it until you're ready. I'll wait for as long as it takes. No guilt."

She turns around in the shower and the water runs over her face. Since I've been here, she had several showers. I know she already had one today, but she's scrubbing herself down again. I know she's trying to get him off her. She's scrubbing her delicate skin red. She called a therapist this morning. She emailed her New York shrink to get the name of someone out here last night, and they already responded to her. The power of Elle.

"Did Sam tell you about rootstock?"

"Tommi and Tabi. Apparently, you had one too many tequilas at Starling one night."

"Shit. I know where their loyalty lies now."

I wrap my arms around her, take the washcloth, and wash her gently, not the harsh scrubbing she was doing before. My dick is a bit more under control now. She turns and kisses me lightly because of the bruising. She licks my lips with her pink and perfect tongue. And now it's not under control at all. My cock desperately wants to be inside of her right now, but I need her to set the pace. I need to feel connected to the most sacred and safe place I know. And Christ, it hurts. She looks down and smiles.

"It is a really beautiful thing to behold." She grabs it, and I moan. I'm going to come right on her if she moves her hand at all.

"Babe, I won't be able to stop myself if you keep a hold. I'm giving you as much time and space as you need, but for me to do that, I'm going to need you to let go. I don't want you to do anything you don't want. Why don't you grab a towel and I'll meet you back in the living room area?" She moves her hand up and down the shaft, and I groan. "Elle. Please. I'm begging you to step away." She smiles her little smile and kisses me while putting conditioner on her hand and returning to my throbbing cock, my orgasm building so quickly as I watch her.

She rubs up and down faster, and I'm holding her shoulders, biting my lip.

"Step away now." I roar. "Oh god. I'm going to finish and come."

"On me."

"What?!"

"I need to be marked by you again. Reclaim my skin." I lean back and let her jack me off. I release all over her with a mighty growl, and she rubs her stomach with my ropes of cum. My fucking Hellcat is still in there somewhere.

I turn her towards the water and rinse her off, kissing her neck from behind.

Despite what I want to do to her, I put shampoo in my hand and apply it to her head. As I wash her hair, I'm reminded of our first night. The night she shifted my entire world. The night I became hers without her knowing. After I rinse the conditioner from her hair, we kiss. Our lips are steamy from the shower. Because of the swelling, there's no hard pressing or tongues. Simply light affirmations of our love. Then we hear a commotion in the living room, and I shut off the water.

We dress quickly and go out to meet Melissa. She pulls on new Ritz Carlton cozy pants and a shirt. I yank on my suit pants and the t-shirt I worked out in. The one I bought downstairs emblazoned with Ritz Carlton. We're going to need clothes.

"Fuck, Noelle or is it Elle now? I like Elle. Noelle was a bit high strung. Jesus H. Christ. You look fucking terrible. I love it! How the hell have you been?" She crosses the room briskly and boldly then pulls her into a strangely intimate hug. Elle clutches on to her.

She backs away from Melissa. "Not so perfect, huh?" She shrugs.

"Nah. Asher? That asshole with the fake name? He put up some bullshit about you on Insta."

She heads over to the table and pulls a pancake off a plate, licking the whipped cream off of it. Then she speaks again with her mouth full. "I went digging. He's a dirtbag, babe. And damn, you're Josh. You *are* fucking hot. Shit. I got no interest in your rootstock, but damn you are all man." My eyebrows raise as she exclaims Elle's nickname for my cock. Elle cringes. "She told Evan about it in an email." I shrug. Mel hugs me as if I'm a long-lost brother. Then she grabs my hand and shakes it hard. I pat her on the back and then she abruptly turns back to Elle. "And damn man, that Asher hates his fucking guts the most. He googles you constantly. He's had a news alert on you for the last ten years."

As she shakes Sammy's hands, she gets gobs of whipped cream all over her fingers too. After shoving a pancake in her mouth, there's whipped cream everywhere.

I want to make sure Melissa knows there's no limit on what I need from her. "Nice to meet you in person. I'm grateful. And of course, my wallet is open to you. Do you have information we don't have?"

"Elle, lick Josh's fingers for him." She rolls her eyes, and I grab a napkin to wipe the whipped cream off them. "Buckle up, bitches. There's a ton of shit you don't know. Might need money later on, but this part is all on the house. It's for this one here with the bashed-in face. Nobody gets away with that shit while I'm watching. Did you guys know that she's one of the only people to ever believe in me? I got this, and I know all about all of you." She winks. It's terrifying how casually she could ruin our lives with a keystroke.

Elle

I sit down at the table with her. "Melissa." In an odd way, I've always found an odd comfort that she's been lurking . She's become a friend and a confidant simply by invading my privacy.

"Mel." I smile at the chocolate stain she's already acquired on her faded vintage Lilith Fair t-shirt.

I look her straight in the eye and rest my hand on her arm. "Okay, Mel. We have a ton for you to do. There's a major winery thing, but my priority is to find a flight manifest that proves Asher was in San Fran at one o'clock yesterday. He claimed—"

She interrupts, "The Indiana alibi?"

"You know?" Sam yells from across the room.

"Police report." She turns to the room and points to Josh. "He knows how good I am. Now I can find it. I know you've got bank. Here's the thing, if it's tech, there's nothing I can't do. But as we go along, I'm going to need complete trust. I can screw you over in a heartbeat, but you can give me up to the FCC as well. This is a two-way street of utter fucking trust. We're all going down together or not at all. And you all need to know there's not much about the four of you I don't know right now. If it's in a text, an email, a phone call, or online, I've already seen it and read the highlights over the past twelve hours. Well, Elle, you know."

"I had a hunch. I'm just boring. So why do you keep reading my email?"

"There's something about you that I've always liked. I wanted to see if you'd crack open and become the interesting person, I thought you were. And you did. Your life is like my favorite binge show. I wait for weeks and then read and listen to it all at once. He's in Santa Barbara, he's back. He loves you; you don't love him. You jump him in the parking lot, wish I could have seen that one. And then you love him. It's a fabulous soap opera but with real sex. I mean those texts from the hospital a while back, those were good. I'm a lesbian, and I thought they were hot."

Elle asks sheepishly, "How did you know about the parking lot?"

"Samantha's text to Sam."

I instantly flush red with embarrassment.

Josh laughs loudly. "Jesus Christ."

Sam walks over, shakes Mel's hand. She throws her arm around Sam's shoulders and addresses the room. "But if you think you're sexting is filthy, you ain't got nothing on this teddy bear muthafucker. You are not what I pictured there, Sam. I did a double-take when I pulled up your DMV pic after I saw your receipt from that little trip to the hardware and then a fabric store. Pulleys, rope and silk? Damn, man. A construction project is a true commitment to kink."

Sam shrugs at us, and Sammy buries her head on the couch. I can't even look at them. Oh my. And Sammy won't look at me, but I'm going to need to know what he built to fuck her. Or does she do something to him with silk? Oh my. This is beyond me.

Mel continues, "Nah, Samantha, don't hide. You're lucky you got a man that will do those things to you and make you feel the way he does. He worships you. And I love that y'all are a switch. He tells Josh all the time how perfect you are. You fit together. And dude you're one lucky mofo that she digs all your oddball shit."

Sammy groans. "Please stop. I'm going to die." I had no idea she was that kinky. And what the hell is a 'switch'? I feel so vanilla and I just did some pretty intense stuff in the shower.

Mel turns back to Sam. "I need one more thing."

Josh answers, "Anything."

"I need Winnie the Pooh to teach me whatever he did to her clit last week that she's still talking about. I got mad skills, but I'm not sure I've ever made a woman bark." Sammy buries her face in a pillow, and my mouth goes agape.

Sam puts his hands on his hips and strikes a pose like Superman. "I'm king of the clitoris!"

"I like this guy. He owns his shit."

Sam turns to Mel and says, "These mad skills you're talking about, who knows a clit better than you, right? How about we grab some beers and exchange labial information. I'm always up for something new."

Mel answers, "I've gathered."

Josh looks to Sam. "You holding out on me?"

Sam raises his eyebrows in a wicked fashion. He's a sex god. Who knew? I mean I'd heard stories from Sammy, but apparently, she's holding back.

I am uncomfortable where this is going and pull it back, "Let's go ahead and eat breakfast."

Mel shoves another pancake in her mouth and talks with her mouth full. "Hey blondie, give me your phone, laptop, etc. The rest of you ante up too. Give me the devices. And as of today, no one's password has their address, relative, pet's name, or your first love's birthday. Think of your locker combination from high school and the teacher you hated. No easy pay apps, no cash apps, and no stored passwords on Google. Sammy, no Starbucks prepay apps. No one banks online anymore. Old school deposits and whatnot for the moment. That's some weak shit, and I think we're playing with someone who thinks they're on my level."

They all sit there stunned, but I get up immediately to grab my things and turn them over. Josh reluctantly hands over his phone. "What are you talking about?"

"Your server in Santa Barbara is awesome. Super hard to hack. That's good. And I couldn't find any trace of someone backing out and covering their tracks. And no one will find me."

"But you pulled the email off it."

"I'm better. We can use that server to keep most of the shit at bay. Josh, hook up anyone and everyone who's involved in this shit with an email address I can route through your server. And it seems as if this asshole is fixated on your farm, but there are others involved. You've all been monitored for quite a while. We're also going to go to burners for a bit. Which one of you pissed off the mob boss again?"

Josh drops a dish in the kitchenette. Mel continues, "Kidding. He's not pissed anymore, but we might need him. Fucking funny man. You're funny how jumpy you can get. Nah. That Sal fucker is totally in line and doing what you told him and what he promised. He just got backed up into some heavy shit that his nephew screwed up. He was just bailing him out. And making sure his sister and her family were safe. The nephew is super fucked up. He's shipped him off to Philly and far away from LA. He's under lock and key. The nephew did a power grab without authorization. But he's in, like, mob jail, I guess. Sal got bitten, so he bit back at you. It got bloody but Mark's still got that whole situation on lock."

"Mark?" I play dumb, knowing I'm not supposed to know about Mark and the FBI. Mel rolls her eyes and laughs hysterically at me.

Again, all of our jaws drop. Mel continues, "Law of the streets. They send one of our guys to the hospital, we send one to the morgue."

Sam puts his head up. "That's *The Untouchables*. And you are talking metaphorically, right? I mean, we're vintners. We're glorified farmers who make hooch."

"Same diff. And Josh is only recently a vintner." We all bust up laughing.

I sit back with my coffee, smiling as this all unfolds. I'm not sure why Mel is on our side, but there might be a way out of this and to nail his ass. "Mel. Can you get into Dasher's computer?"

A couple of keystrokes and she turns my laptop towards me, and I see it's a desktop, but it's not mine. It's a picture of Dasher's mom. Of course, he has daddy and mommy issues. Psycho.

Josh

It's been a week, and our electronics have been scrubbed and deemed safe by Mel. Sam and Sammy head back to Sonoma to work. I should get back, but Elle wants an extra appointment today and then head back to the hospital and see if they can see the ring insignia more clearly. She's obsessing on details, but the control is something she's craving right now. I see subtle shifts in her, but I think it's just her grasping to get back to normal.

I do need to tell my parents what's happened and why Tabi Aganos and Poppy Gelbert are handling things at the winery right now. At different times, we've all filled every role at all five of the wineries. The women are capable of anything and Poppy's mom, Tina, is one of my mom's best friends. She's been managing the tasting room for Sammy and Elle. They think we're all taking a staycation to be together. Like a post-engagement trip.

Hopefully, Mel can figure out what's going on so we can jump on top of it. Sam's going to guys' night tonight and is going to tell them what happened to Elle, with her blessing. We've also handwritten some warnings for them about their devices. Sam didn't get to them last week. I'm glad he stayed here for us.

I'm going to LA at the end of this week to meet with Sal. Elle's coming with me now that they're best of friends. He needs to know that she's ok. He requested she come along. We might just need his help. He reached out yesterday to see if Elle was okay and offered to take care of Dasher. I told him to stand down for now.

I need Sal to stay calm. I'm excellent at strategy, and as much as I want to bury Asher in the dirt, we can't move on him until we know the entire picture. We'll protect her from him, but we need the full spectrum of what we got ourselves into. And when we get our wineries back, it will take a hundred men as large as Lou to pull me back from beating Asher to fucking death.

I call my parents. They're locked away in a controlled clinical trial for now. They need to know what's happening. I don't know how to tell them not to text or use their email without an alarm. I call the hospital room on a burner, and I'm talking to my dad on a landline.

"Son. All is well. Your mom has charmed everyone here and keeps telling me to go away and get back to the winery. Going nowhere without her. Should be a day or two."

"That's amazing news, Dad."

"Figured out how to get our legacy back yet?"

"You're funny, Dad."

"What's up? You sound concerned. Did you sign a contract that gives away a one-hundred-and-forty-eight-year-old property and a profitable business?"

"Glad to hear you're moving on."

"I just feel so stupid. I could throttle that Dasher."

I sigh and don't say anything as I try to calm myself down again. "Dad. I can't explain everything right now, but

I need you and Mom not to text or email anything about Dasher or the wineries that would reveal that we're trying to get them back."

"I'm confused, son."

"There's a lot at play right now. Just promise me. I need you to trust me. I need you..." And then my guilt overtakes me again. My voice cracks as I speak to my dad, "I couldn't protect her. I can't fix what happened. I don't know what to do. I don't know what to do for her or how I'll get past this without doing something terrible." I squeeze out the sudden tears with my thumb and forefinger and try to collect myself.

In an alarmed and quickened tone, he asks, "Is Elle alright?'

"She will be, Dad. Asher attacked her." My new ever-present knot in my stomach tightens up again.

"What the fuck are you talking about?"

"He tried to..."

"Tried to what? Speak, plainly, son. Do you need me? What does she need? Tell me he's locked up."

"No, he's not. I got her, but she doesn't want to see people right now. We're at a hotel downtown. He beat the shit out of her, Dad. The bastard hurt her and tried to rape her. He's spent his lifetime perfecting duplicity, and he's turned it on her. Has an alibi and everything."

I tell my dad the horrible details as I know them.

"Hell yeah, our girl stabbed him?"

"My Hellcat did stab him."

"I'll head home tonight. I can cover things, and Tina can bring your mom home tomorrow. I have to tell her."

I begin to cry silently. I've only ever cried twice before in my adult life that I remember. It was when that old bastard died and recently with my mom's revelation. Just a few tears and I need to be done with this. She's not dead. I still have her.

After a minute or so of my dad just being there for me, he says, "Son."

"Yes?"

"She's stronger than you think."

"I only hope that I am."

"You are. You are both stronger together, and no one can pull you apart. I love you, my son. I see your beautiful soul, and so does she."

I full-on break down and let my father be the one to hold me up for a moment.

Elle

They took excellent pictures of my cheek and lip now that some of the swelling has gone down and you can, in fact, see the dragon. They also swabbed it for metal again. All of this is added to my police report and the restraining order petition. The physical damage is apparently healing miraculously after eight days. The emotional component will take a while.

This is the first time I've been alone since Sam and Sammy showed up at the hotel. Sarah and Will are at the winery, so we don't have to be. Evan started the paperwork to take over my company. I just want to maintain the building in my name, but as for the business, I don't want any part of it. He asked me to stay on as a consultant, and I will, as a figurehead for the clients. I'll be there for him no matter what he needs. He's been the only constant in my life since my parents. Evan is my family. But that business brought Asher into my life, and I can't think about it right now. I need to push forward and dive into my work here.

I've never really been a nervous person, but right now I can't stop fidgeting. I feel terrified and exposed, sitting here outside. He might be anywhere and everywhere. His Instagram has him back from Indiana. If he was ever there. He could be watching me. He could have figured out that I'm hiding out at the Ritz. I've not heard from him. I know the detectives have questioned him.

Sitting here, I can barely breathe as I wait for my therapist to show up. If I were inside, I'd be better. He could see me. And then I don't know what he'd do. He's gotta be pissed off, and he hit me when he was happy. He liked that I was bleeding. I start shaking. That's it, I'm going to go back to the hotel. Then I see a man reading a paper. Who does that in this day and age? No phone, an actual newspaper. He's a huge beefy muscular and tall man.

"Hey."

He looks up at me. "What can I do for you?"

"Josh or Sal?"

"Both."

I exhale. My hands stop shaking. "Thank fucking god."

"They both said you were a ballbuster and if you found me to admit it. I'm Lou."

"Lou! You work at Langerford, right?"

"Yes, sort of, ma'am."

"Lovely to meet you. You're going to make sure while I'm inside that he's not near me."

"No one will get near you, ma'am."

"Elle."

"No one will get near you, Elle." He nods.

"I'll see you in an hour, Lou."

He winks at me as my therapist arrives. I head upstairs to see if I can figure out why I'm so scared. I've lived on the other side of the world, surrounded by all sorts of scary stuff. I've never backed down from a challenge, but this cock weasel has me terrified to stand on the street alone.

* * *

Lou drives me back to the hotel, and I sink down in the safety of the car. I pull on my new giant pair of Gucci sunglasses, a present from my love, and then repeat my new mantra over and over. "I'm strong, and only I have power over me. I'm strong, and only I have power over me. I'm strong, and only I have power over me."

Josh

Tonight, I've invited The Five Families, as Mel has taken to calling us, to gather here at the hotel. She's been through all our computers and phones. The wineries were swept for bugs and cameras. We all had them. Mel's advice was to leave them for now so as not to alert him that we're on to him. The caves and admin buildings all contained serious hardware installed by a professional. Mel hired a friend to go in and pretend he was an actual exterminator to map all the planted bugs while talking about roaches and mice.

The Schroeders think we're nuts, but Baxter came down from Sacramento to be here anyway. My dad and I decided that it should just be my generation in the room until we get the low down. His generation has been meeting weekly to discuss everything and nothing at all. They're coming up with schemes on their own. And my dad will share all the information Mel has obtained with them at Creekside Cafe over Irish Coffee.

There's no digital footprint of this meeting, all invites were hand-delivered. It all sounds like Sal's business, not mine. I needed a consult in hiding things in plain sight. He was gracious, and I'm grateful to him for wanting to help with security. It seems that he's been keeping a bit of an open channel with Poppy, and she keeps talking him off the ledge. Sal desperately wants Dasher to have an unfortunate accident. But we need Dasher to remain the winery steward for now. We need to keep the devil we know for a bit longer so we can find out more about how Vino Groupies operate.

It's been almost two weeks since Dasher attacked my Elle. Her face is still green, blue, and purple, but the cuts are almost healed, and the police promise they're building a case. A DNA order has been approved. Francesca put a substantial restraining order together for Elle, and she had to see him in court the other day to file it. It went uncontested. Which was creepy. He just stared, smiling at her. Lou sat right behind him, looking menacing. I love that guy. We got him a room just down the hall from us here at the Ritz. He's loving room service instead of take-out burgers in his car while on surveillance.

Everyone is milling around the room, some looking at Elle's face from afar and others like Poppy go right up and touch it. Elle's beaming. It's the happiest I've seen her in weeks. I'd like to take credit, but she's a social animal and needs people around her. She's put together a fabulous spread and even created a signature cocktail, The Comeuppance. It's sweet and purple. It's disgusting, but it gave her something to do.

I quiet everyone. "Okay. Everybody got a drink? There will be shots later for anyone who needs. Thanks for coming. We're going to start with some of the information that Mel has found." I look over, and Mel's hitting on Tommi. Good taste, but wrong timing. "Mel! Can we get started?"

"Why didn't you tell me there'd be a hot dyke here?"

Tommi blushes and Mel touches her cheek. Tommi falls hard and fast. Mel should be careful. Melissa steps to the front of the room and addresses my childhood collective, my bros, my friends, my peers, my roots, and my One Perfect Thing.

"I'm Mel. First off, I promise not to tell anyone's secrets. That's not what I was doing with your shit. Thanks for cooperating. I was only looking in places to see who else was looking." She's spent the last four days up in Sonoma combing the wineries after some strange paperwork she found on Dasher's computer.

Jims Langerford, who is now officially Evan's boyfriend, pipes up from the back, "And?"

"Well, pretty boy, you've all been hacked. It looks like for the better part of the last eight years. Some of your wineries are bugged, and others have cameras. Also, all of your laptops have reverse camera access. He's been watching everything you do. And I mean everything there, David Gelbert. Learn to cover the camera if you're going to use the computer for companionship."

David screams, "Fucker."

Tabi screams from the back, "We need to find David a woman." Everyone laughs.

I tell them what I've decided to do. "I'm keeping all that shit running because I don't want to alarm him that we know. It was how Dasher got all his intel to feed to the Vino Groupies to get this elaborate revenge shit done. We need to work on this two-pronged. We need to pursue the assault charges as well as figure out how to get our vines back. But we can't do them one at a time, or it will inform the other. We launch both plans at the same time."

Everyone turns to Elle, and she waves them on like she's

totally cool with this. Poppy and Sam take her hands. Elle's skin instantly goes flush red with the attention.

Becca raises her hand. "Hello. I'm Rebecca Gelbert and full transparency, I'm an attorney, so I don't know if what you're going to say is legal or not, but I don't want to be a part of this if it's going to—"

Mel interrupts her, "No shit, Becca. You think I don't know how much you vetted your boyfriend? Or how you secretly track him sometimes. I'm not trying to freak you out. Don't waste my time with intros. I know you all. Except for the babe over there. That was a surprise. How did I not see Tommi coming? I knew there was an Alicia in the mix, but did not know she was a smoking hot dyke who goes by Tommi. Takes a hell of a lot to surprise me. Nice job there, hotness." She raises an eyebrow at Tommi, who grins back. Tommi is her nickname given to her by her late mother. It's short for Tomboy.

Sammy gets us back on topic by saying, "Becca, I get it. We're in a gray area. You can leave, and your brother can give you the broad strokes."

"I'd feel better about that."

But Sam explains to her, "I know you're already knee-deep in this shit, but there are some legally obtained things you should know that will help you. Let's skip the winery surveillance shit, okay? Then we can move on with the plans to take him down for what he's done."

Becca's cousin, Poppy, pipes up, "Like kicking the shit out of one of our own."

There's a chorus of fuck yeahs, and Elle tears up a bit. I smile at her, and her face lights up. She has an army at her formerly solo back. And so do I. I may have chosen my solo path, but I haven't felt that sense of family in a very long time either.

I quickly hit the main point. "At this point, most of you know that the Vino Groupies wanted nothing more than juice for box wine. LaChappelle and Schroeders' second labels, Chapel and Bellamy's Ghost could have taken care of their juice issue from their joint Lodi vineyards. The rest of you didn't need to be involved. But the juice is a Trojan horse to get the land. That's what they were after all along."

Tabi pipes up, "What the shit are you talking about? They don't want the vines? Or for us to produce wine?"

Mel takes the helm. "They require that you produce wine for the next year. They'll eat up all your profits while they bide their time for building permits, rezoning, and to get your historical status stripped. The Vino Groupies are land developers, not wine guys. Dasher convinced them to create a shell company with the appearance of being wine distributors to get your properties."

"Fuck them. We won't produce," Tommi says.

Becca stands and reads from the contract in her hand. "'All winery and related business must be conducted in good faith and work to full earning capacity while in stewardship for one year from contract signing to the end of the next harvest. Harvest will be concluded on the last day of extraction from the final winery in the association of the Vino Groupies.' If we don't produce, they take everything anyway. Whether it's winery related or not. Everything our families have in savings or private funds, second homes, and personal holdings would all be gone for breach of contract."

Poppy steps to the front of the room. "How do you know this?"

"Melissa found it all."

Mel had me print out a report like she's fucking Robert Mueller, without the redactions. We even fought because she wanted graphics, a curated cover, and full color bound. Elle passes out the information.

Mel continues, "After the last day of next year's harvest, they plan to start the demolition of Gelbert Family Winery, then LC/W."

David says in a terse tone looking at the booklet, "Our winery. Our vineyards are becoming fucking condos?"

I offer up, "High-end retirement condos, but yes. Condos promising the baby boomers and aging Gen X an immersive wine country experience, apparently without any wine. The surviving vines will become landscaping."

"Fuck me."

I continue, "Lucien's hill, my home, and the one-hundred-and-forty-eight-year-old vines, or at least their roots, will become a twelve-unit grotesque McMansion community called The Chapel."

Tabi yells, "Hey Schroeders, what you got? Stafýli Cellars are going to be a strip mall. Dad's going to die. Goldie will be elated, she loves Target. Although TJ Maxx would send her over the edge."

The entire room breaks up. Tabi's always been one of the boldest and funniest women we've ever known. She was my senior prom date and my first, up in her dad's vehicle storage barn.

Baxter straightens himself up and rolls his eyes at Tabi. She's always given him a hard time about his proper manner. In return, he always gave her a hard time about being too loud and brash. We all witnessed every iteration of Tabi growing up. From her punk phase to her garage band to her militant feminist moment. She's tried on everything but has always been just Tabi.

Bax says, "Well, it seems that our elaborate stonework will stand. We're becoming a country club. My childhood bedroom will be the showers of the clubhouse. And our award-winning cabernet blocks will become the back nine."

Everyone laughs hard, and Tommi adds, "Don't forget, brother, we're also going to be a six-room boutique hotel for douchebags."

"Offices, with live workspaces and a special feature retail outlet. Can anyone say LA Fitness?" Sam holds up his prospectus with the plans to ruin Langerford. Everyone laughs. And then they don't. Silence settles over us as the reality of our lives genuinely being dismantled sits down in our souls.

Becca raises her hand again. "Impenetrable ordinances in Sonoma county state that this kind of construction can't be done. And you can't have strip malls and chain franchises within the city limits. That's why we all had to haul our asses to the edge of Boyes Hot Springs to get Taco Bell in high school."

I try to explain what I've learned. "There's a previously unexplored loophole that no doubt Dasher knew about when he approached them. If they own land that's express purpose is for wine and viticulture, and the main profit comes from grapes, they can use the land for anything they want. It's basically why we're allowed to sell commercial merchandise. As long as the largest profit on their ledger is from wine production, they're untouchable."

Jims says, "Then how the fuck can they get rid of all of our grapes then?"

Elle answers from the back. "Chapel and Bellamy's Ghost." My grandfather and Helmut Schroeder bought massive pieces of land in Lodi in the early '90s. It's proven very lucrative for both families and a partnership that remains intact today between the two wineries.

Elle explains further. She did this piece of the research

at the library using their computers over the past couple of days. "They won't destroy the high-yield Lodi vineyards and won't be concerned with stems and seeds. They'll squeeze it all and not sell a drop of juice to anyone else. They can cut the production corners to produce a massive amount of box wine with a large-scale marketing launch. No glass, no labels, fewer taxes. They go to market at a higher price point, citing the history and prestige of your wineries as the justification. They could feasibly capture the market and make a shit ton of money. Just a few dollars more a box will do it. It will be more than enough to use the land any way they please. They only need next year's harvest to make all of this happen. And then none of your grapes will matter except Lodi."

David clarifies, "So if the juice box profits are large enough, they can bulldoze our wineries. Theoretically, they don't have to do anything with the land. And their only obstacles are the zoning commissions. Which is why some of us are strip malls, and some of us will end up residence, right?"

Elle pipes back up. "Yes. And all of your varietals won't matter because no one will know what a Cabernet should taste like after people swill the new unfinished and unre-fined thin-ass Chapel and B's Ghost. And all of your labels will get slapped on to box wine as well. They bought the high-end name recognition, so it won't matter that it's not your wine in those labels. They own your names."

Everyone laughs, and I'm so proud of my girl who less than a year ago knew nothing about wine. Less than a year ago, she was alone still waiting for her world to crack open. I was waiting too, just didn't realize I was waiting for her. Here she is surrounded by a community I abandoned without a second thought. I took for granted how essential roots can be. I listen to her finish up her explanation.

"But the profits from their box empire will pull in more money than even the newly developed businesses they're planning for our properties. Once we all signed, all the properties came under one ownership, linked. They only need the juice from one or two of us because we're all considered one large property. One owner."

Sam smirks. "Like David said, we're fucked."

Becca looks at him, slyly. "Not necessarily, little brother. There's always a hole in a plan. Give me a minute to find it."

Before everyone leaves, Mel hands out a burner network. The Five have agreed to split the cost of her fee, which is NOT small. I'm sure it's less than she could charge, but it's not nearly as much as she's worth.

The phones are only linked to each other. You can dial out, but you can't add a new number to contacts. Everyone in our 'Village' has a burner connected to Mel's network, even Evan. Although Mel will be paid well, I think she just likes the covert spy crap. I'm not sure how my straightforward life got this convoluted.

Elle

Everyone decided to try and meet next week. Mel's going to work on a solution to the bugging. Becca is going to pour over the contracts to see if she can find something. Becca's a corporate lawyer, not criminal, so Francesca will keep building my criminal case against Asher. Becca used to practice criminal law but chose to go a less gritty path when she and Frannie opened their practice.

We're all moving forward into the holidays and super-busy time around the winery. I feel stronger every day, and the nightmares aren't as bad. I'm not ready to give up Lou yet, but at least Asher's remained quiet. That's both comforting and terrifying. He can't legally come anywhere near me. But I'm not sure he's one to respect the law.

Josh's parents are headed to Europe after Christmas. Sarah wants to travel to where Emma was born. She was there once as a little girl with her father and mother. But her goal is to be there for Josh's birthday.

I was going to surprise him with the trip for Christmas and join them at the end of February. I'm not so sure anymore. I feel better physically, but emotionally I can't help but backslide. I've made great efforts for no one to notice, but I've started to do little things to make me feel more protected. I don't want Josh to know I don't feel safe. My therapist said I should get back to my routines as soon as possible. I don't have a whole lot of routine with the winery so I'm creating my own. I just make sure all doors are locked a couple more times than normal. The fear will fade. I know it will.

I need to get my head back into the game and work. And probably move out of the hotel. I sit down on the couch and text my business partner and best friend, Evan. Mel said it was okay to correspond with him now. I promised to use the burner.

ELLE: Hey. The payout schedule looks fine. But you don't have to rush. Take whatever time you need. The contract should stipulate that the building still belongs to me. And that the LLC is in your name now.

EVAN: Babydoll. How's the shiner?

ELLE: Purple but healing.

EVAN: Jims said it was gruesome. Seen Asher?

ELLE: Let's talk about something else.

EVAN: We lost Homesick and Xfinity.

ELLE: Sorry. I can bring them back, but they'll leave when I do. Get your own damn business.

EVAN: HA! We'll be fine.

ELLE: I know. I promise I'll help you out whenever, forever. I can try to persuade them to stay if you want me to.

EVAN: No, I got it. Whenever, Forever. That's us. Must go, have to Skype a certain gentleman.

ELLE: Hey, give it a rest tonight.

EVAN: Can't. You've seen him. Way too hot. Night love.

All our correspondence is monitored by Mel, and the two of them could care less. They're still going to Facetime cyber fuck.

Josh is finishing up drinks with Bax and the guys outside around the firepit. Damn, I will miss this setup. I see them through the windows. Baxter Schroeder is a built and blond man who stands regal in a room of dusty jeans. His perfectly pressed khakis and a pink polo shirt are an anomaly and adorable. He's an environmental lobbyist and a partner in the new boutique organic label with Sam Langerford and David Gelbert. I suspect he has more extensive plans, but who knows.

Bax is headed back to Washington tomorrow for a big vote on the precursor to some groundbreaking climate change legislation. Josh wants to make sure he knows as much of this situation as possible before he leaves. We have no solutions, but we at least see the problem.

My cut lip has healed, and the bruising is minimal. I can still feel where the cut was, even if people can't see it. I can still hear the sound of the ring slicing my lip. I realize that I'm still giving Asher power. I can't stop. I keep putting on white noise at night, but I can't shake it just yet.

I jump in the shower. A new element to my routine schedule. I like it because it's a contained space that I have complete control over. I haven't kissed Josh in almost two weeks. Something crept up on me, and now I worry about being too audacious. Too happy. I wonder in a fucked up cosmic way that this all happened because I was too happy. Like the universe is balancing out my joy. I worry about Asher seeing us kiss. I don't want him angrier than he already is.

I've been attempting to remain even keel. I just need to

maintain. No spikes in emotions or desires. That way, I keep the ugliness from flooding back. I can put it in its place if I'm not stirred.

But I rub my finger over my lips and want Josh there desperately. I'm not sure about the rest of it, but if I can take back my kiss, maybe the rest should follow. Maybe that will be the thing that will keep Asher and thoughts of him at bay.

I squeeze my eyes together, so I don't cry. Fucker. I want to destroy him so badly. I have to keep trying to remember that the assault had nothing to do with me but his pathological, psychotic need to destroy Josh. It's about power, not about me. I know this, but I can't help how it affects me emotionally. I'm still slipping into a different person each day. We're going back to the Emma Farm tomorrow. Josh offered to pay our insanely high hotel bill. Thank god. It would have tapped me for life. So crazy expensive. It's like a starting teacher's salary. Sam and Sammy stayed here on and off but are back in Sonoma. Tonight, it's just us.

I hear the last of the guys leave—well, Tommi—and I'm in the bedroom. I've been turning one thought in my head over and over. It's wearing on me. I need to kiss him. I need to get past just this moment, and everything else will just go back to normal.

I'm wearing his Stanford T-shirt and some teal boy shorts that I know he likes. I walk out barefoot to the living room, and he's at his computer looking terribly stressed. I see that the moon is out. I take his enormous and steady hand, and he follows me to the patio. I need to bring back our kiss. Just my lips for right now. He flips a switch, turning the firepit back on. I stand in front of it for warmth. He squeezes my hand as he sits down. He's been so patient and kind. I can't imagine how helpless he feels. I pull him back to standing, feeling his hard and smooth biceps around me. His hands grip my hips as I stare at him with a little smile. I'm flooded with sunshine on the inside. His azure eyes stare sweetly at me. I can feel him push back the encroaching darkness that's been swallowing me slowly.

We've both wanted revenge and have had the darkest of thoughts. I want Asher to suffer, but as he holds me, I remember this quote. I say it to him as he faces me, "'Darkness cannot drive out darkness, only light can do that.' You're my light. I want to move through this. I want to be yours again."

"Cosmo, you're always mine." I lift my chin and go up on my tiptoes. He reflexively pulls back a bit. "My love, are you sure? Don't kiss me for me."

"Why not? Can't it be for me and you? I am doing this for us. I'm not ready for a lot of things, but I do know that I want to take back the power of our kiss."

He touches my face, then lightly brushes my lips. It's the softest, most healing moment of my life. I lean into the kiss, neither of us parting our lips. It's enough to be connected again. I pull my head back and sigh. I feel it in my toes. Then he suddenly scoops me up in his incredibly hot manly way and pulls me on his lap as he sits. I curl up like a cat as he whispers wonderful things. I kiss him again softly. And then he nods to me. I return his hungry gaze. He slants his mouth over mine and tangles his hand in my hair and angles me perfectly so he can tease my mouth with his tongue. It's flicking and licking the inside of my mouth, and my stomach flips. It's so fucking delicious, but I taste his concern, worry, and desire. It ebbs from him, and as the kiss progresses, I only taste how much he loves me. I forgot how absolutely yummy this man is. I won't forget again.

Josh

Christmas has come and gone. As has Valentine's day, where we spent a very chaste night catching up with Netflix.

We agreed not to get anything for each other because living at the Ritz was so fucking expensive. I wanted to give her all the things for both holidays, but she insisted. I'm trying to listen to her more. Other than making out occasionally, she's still working through the Dasher issues. I feel as if we're going backward instead of forward.

She seemed stronger in the days following the assault than now. We work all the time. She's always making plans. There are a ton of papers and folders. She's continually cleaning up the office. Reorganizing. All the marks are gone, and her restraining order is in place. We haven't heard from him. But there was a rumor that he was at dinner in town at some new restaurant. Now she won't even go to Poppy's. She claims it's all because she wants to learn to cook. She does run around the winery with authority, but honestly, I don't know the last time she set foot off the property.

* * *

I walk Elle across the parking lot to the offices. She and Lou have an outing today. I told him to take her anywhere, just get her away from here for a second. She's been leaning on him more and more. And if he gets her off the property, all the better.

But it fucking eats at me. I fucking hate that Lou makes her feel safe. That she'll leave the property with him, but I'm only able to escort her from the couch to our bedroom. It's fucking grim, and she fades a little more each day. It's like I'm trying to hold onto sand and it's just slowly sifting through my fingers.

Every other day seems to be a different relationship between us. And then when I get used to what we are now, or her new quirks, they shift again. I can't quite get to her anymore. She gets just beyond my grasp, and then suddenly she'll plunk herself onto my lap or pull me up to the roof to look at the stars. In those moments, she's my Elle. Those flashes of her are getting few and far between. My mom tried to get through to her. She sees her therapist twice a week, but I'm afraid her gift for compartmentalizing will eventually include me. She'll file me away in some dark place in her brain and take me out only for certain activities, but I don't get to participate in her life as a whole. She's a stunning shell of organization and work that never quite seems to get done. It's like she's running in place.

I watch as she goes to her desk and closes the door. We all hear it lock. She locks the door to an office that's in the back of a private building, surrounded by people she knows, and not on a main road.

Lou sits down at his spot in a cubicle outside the door and pulls out his morning paper. I'm standing there getting ready to pull my hair out. I've ranted, begged, been under-standing, been patient, asked sweetly, asked pointedly, listened, and waited for her to come back to any semblance of herself. Fucking Dasher stole her fire, her soul from me. He did exactly what he set out to do, take what's mine. I have an extreme plan to fix her, but I can't quite get to a point to pull the trigger on it.

And now the burner is blowing up in my office. It's several separate text chains.

SAL: *He's MIA*

SAL: *Plan B. Get her away from you and Sonoma. We can't protect her. He's rogue.*

* * *

MEL: *Surveillance compromised! Call me.*

MEL: *He wants her. I intercepted a text to her, and there are multiple messages. I sent them to the police. She needs to know I did this, but I don't think she should see the fucked-up shit he wrote.*

MEL: *He threatened to keep her locked up until she submits to him forever.*

* * *

BAXTER: *Colleagues in San Fran today said they ran into Dasher, and he mentioned he's engaged to Elle. WTF.*

* * *

POPPY: *He was just here looking for her, like twenty minutes ago. Bill, the giant, just escorted him out, but he eluded him. Thank you for watching out for all of us, Sal.*

SAL: NOW. Elle goes to Santa Rosa Airport, NOT Napa like he'd expect. ASAP. He fucking threatened Poppy. He said Poppy was good enough to keep after he had Elle. He's unhinged.

The threads leave me cold. I need to move forward with Plan B. There's one last text to catch up on that scares the shit out of me. My FBI friend, Mark.

* * *

MARK: Hey, Josh. You know that guy you and Sal wanted me to look into, the wine guy with the double name? I can't tell you specifics, but he was surveillance Special Ops and was dishonorably discharged. Those are the only declassified things in his file.

I have no feeling in my body. I'm frozen with fear. I will do anything to protect Elle and somehow bring her back from the brink he's put her on. Fucking Special Ops. Fuck. Fuck. We're so unprepared for this shit. We're idiot children playing hide-and-seek with a professional. We need to get her the fuck out of here. Then we can regroup and see if Mark can give us insight. Becca and Francesca need to put his ass in jail now. We push on the assault and figure out the winery shit later. Fuck. I message Sal and Mel.

JOSH: We're on our way to Santa Rosa. FYI- Dasher was Special Ops.

SAL: Mark told me. Tell everyone PLAN B.

JOSH: The threat is real, and I need her whole to help me fight this. I can't reach her anymore. She's shut down inside her own fear.

JOSH: Sam- Plan B. Tell everyone to lay low. LH meeting tonight @ 7:00 p.m. mandatory.

MEL: I'll be there.

* * *

Sam texts me privately.

SAM: You okay, man?

JOSH: NO. I'm fucking raging.

SAM: DO nothing.

* * *

Now to tell everyone else.

JOSH: Everyone, we're into Plan B. She goes in the next hour. Sammy, you're up.

SAMMY: For the record, I am totally against this.

JOSH: Just do your part. Jims- Evan's already on board. You'll be up next.

JIMS: Fine.

SAMMY: Just talk to her.

JOSH: There's nothing more to say. She needs fucking shock therapy. Or my version of it. I cannot watch her give herself over to fear and this asshole anymore. This is not up for debate. Dasher is missing. He harassed Poppy. We don't have eyes on him. He texted her that he's coming for her. She goes. NOW.

BECCA: I feel like you don't trust well. We can protect her. This is too drastic.

JOSH: I am sorry, everyone but shut the fuck up. You've talked to her. You see her. Is this your friend? No, it's not. This is my decision. You can either support me or get the fuck out of my way as I try to do what's best for Elle.

POPPY: We just don't want her to go.

JOSH: She's already disappeared from our lives. This conversation is over.

DAVID: We're here for you, man.

BAXTER: *This is not a good idea. But I support you, Josh.*

TOMMI: *I'm a go on Plan B.*

TABI: *I agree with Josh. I don't know who the fuck this girl is, but it's not Elle. And if she's out of here, maybe we can get back to the business of burying this asshole.*

DAVID: *Offensive, not Defensive.*

TABI: *Exactly.*

SAM: *Okay.*

BAX: *Okay.*

SAMMY: *I am still against this.*

POPPY: *Me too.*

BECCA: *I don't like this either.*

JOSH: *Again. Get on board or get the fuck out of the way. 7:00 p.m. tonight at Longhouse and this will not be a topic of discussion. Also, it's come to light that Dasher has Special Ops training. Please be vigilant.*

I turn my phone off. Pissed off that they even question me concerning Elle. They don't see the subtle shifts she has made to accommodate fear. She makes more room for fear everyday, stealing pieces of herself to give over to it. I know she doesn't think I've noticed. She checks all the bathrooms and closets before she'll get into bed. She does it like brushing her teeth each night. She locks her car after she gets into it. Then scans the back in case anyone is going to hide back there. She takes her car in for maintenance once a week. The shop has told her the car is in perfect condition, but she brings it every Thursday. She told me it's in case she has to make another getaway. But she doesn't think I know about her standing appointment.

She carries mace, an extra phone battery, a small taser, and cuticle scissors wherever she goes. They're in a small discreet crossbody bag that never leaves her body. She could be walking from the Farmhouse to the tasting room, and she has it. Most days she works with it slung around her back as she finalizes tasting room schedules or approves payroll. It's only off her body if she's with me, but it's always within reach. She sleeps with it on the nightstand.

I will protect her. She can't protect herself right now. That sounds sexist, but I am operating on a gut reaction now, no more fucking talking. Action. Protect what's mine at all costs. Sal understands me.

Elle's made many grand plans for the other outbuildings, new tours, and education vacations in the works. But no dinners. No plans where she might not be close to home. We order out or cook. Lou is never far from us. Hell, he lives in the Cooperage. She converted an old office for him. Ordered bedding and everything on Amazon, of course. It wasn't like she was going to Target like normal people.

She's begun trying to control every single aspect of her life, and I need her to come unhinged. She must unravel. She has to remember who she is and build herself back up. Right now, she's Noelle dialed to 11. She sets out her breakfast in the fridge the night before. She has a standing order from Whole Foods delivered to the tasting room so that she doesn't have to deal with a stranger delivering food. She never has more than one glass of wine anymore. Her Google calendar is updated to the minute when things happen, so she knows I'll know where she is if she goes missing. My phone pings up to fifteen times a day as she makes sure my phone is connected to hers. She rarely works the tasting room, and if she does, it's in the back, usually not talking to customers.

I wish to fucking god I could think of a better way because Plan B will break me. I discussed it with a therapist. And her therapist agrees that her OCD, controlling tendencies are off the charts. But they don't usually rule her, so it's her way of ensuring he never gets to her again. She thinks she's prepared for all outcomes and there are no surprises.

She won't medicate, and I frankly don't want her too, but if this doesn't work then meds are the next step. She needs to get away from Sonoma. Especially with this new threat that I can't tell her about. I promised her that I'd hide nothing from her again. I promised I wouldn't disappear for her safety again. With my parents in Europe, she's all I have. She's the best of me, and I will go down ridding the world of him. She can't know.

Josh

S he's in the shower when I pack a bag for her as fast as possible. I load her favorite leather market tote with a phone charger and a Mel-approved laptop. Then I make sure Daphne, the Birkin bag, is loaded with her wallet and all the things she'll need. I find three new packages of cuticle nippers tucked inside Daphne and two in her market tote. I dress in jeans and a black tee. I take her bag, purse, and run downstairs. I will fucking kill him with my bare hands if he shows up here. How can this one man be such a fucking menace?

Evan picks up my call immediately. "Oooh, the batphone. What's up? Is Elle okay?"

To fight off Dasher, I need my partner back and this is step one.

"She's fine but getting worse about the paranoia and fear stuff. She discusses nothing else. It's time. He's too close, and there's no way she can handle any of this without snapping back to who she is deep down."

"Alas, Plan B," he says resolutely.

"Yes."

"She won't leave you."

"She will if she thinks she's coming back. But you, Evan, are the only reason she'd ever leave Emma Farm. You're her whenever, forever."

Evan's voice cracks a bit as he speaks, but there's steel in his veins. He's a good fucking guy. "I'll get our girl back. She's my family, and I can do this. I'm her only family. I get that."

"That's not true anymore, but it just means there are more people on her side. You're not alone in this, but we're all counting on you, Ev."

"I'll shoulder your burden. The upshot is, I get to see Jims sooner, and he'll be safe. You do know I hate him there. Can't you people solve this shit yet? Keep my man safe."

That's so fucking cute, my heart hurts.

I ease his mind but caution him. "The upshot is we get Elle back, and that asshole has no more hold on our lives. And your man is safe."

"You know she might not forgive you for this?"

"I know."

"And she means that much to you that you're willing to risk her?"

"I am. She's everything, and if she never speaks to me again after all this, it will be worth it if she finds herself again."

"And everyone's on board?"

"The Village is ready."

"Y'all are more like a small uncorked army."

"Shit's about to uncork, that's for sure. Be safe. Thank you. Thank you so much, Evan. I owe you everything. I know you're doing it for her and not me. I want you to know that I am eternally grateful. I'm sending you my heart and soul, keep it safe. Keep her in New York until she breaks open. Until she remembers how fucking fierce, fearless, and beautiful she is. If we do this right, she'll be back to me in no time."

"I promise I'll do my best. We do have a giant new client coming next week that could be lots of potential. I could use her special brand of Parkerness to close this. Luxury living with a wine country slant. Right up her alley. I'll set the meeting ASAP. Pitching and selling should surely pull out the old Noelle and hopefully spark Elle back to life."

"Perfect. Send her the research. I'll be in touch."

I put my face in my hands. Now that it's happening, I want to lock Elle up and hold her.

She enters the kitchen, breathtaking in a simple wrap dress. I haven't seen her in a dress in a while, and it's this beautiful shade of dark pink that makes her green eyes sparkle. This will be my undoing until she comes back to me. I believe in you, Elle. Please believe in me.

"Josh? Have you seen my—"

I hear her phone ring. That's a good boy, Evan. She exits the Farmhouse to the parking lot to answer the call. When the sunlight hits her face she becomes even more breathtaking. It kills me she's never really come back after what he did to her. I can't let him take another part of her.

She will find her spark again. It was dulled by her loss of control.

Tabi confronted me, making sure this plan wasn't about getting sex back. For me, this plan has nothing to do with that. I'd wait for a lifetime. It's not easy, but it's not about that at all. It's her heart and spirit and soul I need back, her body will follow.

It was being struck by him repeatedly. I believe it was the shock more than the actual injuries that did the most damage. There's a large part of her spirit that never got up off that floor once he knocked her down. The girl who went to Bali by herself, who fought misogyny in Manhattan to create two successful businesses, who survived her parents death, who came here knowing no one and wouldn't leave until I realized that my heart belonged to her. That beautifully stubborn Hellcat of a woman who saw me from the very beginning even behind my walls is unreachable right now. I'd do anything to help her find her way back. Even if it means sending her away.

I need her whole, and that can't happen until she finds it for herself. I can't do it for her, and that's the part that kills me. Her skin doesn't even blush the same anymore. It's like she's controlling all of her reactions in a measured and catatonic way. She agrees to everything anyone asks her. As much as I fucking hated her stubborn nature, I now desperately miss it.

I've tried everything: vacations, therapy, patience, debourbage, even tried to fight with her, but she's slightly altered. I pretend I don't notice a difference, and she pretends to be normal. Just like we pretend we're Josh and Elle, but we're not.

I will never forgive that fucking piece of shit for dousing her light a bit. It's not gone, but until she can stoke that fire again, her whole heart and soul remains just beyond my reach. She found herself once in New York, after her parents' death. I hope lightning strikes twice. I'm betting on her to find that sparkle that usually dances in her eyes.

Nine more months, he lives, and if he wiggles out of all the charges against him, then Sal can do whatever the fuck he wants. But for now, she goes.

She smiles and calls out, "Hey. There you are." I take

her in my arms, she moves her crossbody bag to the back, and I kiss her, in our now chaste way.

I ask, "Are you okay?"

"Why? Kiss not good enough for you?" I grin. "You have your Joshua face on." I laugh at her, and she says, "It's probably for the best. I need to go to New York."

I exhale. I'm so relieved she's going. Now if I can get her to stay there.

"Why? No. I will not let you go. Nope. That's too far from me," I say, playing my part in the plot. I pull her closer, trying to cover my tracks.

"There are two clients about to walk and a new one that Ev needs me to nail down. And I am still a silent partner. Evan thinks I'm the only one who can save them. I owe it to him. He played the, 'I covered for you while you were falling in love with California' card."

I force a laugh, but that's the script Evan and I came up with. I knew it would persuade her. If nothing else, she's fiercely loyal and fair.

"It's only a couple of days. I think I could use a change of scenery for a moment, maybe clear my head a bit. I can talk to the realtor about putting my place on the market."

"Sounds like a great idea. Go be brilliant. I was taking you on a surprise trip for the night to Palm Springs. Sal's jet is gassed up in Santa Rosa. I'll see if he can reroute the flight plan if you want to go right now."

"Really? I love me some Sally Pipes."

"You know you can't call him that."

"You can't, but I can. And that way I'll be safe. The thought of the airport had me a little freaked. I mean, Dasher flies all the time. What if I ran into him? He'll think I'm here, right?" She bites her bottom lip.

"I don't see why not. You don't post on social media.

And no one posts about you except him. Evan and I are the only ones who know you're going. Mel will figure it out, of course."

"Of course, she will. Okay. A private jet. I'll take that. Come with me?" She kisses me, and it's taking every piece of me not to go.

My tongue gently slides into her mouth. For the first time in months, it's met without resistance. I push it a little further, and she backs up out of the kiss. I feel secure in my choice. As painful as it is. It's all for the greater good. Lie, cheat, steal, kill. There is nothing I wouldn't do to keep my woman safe. The end justifies the means.

"Baby. You go. Be brilliant. You haven't gotten to do that shit in a while. All winery plans all the time. This is the business that's in your blood, go. Should be fun."

She says quietly, "I'll step into that world for a second. But this is my business now. Our business." She bites her lip again.

I put my hands on her shoulders. "Our business. Got it. You're safe. New York will be good for you."

"I don't know if I can sleep alone." Tears well up in her eyes.

"If you get freaked out, check into the Ritz Carlton. It's my treat. Don't be silly though, you can do this. Call me anytime. And Sal can have someone meet you there if you want a New York Lou."

She exhales. "I don't need a Lou in my city. New York is my city. It always will be. I can do this, right?"

"He's here. Mel is watching his every move." I say this knowing that he's currently missing, but I need her to get the hell out of here as soon as possible. "You have your restraining order. He's not going to come near you. You can do this. I will tell no one where you went. I promise.

143

Clearly, Evan needs you. Use the burner network. You'll be fine. In fact, leave your iPhone here, so if he tracks it, then it will look like you're here. I'll carry it around, so it looks like you're moving around."

She cries silently into me, and I hold her. I kiss the top of her head. I want to scream. That's enough tears wasted on that piece of shit. I need her to get on that plane and fly far away from me and all of this. I need to give her perspective to remember who she really is. And hide her from Asher. New York should do all of this for her.

"I love you."

"I love you too, my Elle. I love you so fucking much. Hold onto that, okay? I need you to remember that above everything."

"I will."

And now it's time to begin my part. I'm going to crumple on the ground when she leaves. I breathe in a big breath and say, "I'll use the time you're gone to take care of Magnus things I've been ignoring. I'll jet down to Santa Barbara for a couple of days. Magnus wants me to meet about upcoming projects."

"New ones? I thought you only had Sal's projects."

"We'll see."

Step one. Make her think I don't want to go with her, and Joshua is returning. I hold her close and then release her.

Please let this work. I say a silent prayer to Emma. I'm not sure I believe in God most days. But when I was little, I was told Emma was in the soil watching over us. My great-times-four grandmother, founder of our winery, became the face of whatever lies beyond this world for me.

Emma, please take care of my heart. Show her a path through this and back to me. Amen.

Elle

My two phone conversations with Josh since I left have been brief and stilted. He's been busy. I've been busy. There actually was a lot of stuff for me to do here. I used to know that beast work mode, so I don't blame him. It's hard, though. I did sleep at the Ritz the first two nights in town, but the last five nights have been in my apartment. Sal's checked on me every day to see if I want someone with me. I don't. I think I got this for the moment. Each day I walk a little further without taking a Lyft. Yesterday I got on the subway. And I'm pretty sure Sal and Josh have a secret Lou following me anyway. At least I'm going to believe that.

I've been nightmare-free a couple of nights in my own space. I usually don't go to sleep without hearing the memory of his voice or imagining his sweet sickening scent so close to me. But it's finally fading.

Seven full days in New York so far and they've been kind of glorious. Langerford Chardonnay helped with homesickness and anxiety. I've ended up staying longer than a couple of days, but Evan needs me. It's been nice to dive into research and familiar work. The office is a haven for me as is my closet.

Evan is all about Jims Langerford these days. I don't know him as well as Sam, but they seem well-suited and incredibly happy. I'm thrilled there will be a clash of my worlds this week. Jims comes to town in a couple of days to visit his Evan. I am excited to see him. Maybe he can tell me why Josh is so odd lately. Or what Tabi has checked off the 'Fuck It List.' Or if David ever got that girl from Napa to go out on a second date. I just want the gossip and to feel close to those people again.

I miss the winery. With some distance, I can see that I've been making plans for far too long without following through. Very unlike me in retrospect. I don't usually let an email go more than twenty minutes without an answer. It's like I was just moving papers around on a messy desk. I was just reallocating piles but never cleaned or threw anything away. I didn't realize I was doing it until I dove in here and called a bunch of companies to begin scheduling education vacations for the winery. I'd been over-analyzing it for months. Paralyzed and second-guessing every decision I could make.

I texted Mel about her scanning my laptop for any Asher invasions. I worry he'll find a Manhattan IP address attached to something. She mentioned she noticed I was no longer cart shopping. I guess I had gotten back in the habit of cart-hoarding again. I've been stuck in all aspects of my life for the past couple of months without realizing it.

It seems as if I have been vamping and standing still in Sonoma. Is that what that asshole did? Take away my drive to succeed? I didn't even notice. I was too busy checking closets and bathrooms, I guess. I've been seeing my New York therapist every other day, and he's been fantastic. No nonsense about the whole thing versus my touchy-feely California one. I needed a dose of wake-the-fuck-up-you're-disappearing. I didn't realize I'd lost touch this much since it happened so slowly.

I'm desperate to tell Josh my revelations, but he seems extremely busy, I guess. I've emailed a lot of things I want to expand upon, but he hasn't responded except once.

He wrote:

E

I will read emails when I have time.

Love ya.

J

'Love ya.' What the hell is that about? We've made fun of people who use that phrase. He used to say it was a cop-out. There's a country song he likes by Tyler Rich called *The Difference*. It talks about the difference between "love ya" and "I love you." I don't know why he's using that phrase with me.

I just chatted with Mel about specific website changes to be implemented and then she said the craziest thing. She suggested that I present them to Josh and see if he'd approve my copy for the new merch brochures pages on the site. Funny girl. Of course, he will. Next, I make arrangements for the secondary Cooperage and storage shack at the end of the property to begin construction. Again, I was told they'd need Josh's approval. That's getting annoying. I never required authorization to do anything before. Especially since we got engaged.

I flip Emma's ring around my finger and look out at my view of the tree-lined street below. It's strange to feel completely safe in a city of millions of people, but it's my city. Dasher fucked me up even though he didn't fuck me. Josh has been so sweet as I adjust to my new reality. My therapist told me that this is the new basecamp, that I shouldn't try to emulate who I used to be, just be who I am now. Similar advice when my parents died. Adjust. I'm Elle, and this happened. I'm the same person, but I'm all that and what happened since. Nothing is missing or changed, just added on to.

Walking these streets, drinking late with Evan and noise all around me are making me remember myself. Almost like muscle memory of who I was before the incident conflicting with who I've become after. Have I become this other person? Are there really two different realities? I don't know who I am now without Josh by my side or post-Dasher, but I know I'm not that naive fool from before. But I did like that she was fearless.

* * *

SAMMY: *Hey.*

ELLE: *HI!!!! What's happening?!*

SAMMY: *Have you talked to Josh?*

ELLE: *Briefly. Why?*

SAMMY: *He closed the tasting room and went to Santa Barbara.*

ELLE: *WHAT? Huh? He's drunk. I'll call him. Tell the staff not to worry. In fact, go ahead and open tomorrow. Do you want me to call the team?*

SAMMY: *I got it. Just thought I'd tell you since you're the one who was technically in charge of that aspect of the business.*

ELLE: *Was?*

SAMMY: *Josh said that wine club, events, tasting room, and marketing are to report to this new chick, Gina. Are you good?*

ELLE: Huh? I'm fine, but who is Gina?

SAMMY: Used to work at Schroeder but has been down in Santa Ynez for the last couple of years. She's this willowy dark-skinned Latina. Gorgeous but annoying and kind of grating.

ELLE: I will to call Josh and see what's happening.

SAMMY: Okay. Call me later.

ELLE: Sure.

What the fuck? I thought he was joking about Santa Barbara. And why close down the tasting room? I dial, and it gets sent to voicemail. It doesn't automatically go there; he sent it to voicemail. Any girl I know Josh has been with besides Tabi and myself looks willowy and has dark skin. I don't like this one bit. I redial, and the same thing happens. Jackass.

ELLE: Hey, babe. Got an odd message from Sammy. Are you okay?

JOSH: She should mind her own business.

ELLE: Where are you?

JOSH: Sammy fucking told you, didn't she? Why bother asking?

ELLE: Stop being so strange, please. Who is Gina?

JOSH: A new hire. You're not here. We needed help. I knew her in Santa Barbara.

ELLE: Sammy said she used to work at Schroeder.

JOSH: Yeah, I don't have time for this. I have to get back to this client.

ELLE: Is she just filling in? I mean marketing, really? HA. HA. That's funny.

JOSH: Okay. I'm busy. Talk later.

ELLE: I guess. I love you.

What is happening? He never answered me. I have a meeting this week for Evan's new significant lead, but then

I'm going to nonstop keep calling him until we talk. I ache to have him with me, and now he's strange. Although, in the last week it's been nice to remember I can rely on myself too. But I miss the smell and feel of him. I miss his rough, raspy growl when he's exasperated by me. I miss Josh. I call Tommi Schroeder. Surely, she'll talk to me.

"What's up, buttercup?" She sounds strange too.

"Hey, who's Gina?"

"How did you hear about Gina?"

I demand, "What is happening at my winery?"

Tommi exhales loudly, and all in one breath gives me the information. "Gina used to work for us and dated Josh for a while when he first moved down to Santa Barbara, and she went to Santa Ynez for a while—"

I interrupt her. "Hold up! Dated?"

"Yes, but nothing is going on now. It was only like a month or two, maybe. She's really good at what she does." Tommi is covering up something.

"At doing my job?'

"Aren't you doing your job in New York? Josh said you were back at work full time. I'm not sure what Gina's doing. Ask Josh."

"He won't answer his phone. Did he go Wednesday night?"

"Yeah. He brought Gina. It was nice to catch up with her. The two of them jetted out the next day, though. He said he'd be gone awhile."

"A while? Both of them? And I'm just helping out here. I'm not back in New York. Or I didn't think I was. Tommi, what the fuck is going on?"

"Not sure. But honestly, I haven't seen much of him. Bax said he's kind of being an asshole this week. Ask Jims about it. Isn't he coming out there soon? They were all at a dinner the two nights before he went to Santa Barbara."

"What dinner?"

"Some high-end wine tasting event Gina set up with regional distributors."

"A marketing dinner? She's actually doing my job."

"I don't know. Ask Jims."

"I sure as shit will."

"Thanks, Tommi. Take care."

"See ya, Elle."

Fuck. Am I alone again? Does no one have my back? The moment Gina stepped on to the property, everyone should have called him out on this. And then called me. And continued to yell at him until he called me back.

Sammy said nothing. And then they all drank with her like that was totally normal. What the hell?

Josh

I can't sleep. I can't function. Snippets of information from Evan or Tommi are not enough. Hell, I had Evan send me a picture of her yesterday. She was all decked out in a jumpsuit with a blazer. She looks stronger. I hope she's stronger. Her New York therapist and I talked. I had a session with him but he, of course, could say very little about her. Just that she was improving and looked better today than in their first sessions. He said that he felt that their work together was in compliment to her California shrink and it was all coming together.

He's helping me deal with my own shit. The guy's pretty good. He did mention that maybe the pieces are falling into place for her. That the scattered fragments of her emotions are clicking into a breakthrough, but he can't be sure, and he can't be more specific. He knows all about our alienation plan but is not allowed to tell me if it's working.

I head out for a run. I'm getting strangely thin. My abs are insanely cut. I'm all muscle. All I can do to release my fucking rage—not to mention the back up of sexual frustration—is work out. I run to keep my mind off her and how she's doing and how we're tearing at the seams of what she feels she's built here. Running.

Elle

I text Josh, hoping he'll answer. I know it's insanely early there, but I can't wait. It's 5:00 a.m. here, but I hope he's up. Instead of texting back, he calls. My adrenaline soars at the thought of hearing his voice. I'm so excited. I've missed him so much. The longing is tearing at profound pieces of my soul. That small knot of fear of being left again builds every day. I push it away, knowing that can't be true. Holding onto the words, he said to me as I left for New York.

It's only been ten days away, but we've only had two phone conversations. We're starting to have days and routines that don't include each other. It feels like a lifetime away from the heat of his body. From the voice that soothes my soul. I'm hoping all the strangeness can get cleared up. He won't Facetime or Skype with me, so I'm overjoyed he's calling.

"Good morning! Are you up late or early?" I say with all the brightness that is starting to return to my soul. It's 2:00 a.m. his time. I like that he needed to talk to me right now. I want to share what I've been up to and how I feel. And how much I love and miss him. Distance sucks. And it seems as if we're divided right now. I don't like it.

"Who the fuck do you think you are?" He barks at me. He is freaking barking at me. It's not Josh who called me; Joshua seems to have reared his ugly head again.

"I'm sorry, what?"

"You have no authority to reopen the tasting room."

"I do, actually. Or I did. And I tried to call you and ask you about it, but you didn't answer me."

"And it's my right to do whatever the fuck I want. And last night I didn't want to talk to you."

And that familiar knot of fear, the one that says I'm going to be left, grows in my stomach, one I thought it was gone forever. Joshua found it again. I want to hang up, but I feel compelled to talk to him. My body begins to go numb. This can't be happening again. We are not that anymore. He's retreating into his jackass persona, and I'm baffled how this happened.

He continues his rant. "This is my winery for all intents and purposes until harvest and you overriding my authority is unacceptable. You do not make unilateral decisions that affect *my* business. How could you be that presumptuous? It's mine and mine alone to do with what and when I please."

"Josh. Calm down. Tell me what's bothering you, babe."

"Don't patronize me. The wine club is fucking done too."

"I'm not patronizing you. I'm trying to figure out why you're so mad at me."

"I fucking told you why. But again, you're not listening. I know what's best in the business world. My business, my decisions. If I'm forced to run this godforsaken place, then I'll do it my way."

"Oh."

I am fighting tears. He chose to stay with me and run the winery. What happened? I try to compose myself. His business. I thought it was ours. I felt that the pieces that I ran were mine and the ones he ran were his, but it was ours. I can't breathe. I almost don't remember how to breathe. He said the winery is my business too until our next chapter. But I'm not sure what's happening. He's not trusting me with anything. He's not himself. He's pushed me away, and I am going to crumble if he keeps talking to me like this.

"That's your response? Oh." His tone of voice is cutting and chilling.

I settle my nerves to stop my voice from cracking. "Did I do something?"

"You made decisions that you had no authority to make. It's not your ass on the line, it's mine."

"Wait. When did you make this choice to do all of this without me?" I ask.

"My head is a lot clearer when you're not here."

"That's funny, mine seems to be increasingly fuzzier about you."

How is this happening? He's speaking to me with an edge of cruelty. Like he's a different person. Even when we hated each other, he never spoke this dismissively. He's chipping away at everything I thought we'd built. The winery, us, a future.

"Well, you're a lot more emotional than I am."

"Hold up. Stop. I'm going to get ready to go to my meeting now, and can you have Josh call me later? I have no fucking desire to speak to Joshua again." I feel sick to my stomach as I defend myself. Not something I've done lately.

"This is me, take it or leave it. I have clients to see, lunches and a dinner. Calling you back will be hard. I have to haul my ass back up to Sonoma tomorrow night for a quick meeting. I'll see if I can call you then."

"You're still in Santa Barbara?"

"It's where I live. Why not?"

"I guess it's a good thing I didn't sell my place in New York," I joke, but not really.

He says casually, "About that. Don't sell it."

"Are you kidding me right now? What the hell has gotten into you?"

"Don't you talk to me like that. I'm not yours to command. Jesus, Noelle. Talk to you later."

He hangs up. He called me Noelle.

Josh

Sam is sitting next to me. I asked him to stay the night at the Farmhouse in anticipation of this fucking call. He got up with me at 2:00 a.m. knowing I would have to take her call today like it's urgent. This is the morning I ruin her day. I walk outside and puke. I've been nauseated for two days thinking about that phone call. It's the last part of the plan, and if it doesn't work, I'll die. I'm all by myself on this limb. No one believes this will work but me. It's been too long, according to most of my friends.

Hopefully, I can get an update on her today from Tabi or Tommi. But they're not happy with me these days.

"Jesus, Josh. That was fucking brutal. How can you be that cruel to her?"

"Because I love her so fucking much. But it's working. She pushed back. The point was to push her until she pushed back. Take away the things she loves so she fights to reclaim them."

"What if you push too far and she breaks?"

"She can't. She won't. That's not who she is. But if she breaks, then so will I."

Sam paces the kitchen, running his hand through his beard. "This is fucking crazy. How do you know it's working?"

"That was her on the phone. Not with the same Elle veracity, but it's there. She's emerging. I need all of her to return to me. This vibrant woman needs to step out of the gray."

"You know she's going to dump your ass? And I might flip to Team Elle if that happens. She deserves better than this."

"She's not going to dump me before she knows what I've done. I won't let her leave me. I will not let her step away from me ever. I know that now. These last ten days of true separation are killing me. Like honestly chipping away at my brain and body. She's my flesh and my soul. I never thought I'd be lucky enough to feel an eighth of what my parents have. And here it is, and there's no fucking way she will be away from me like this again. I think that phone call might just be enough to tip her over."

"You better fucking hope so because it's killing Sammy too. I know she had one more part to play. But Poppy's sending her the fake picture of you and the girl. She really doesn't want to do it."

I growl at Sam. "It has to be Sammy."

"Don't fucking order me around. You take your shitty mind game and finish it yourself. Sammy's out."

"Fine. Have Poppy send it," I growl and snap at my best friend.

"I'm your friend, but I won't be ordered around in your theater of pain."

He stands up to leave, and I stop him. I don't know if I can do this anymore either. If she doesn't crack today, I'm on the next plane to New York. Even if she's different, even if she's not the Elle I fell in love with, she's still Elle. I can't live another agonizing day without her. I can't do it.

"Sorry, man. I'm just..."

"Processing. Okay. Get your shit together so we can get this asshole out of our lives and minds." Sam seems exasperated.

"Yeah, I guess."

Sam turns back to me and takes on a stern tone. "A lot of shit has gone down in a relatively short amount of time. You're not the only one who lost a winery. Fuck. But think about this man, your life is really freaking different. Hell, two years ago you were engaged and bought that glass monstrosity of a house on the ocean. Now you've got dirt under your nails again, and you're engaged to the right woman, your mom is sick, and Dasher. All of it. That's a fuck of a lot. Christ, you had the mob mad at you not too long ago. I mean, damn, that is a lot, bro. Let some of it go, or if this works, there will be nothing left of you for her to come home to. You're not responsible for any of the shitty stuff that's gone down. Not Dasher, your mom, Elle, the winery shit. None of it, man. It's not your job to clean it up or fix all of our problems. We're all here to do that. Cut yourself a break, Lucien."

I smack him on his arm. "Point taken."

"Damn, you are such an alpha male."

I put my arm around him, grateful he's around. "You know that makes you a beta."

"I'm cool with that everywhere but one place."

"The winery?"

"Hells no." His eyebrows flip-up. "The bedroom." I laugh, knowing his predilection for dominance in that arena.

I leave Sam sitting, sipping coffee at the kitchen island.

The one where I desperately want to see Elle again. I want her sipping coffee or reliving the memory of the night I told her I loved her. Her perfect skin contrasted with the dark marble of the island. The memory of her feel and sweet words and smell haunt me. I'm going to do a sweep of the caves early this morning with Alena. She's testing to see if some of the good reserve stuff is ready for bottling. Then breakfast with Tabi. Then I have to run. I will head out to the blocks. I need the soil today.

"I'll be back," I say.

"I'm headed out. I'm going to climb into bed with the woman who matters the most in my life, who knows that, no games. I was here for you, but we all have bottling to do and wineries to pretend to run. Fruit to manage. All of us are done with your little 'get Elle back project.' We all need to focus on our own lives. Would love it if you'd join us and remember that we need you too."

"I hear you. I do. I'll call you later."

"No more shit from us. I still got your back. I'll see you at the Longhouse tomorrow night." We have a meeting of The Five called by the moms and dads. Should be a thing. I desperately want to tell Elle about it, but for now, I need to be Joshua the bastard.

"Thank fucking god for you, man. I don't know what I'd do without you."

"Soon. I'm going to need you to be there for me. Just once. It's all take, take, take with you."

I flip off Sam, and I head for the caves.

* * *

I meet Tabitha for breakfast. Tabi's all pissed off at her dad again. He won't increase her workload or give her any power. He keeps telling her to find the patience that her time is coming. Costas doesn't trust her yet. She's starting to doubt he'll ever let her run the winery. He keeps bringing in distant cousins from Greece to see if they're the perfect fit to run the vineyards. They all fail, and she stands there being passed over. She's pissed. She blathers on and on about it. Then she yells at me about the Elle thing.

"You know she will *never* get over this, asshole. I was on board with this, but it's a bit far. She won't trust you again."

"She will, and I'm exhausted from all of you fucking people yelling at me."

"You're diabolical with this shit. And I still can't believe you talked us all into ditching her."

"We didn't ditch her."

"I have sent no fewer than six calls to voicemail. I've never called her back. I suck. And if I didn't love you like a brother, I would fly her back here myself. And what's with your hair?"

"What?"

"Looks shitty. Like all the time now."

"Jesus. Tab. I gotta go."

* * *

I wake up a full twenty-four hours after the cruelty phone call. Well, wake up is a relative term. I napped. I can't sleep without her. I want to talk to no one. Not one fucking syllable. After the Longhouse meeting tonight, I'm going to get her. Enough. But today, I have to disappear. Coffee, quick emails, and possibly another horrible conversation with Elle.

I don't need anyone to tell me anything anymore. I head out for the longest run of my life. I'm going to run until I have clarity. I'll stop along the way and eat if I get hungry, but I'm not coming back to the winery if it still hurts this much.

I'll fill my day. No phone. No people. No demands. Just me and the road or the trails. The sound of my footfalls and heartbeat until I can only see her face clearly without guilt or pain. Fuck me. This has to work. Come back to me, my One Perfect Thing.

It's still the middle of the night. Shit. I'm just staring at the ceiling trying to settle my entire being. But I will disappear today for the day. I have to disappear.

Elle

He returns only one text in the last day.

JOSH: Told you, busy! I will call you when I have a moment in a couple of days.

I need something amazing to take my mind off of Joshua. I need armor. I forgot how much I like my clothes. I've never used my second bedroom except for an elaborate closet. That's a part of me I let go. I've dressed up for each day that I've been here, and my dusty jeans have sat in my hamper since I unpacked after the first day in the office.

Today is devoted to Chanel. I step through a cloud of *Chanel No. 5* after I dry off from my shower. I grab my pale pink Chanel leather-edged suit. There's a soft white shell underneath the jacket that zips up. I pull up cream, sheer knee-highs. The stockings making me feel sexy and strong. I love that my suit is hard and soft at the same time. I choose stacked heel oxford slingbacks in black—Chanel, of course. As I slip into these luxurious clothes, I'm reminded of how far I've slipped from this girl. I also purchased Chanel lipstick with my new favorite name, *Epitome*. I know I'm both girls, but it seems as if my yang has overpowered my yin for a little too long.

I got a strange picture from Poppy last night of Josh eating dinner with a gorgeous raven-haired woman, who I assume is Gina. But I guess it wasn't from last night because Tabi texted that he's still in Santa Barbara, unless she's there too. I dial Josh, hoping for the best. It's a little over twenty-four hours since he was an asshole. And I am baffled and bewildered. I call to leave a friendly voicemail message for him to wake up to this morning. It's 7:00 a.m. my time, he should be fast asleep. But he answered yesterday, maybe I can reach him this morning.

"What?" he bites out.

"You're awake. Is that how we greet each other now?" I ask bluntly.

"What do you need, Noelle?" My full name stabs at my heart.

"I can't believe you're awake."

"I am now that someone has woken me up."

"I was just calling to see how you were doing. Are you back in Sonoma? How are your parents?"

"I'm fine. No. They're fine. And I feel as if you should stay put for a while in New York. It's easier this way." His voice is callow and cold. He's not sleepy or annoyed, just disjointed. I did not just wake him up. He's fucking waiting to pounce on me.

"What is easier?" I ask.

"Everything."

Oh god. He's breaking up with me. On the phone. And I called him. I need to get off the fucking phone and push this down. I can't deal with this right now. I have to nail this pitch meeting for Evan today, and then I can deal with this freaking *Twilight Zone* episode that's happening.

"What the fuck is happening to you? You're a coward. Deal with me. Don't hide behind whatever persona you've decided to adopt."

"Not persona, reality, honey. If you can't deal with it, you know what to do."

"Hold up. You can say your cruel things to me later. I have to go. I need my game face on today to close this client for Evan. But you're fucking deluded if you think this is the way you get rid of me. I thought you were more of a man."

He begins to roar, and I hang up on him. I don't want to talk to this person. I don't even know this person. You'd think I'd be crying, but I'm furious at this jackass. He calls back immediately.

I pick it up and before he can anything I yell, "NOPE. Not now, Jackass."

He calls back again. I'm sure to yell at me. I ignore him and send him to voicemail. Which I know pisses him off even more.

JOSH: DON'T YOU EVER FUCKING HANG UP ON ME. HOW DARE YOU?

ELLE: Told you, busy! I will call you when I have a moment in a couple of days.

I just copied and pasted his words back to him. Jackass. I'm standing in a ridiculously expensive suit, holding gorgeous shoes, and I've just had one of the ugliest conversations of my life. I'm so tired of crying. My whole life just shifted again. I feel like Alice falling through the rabbit hole. I have no idea where it stops. But maybe I've been falling all this time and didn't realize it.

I take a shot of Basil Hayden at 7:15 a.m. in my kitchen and exhale loudly. Why the hell did he answer at four a.m. his time? Just to yell at me. I tamp down all the Josh stuff, fix my lipstick and head to the office. Work can be my salvation right now, as it always has been. I leave my apartment with this mantra in my head, "nail the deal, conquer the client, and reclaim the shark." Then it will be time to put Joshua in his place. I get a slight excited chill at the thought of being a shark this morning.

* * *

I've done my homework on the luxury brand appliance company we're pitching today. Josh has been compartmentalized. They make things like wine fridges and frosé machines. I'm in control of myself. I adjust my skirt and suit jacket, with a real fucking cup of coffee in my hand. No tepid mess like that stupid ass ginger-haired Sonoma barista pushes on me. New York coffee. I'm going to slay this meeting. I pop into Evan's office, thrilled to see the back of a familiar head. Josh and Sonoma pang in my stomach for a moment. I breathe through it. Later. I can deal with him later.

"Morning, Jims." I kiss his cheek, and he looks up from his laptop. He leaps up and pulls me into a full-body hug. He's perched on Evan's office couch. It's my former office but Evan redecorated. Although he did keep my pink chair.

The two of them seem to be so domestic around each other. I love that Evan feels like he has someone who doesn't mind how much he works. Evan loves to work. It's his dream scenario that Jims lives in California. He says their sex life is hotter because of the distance. He'll have to teach me since apparently mine is nonexistent. I suck at doing distance. Or Josh does. No. I push the thought of him down again.

But then suddenly the thought of that little area above Josh's waistband flashes in my mind. I'm starting to heat myself up a bit at the thought of licking it. My chest and cheek flush pink. This is the first time I've thought about him this way in a very long time. I clamp my thighs together at the thought of his rootstock. Damn, I'm hot for him right now. It's a shame he doesn't want to talk to me because I'm suddenly thinking incredibly filthy thoughts, I'd like to share with him. Who knew that this would be the way my libido would return? He just had to be a jackass. What is wrong with me?

"Cosmo. Darling. You look stunning. But troubled." My Sonoma nickname stings just a bit. What the hell is wrong with Josh? I want to know what's going on. Later. Later. Focus Elle.

"You look gorgeous yourself. I'm fine. Where's your man?"

"They're in the conference room up here. You got this."

"I do got this. I haven't had things together in a while, but I really do now."

"I *see* you. And you know what, darling? It's nice to see the real Elle again."

"Nice to be me again. Have you seen Josh?" It pops out. Dammit.

He pauses and looks me directly in the face. "My darling. No one's seen him really. He's been in Santa Barbara, and when he is in town, he's locked away with that woman he hired."

Jealousy curls around my heart like an icicle. "Locked away with her?"

"I'm sure it all means nothing. Perhaps he's an asshole again because you're out of town. Just call him."

"He won't talk to me."

"Try him again. And who cares about Josh right now

when you are *serving* Chanel to me." Shake it off. Josh later, shark now.

Jims' lips curl approvingly. He stands and hugs me, and I need it. Then I nod to him and drop my big Chanel bag on the couch with my laptop in it. Then I place Daphne carefully on her designated shelf.

"I'll watch her, don't worry." Jims winks at me.

I strut down the hallway with my folder and favorite pen in my hand. I grace the door and survey the room to figure out my target. It's what I always do. I seek out the one person in the room that I know I can convince. Then that one person will do the rest of the work by convincing everyone else in the meeting for me. It's like reading a jury. I'm really fucking good at this. I need to get that one unsuspecting person on my side, and then the rest of the deal is done.

My eyes scan the room, and my body goes cold. Bile rises as I land on the face of my nightmares. My eyes go as wide as possible. Evan's talking, but there's blood thundering in my ears, but I don't break his gaze. I attempt not to react as the devil stares coldly back at me with his lips lifting a little. Oh. My. God. There's activity all around us, but we're suspended in this deadly stare.

Evan's introducing everyone, and then he says, "And this is Robert Doyle." Slimy fuck. That was my father's name.

Elle

He stands and reaches out his hand to shake mine. I drop my pen, so I don't have to touch him. He nods and sits back down as I retrieve it.

I fixate on his ring with the stupid dragon on it. I'm staring at just that, and something snaps in me like a rubber band pulled too tightly. My mind clicks into some kind of rational plan I didn't think possible. My thoughts race.

This will not paralyze me. He will not break me or stop me. He has no control. He is nothing and will not take one more fucking thing from me. He will not hurt Evan. NOT one more second. He gets not another second of my life or anyone's life that I love. Today he takes nothing else.

Even though I don't have my ever-present cuticle nippers, I'm eerily calm. I will myself to shake his hand and then I'll escape. NO. Not escape. Not this time. This time I stand instead of falling on my ass. This time I will fight. These other people need to be away from this monster, though. It's not their fight. It's mine, and I'm fucking ready for it. I need Evan safe.

I direct my voice to him. "Good to meet you. Interesting name."

"I've always liked it." My stomach turns as his voice drips with slime.

I turn to Evan and put on my best act, "Hello, everyone so nice to meet you. I'm Elle Parker. I think you will all be so much more comfortable downstairs in the bigger conference room. I've set up a coffee service and baskets of yummy pastries from Maison Kayser. It was for later, but I think we should all nibble while we talk. There's also a ton of fresh-cut fruit. We'll be right down to join you. I'd like to have a moment alone with Mr. Doyle." I give away nothing in my demeanor. I give him nothing more.

He licks his lips, and my skin crawls. But muthafucker, you have no idea who I am now. Or what Becca and Francesca did for me. Basecamp. I'm Elle plus this now. Not in spite of, not less than. I look at him and want to let him know that he added to me, not subtracted. I just didn't realize it until right now. Best of the old incorporating the new. Evan seems confused, but he trusts me.

Evan stands. "Come on, everyone, best pastries in the city await us. Do you need anything else, Elle?" I have not looked away from Dasher. He's adjusting the crease in his pants like the pig he is. He's dressed the part in a high-end suit and looking as smug as he can. It turns my insides into rage for all the shit I've given to him. All the things I haven't been since that day, he gets not one more moment from me that I don't control. Not one more tear or regret or second guess or minute of my emotional life. I am resolved and fucking evolved. Staring in the face I built up as a monster, I know he is worth nothing.

I say sweetly and with an even fucking keel, "Actually Ev, could you have our associate in your office join Robert and me in here? And have him bring my laptop, please. I need to print something for this meeting. Oh, and I'm so sorry, they were out of kiwi."

Evan hates kiwi. It's his safe word. It's the word we used to joke that if we used it meant we were kidnapped. Or one of us was tied up in bed and needed a rescue. I pray he remembers and calls the fucking police. I'm going to throw his ass in jail. Even though I've got him on bail jumping, I have more planned. I am guessing he didn't read the fine print.

"Oh, well then, I guess it's melon for me. I'll see you in a moment, Robert. Elle." Evan nods slowly as he closes the door behind him.

I turn to him. "How are you here?"

The cold chill of his voice begins to speak. "My darling, angel face, Noelle. It's been a while. You've been hiding from me. Naughty, naughty. I don't like games. You even had me fooled that you were tucked away safely at Emma Farm. I recommended Bixby and Parker to my friends at Allavino when they asked for help finding a marketing firm for their new line of wine refrigerators. I was simply consulting on this meeting to size up Evan. I was supposed to Skype in but what a delight to find out yesterday you'd be running the meeting. I couldn't help myself. I jumped on a plane to see you."

"Asher. You are a surprise. Are you in town to see a show or just to try and beat the shit out of me again?"

He laughs a titter that turns my stomach. I have no idea where this fire is coming from, but my chest and face color red with rage. I will not run from this asshole anymore.

"Let's not pretend, shall we?" He steps toward me. "You like a good beating. I've seen it with my own eyes. Even now, your face flushes at the thought."

"You don't know me as well as you think. That's just plain fury."

He waves his scarred hand in a flourish at me. "We have unfinished business between the two of us. And there is the small matter of the stabbing, but I'll write it off as foreplay. Now aside from you being the key to taking down the unsavory set of assholes from 'The Five' wineries, once I saw you get up after what I did to you, I knew you could handle all I wanted to dish out. Look how beautifully your face has healed. Although pity it didn't leave a permanent branding on my woman. To answer your inevitable question: it's time for you to be at my side. We go now."

"You think I'm leaving here with you?"

"I know you are. What—is Evan going to stop me? You can't stop me. Unless you have cuticle nippers. No one can stop me. From what I know, you've been cowering, waiting for me to swoop in and save you from a life with that tedious man. You never go out. You rarely leave the property. You hide away, waiting for me to rescue you. And I have arranged for us to head far, far out of town. A place where we can relax and get used to each other. And you can learn some fucking manners. Maybe learn to do what is asked of you."

"I've never been really good at doing what someone tells me to do."

Jims enters the room, irritated at being summoned. "Elle? What is it...What the *FUCK?*" He lunges at Asher, and I pull him back.

Asher looks rattled but quickly recovers. "This is another surprise. I make it my business to know everything about everything. I did not see little Jimmy Langerford here today. I am shocked. But there's nothing this little poof can do."

"Gay slur? That's your move? Thought you were Special Ops?" Both Asher and I look at Jims with shock.

"What?" I spit out.

Jims continues, "Yes. Seemingly, he's a surveillance expert."

"Since that's classified information, I'm a little put out that I didn't know you had access to that. But I can't confirm or deny."

I pull Jims' focus. "Why am I in the dark on this? This seems like something that should have been shared with me. Fuck you guys."

Jims looks at me. "Not now, Elle." He takes his phone out of his pocket.

Asher calmly leans down to the bottom of his pants and slams his hands on the conference table. There's a large knife in his left hand. The handle makes a terrible clinking sound as it slams with incredible force onto the table.

"No PHONES. Slide them to me. Oh, wait. Of course. Whittier has your phone, doesn't he? Fuck. That was clever. That's why I didn't know you were here."

My Five Families burner phone is in my purse in Evan's office. And Jims' phone isn't his burner. Thank god. I only pray that he doesn't have it on him. Asher can't know how we've been dodging him.

I nod. He throws Jims' phone with tremendous force against the wall and it skitters to the floor, pieces flying in every direction. I jump but quickly compose myself.

Asher speaks again in a calm and creepy tone, "I'm here for Noelle, and she's not going to fight me, or I'll make sure the people she cares most suffer. What's interesting is that when I met you, you only had Evan. He would have been the only one I chose to hurt. But since you had to go and care about the fucking Whittiers and their selfish friends, it now extends to quite a few people. The choice is yours, my angel. But it seems those people have been pulling back from you as of late. They've cast you out. Maybe I'm all you really have. I've never abandoned you. I'm here to save you."

He's right. They have pulled back.

Jims puts his hand on my arm. "It's not what you think. Do NOT listen to him." I know Jims is trying to clue me in on a reality I'm not privy. Clearly, there's a hell of a lot going on in Sonoma, and they haven't been sharing with me. What the hell have I been doing? I was so checked out or too busy checking under beds to notice anything.

I let Asher put a wedge between those who care about me and myself. I put up rigid steel walls around myself. And then topped them off with cuticle nippers. I should have stock in cuticle nippers at this point. I've hidden them all over Emma Farm. There must be like a hundred pairs. I was never more than a foot from a pair. Wow. I really went crazy, didn't I? But none of them really pulled back from me. I pushed them away. I let Dasher rule my head. Fuck him. I take those people back today. I take my people back from him today. And every damn one of them gets a free pair of nippers.

I ignore Jims as part of my strategy and smile at Dasher. "Let me cancel my day before people notice." He nods in approval. I open the laptop that Jims brought in.

"Good, little Noelle. You'll learn that you belong to me. And you'll learn that being this sweet and docile is the only way you'll survive."

"Fucking hell. Shut up, Dasher. She's going nowhere with you."

"And you're going to stop me? I don't have to force her now. Do I, Noelle? I'm the only one who cares for you. I know what's best for both of us. My princess, my queen Noelle. You'll want for nothing. You'll come now, or you'll learn a new definition of suffering."

Jims puts his hand on my back as I print a document he can clearly read. I print many copies, so Evan will be alerted that the printer needs ink or has run out of paper. The printer downstairs is networked into his laptop, which is with him for the presentation. I need Evan to find five hundred copies of my restraining order. The one Becca and Francesca made sure was ironclad.

I close the document and my laptop. And Asher gestures for me to slide that over as well. Then he shoves it from the table and it smashes against the wall.. Then Dasher retrieves it from the floor and opens it, I pray the document isn't still up, and he pours a cup of coffee onto the keyboard and into the ports. I don't know why he feels the need to murder my computer. Then again, I get nothing about this monster.

Jims tucks me into his side. His long arms snaking around my waist in protection. We all stand there, staring at each other for a moment like a strange stalemate. I break free from Jims and lean down onto the conference table. No one fucks with my friends and family. I only just got them. No one threatens my loved ones or business. Not even this psycho.

"Dasher."

"Darren."

"Dasher, I'm not going anywhere. And not only am I not cowering, but I will make it my fucking mission until my last breath, whenever that may be, to make sure you never rape or hit another person. If I even hear a whisper of a woman with a dragon signet ring scar, I will chop you up."

"Is this flirting? You've always known how to get me

hard. I look forward to breaking your stubborn will." He grabs himself, and I see that he's disgustingly erect.

Jims can't help himself. "You're such a piece of shit. I mean damn, bitch. How dark are you?"

Without warning, he's behind Jims with the knife at his throat. I yelp.

"You have no fucking idea how dark. Noelle, that is quite enough, dear. I need you to start walking out of here and down the stairs. You go slowly. You don't need to see me gut this useless fish. It's time to go, our life is calling. If you start moving, then I might not leave this smug colorful asshole's blood all over the carpet. I'll cut him cleanly, so he dies instantly instead of letting him suffer. But tick tock, your decision."

I steel myself, hoping Evan did what I need. I need to stall a little bit. I outstretch my hand and say as sweetly as possible. "Only if you come with me. Leave him, come with me now."

Dasher doesn't move or take the bait. I have no other recourse. I put my hands on my hips, lowering my voice. But it gets gradually louder as I end in a roar. It's everything in my soul spilling out of me.

"Get the fucking knife off his throat. Or you'll never have me. This is not the way in. Leave him alone, you small dicked unremarkable fucking cocksucking piece of shit. I will go with you downstairs. I will leave with you. Under one nonnegotiable fucking condition. Take that knife off Jims' throat right now. I'll never go back to Josh or Sonoma if you step the fuck away from Jims. Use the knife to cajole me down the stairs. It's the only way we're leaving together. Because if you're going to kill him anyway, what's my motivation?"

"There's that fire I can't wait to douse, darling Noelle.

I'm going to make you as obedient as a lap dog. You've already had your first lesson. The next lesson won't be as gentle."

He puts the knife down from his throat, and I exhale. I know he won't hurt me here. I needed Jims safe so he can call the families as I go downstairs. I need him to be safe because he's my family.

He throws Jims to the ground hard. He's behind me in an instant, and I'm aware the knife is in my back as we walk slowly towards the stairs. His hand on my shoulder, guiding me. I lower my shoulders.

I stall some more. I stop and turn around. Now with the knife at my stomach, I look at my devil in his cold mottled beige eyes. "I can walk by myself."

"Yes, you can, my princess Noelle." He brushes his sickening hand over my cheek that's healed. "I can't wait to see my handiwork on your face again." He digs his hand into my shoulder as he puts the knife back into his leg holster. "See we already have a new level of trust between us, angel."

I nod, and we slowly walk down the stairs, his hand digging into my shoulder. At least it's not a knife. We turn the corner to see Evan standing there with three police officers. I almost crumble at the sight of them. They're all holding copies of my restraining orders, which Becca and Francesca made sure was valid in all fifty states. I turn to him as he rounds the corner. His face betrays him as he scans around for a victim or an escape.

Jims hurries down the stairs, and Evan's hand goes to his heart now that he knows he's okay. I turn to Asher.

"My dear, we're not in California. And you are standing with me on your own accord. There's no coercion. But with the present company being what it is, I think I'll be going. We'll meet again soon."

The large officer speaks, "Actually Mr. Marcus, it appears her lawyer registered the order in all fifty states. Which makes you in direct violation. You'll have to come with us. You're also trespassing on private property according to this gentleman. And it appears you've jumped bail in California."

Jims yells from the staircase, "He has a knife holster on the left leg. A concealed weapon. One he just put to my neck!"

I turn to Dasher before the officers get to him. "Read the fine print. You may have thought you doused my fire, but the truth is, by coming back, you just fanned the flames. I'm a goddamned phoenix rising, and you're going to rot in jail. Then it's your turn to find out what it's like to be raped and beaten and taught to behave."

He puts his hands out to the officer and tosses a comment back as he's led out in zip ties. "Be well, my angel. I'll always come for you."

The door closes, and my knees go out from under me. Jims catches me and Evan's instantly at my back. Both men sandwich me with support and love.

I curl into them, sobbing. Not because I'm scared but because of gratitude that I was able to face the devil and win the battle. I kept myself and these men safe. But I still have shit to do. There are things to be said. I have more fucking people to put in their place today. I'm just getting started. I need Sal, and I need him now.

Josh

It's well after six and it's time to face the world. I was absent from everything today. I ran until my legs buckled and burned. I ran until my lungs began to betray me. I grabbed a sandwich at Broadway Market and some Gatorade. Then I walked the trails home. I rode an ATV along every path I could find. I checked on our bottling. I went to the warehouse and packed up some wine club shipments. Anything to get lost today. I have been removed, even from myself all day. I don't feel any better, but I made it through the day. My stomach is still a mess thinking about her.

After my shower, I leave my phone off. It's easier to ignore Elle if the phone is just off. I'm headed to the Longhouse for a strategy session because the parents have a plan. We'll see. It's an all hands-on deck. Bax is in town as well as Ingrid, his decade-younger hipster sister. Her actual job is being an Instagram influencer in Los Angeles. She was on that yacht with Bella Hadid in the Fyre Festival ads and has one-point-two million followers. I don't get it, but she's happy.

We've all been commanded by our parents to bring bottles and our winemakers. Alena's bringing a new Syrah blend that Elle loved in the barrel. My day of solitude didn't bring any peace, just frustration. I'm headed to get her tonight. I booked a plane. Twelve days and I've hit my breaking point. We'll figure out something, but Plan B is a bust. Alienating her didn't bring her back, it just made it all worse. Fuck. I can't be away from her for one more second. Let's see what medication can do. This is too fucking painful. I'm a husk of a human without her.

As I enter the Longhouse, I turn on both phones. They pop off with crazy notifications. I see they're from everyone as I head into the big room. Sal's looming in the corner, and I don't remember him being invited to the meeting. Mark is here with his arms around my mother. He grins at me and then nods with his chin towards the other side of the room. Then my heart drops, and my breath catches. Standing in the middle of this overcrowded room is a beacon of light in a badass pink Chanel suit. My beacon of light.

She sees me, but her face doesn't look like this is a good reunion. But she's here. She's here with me. Her emerald eyes flare at me, but the dancing gold flecks are in place. Her eyes are shimmering from across the room. A shimmer I haven't seen in months. I feel lightened and unburdened just by being in her proximity. My chest eases, and my lips pull into the most massive smile possible.

Her chest and face flame red, and I know that's rage and frustration, not warm fuzzy love. But it's a marvelous sight. Her blush is back. Her emotions and passion. Her anger is back. I want to run to her, but there are twenty-six people, stacked cases of wine, and lots of chairs separating us. She sees that she can't get to me either, but that has never stopped my Hellcat before.

She steps on a chair heading for the top of the long farm table in her kick-ass and sexy heels. Sam helps her up. She pops her left hip and puts her hands on her waist. Everyone goes quiet as she commands the room without saying a word while standing on the table. Caught off-guard. I'm off-kilter and uncertain of what to say or do. What the hell is she doing here? When did she get here? My heart is beating out of my chest. How did she get here? She's my fucking caught off-guard girl. I look at her directly in her gorgeous eyes and say, "Hey there, Cosmo."

The crowd laughs and cheers a bit. And then she lets loose at full Elle volume, and everyone goes silent again.

"YOU! Shut the fuck up, Joshua Whittier! Do you even *know* what the fuck I've been through today? You would if you turned any of your fucking phones on or read an email. Or told anyone where you were today. Jackass. No one could find you."

"Elle," I say, leading and trying to calm her down. I want to explain why I went dark today.

She screams at a deafening volume, "NO. NO. NO. I talk now. You listen. This is *my* business." She's wildly gesturing to the winery around her. Then her laser focus returns to me. "My winery. Mine. We may share it, but you cannot fuck with my business. Closing the tasting room and canceling the wine club is not your call despite what your cock and cocky attitude tell you to do. You don't mess with my business. I thought you already learned that fucking lesson. And this whore, Gina, she's fictitious, no?"

"Yes! She is totally made up!" Tommi yells too loudly and giddily. And everyone laughs until Elle silences them with a flick of her wrist. She never turns away from me. I'm kind of scared of her right now.

"Think with your fucking head, Josh. You thought I'd

believe you hired a marketing person and instantly fell in love with her? That only happens once in a lifetime, asshat. And you know what? It's already happened. And another thing, you don't live in Santa Barbara..."

She slowly walks towards me on top of the table as her face flashes with rage. Gloriously beaming in a red rage, and my heart fills with every step she takes towards me. She hasn't been angry in months. She hasn't pushed any limits, my buttons, or demanded any attention. She's been agreeable at best but mostly simply existed. Her entire existence shrunk. And now she's larger than life.

"You live *here*. With *me*. Joshua is dead. And did you make poor Poppy send that fake romantic picture? That was a shitty thing to do to all of them. You're mine, and there's nothing and no one that can change that motherfucking fact."

Everyone cheers her on, and I try to open my mouth. But then she gives the crowd and me a look with her wide bright eyes and cocks her head. I know she's not done.

"I don't know what you were trying to do with those phone calls, whether that was your shit or mine, but that cruel tone won't be tolerated ever again. You'll have to tell me who's dumbass plan this was later."

Sammy begins clapping, and everyone joins her. I wink at her, but Elle has even more to say. I need to touch her right now. Everyone settles down, and she continues in a calmer but still stern tone of voice.

"You mean the plan that seems to have worked." I crook my eyebrow at her and nod to Sammy, Tabi, and Baxter. But my focus is immediately pulled back.

"Hey! Me. Focus on me. Next order of business: my jackass of a fiancé, I had Dasher arrested today."

I explode at her. "What the *FUCK* are you talking about?"

Sam looks over at me. "Dude. You gotta turn on your phones." Everyone is silent and staring at me. Even my dad nods that he knew.

James Sr., speaks next, "He held a knife to Jims' throat at her New York office this morning. Apparently, Cosmo was the cavalry. She convinced him to turn the knife on her rather than cutting my son's throat. She secretly signaled Evan to get the police to arrive while she stalled him in the conference room. Then she had his ass thrown in jail for violating her restraining order, bail jumping, attempted assault and battery, concealed weapon charge, and trespassing." He bows to her and blows her a kiss. She smiles and bows her head to James Sr. and Theresa Langerford.

I'm white as a sheet with shock. I thunder, "Did he touch you? Hurt you? I am going to fucking kill him. It's time to end him." My gaze shoots to the one man in the room I know who can carry out that kind of order. Sal shakes his head from the corner and nods back to Elle.

She took care of him by herself. Sal must have flown her back to me. I nod to Sal as a thank you. He puts his hand on his heart. He loves her like a little sister. If Dasher did touch her, no one could stop Sal. This is how I ended up with a mob boss as one of my closest allies. He loves my girl as much as I do. Off-kilter. Our caught off-guard girl.

Elle turns her attention back directly to me. As the crowd begins to murmur, she raises her hand to silence them again. "He's not going to be too happy with me when they let him go so whatever plan the adults have cooked up, we follow it. You will not make unilateral decisions for me or anyone in my family that stands in this fucking room.

We're a team, and we're done marching to your arrogant beat. Got that, Suit?"

The room claps and cheers. I see that my ego may be larger than most. It's time to take a backseat.

My Elle stands still too far away, on the table, glaring down at me. She's magnificent. All of her. I jump onto the table, snatch her into my arms, my hand sliding up her back between her shoulder blades and melding her body to mine. My life snaps back into place as I see the gold dancing in her emerald eyes again. We're face-to-face on even ground again.

"Anything you say Cosmo." I kiss her like no one else is in the room, all of me twitching at the thought of having her. But I must be patient. I'm not sure she's all the way back to me. People are cheering as we kiss. And I could care less.

Her pink perfect lips part, and I slip my tongue into her mouth, finding hers. No hesitation, no retreat on her part. She leans into me, and I know that she's close to whole again. Her tongue is a drug to me, healing every piece of my body and soul. I've always said I was addicted to her, but this is something different. This is a period at the end of our courtship and the beginning of the rest of our lives. Her tongue is swirling, matching me stroke for stroke. Each flick of our mouths stoking a fire we can't quite put out in this room.

I will never be separated from her again, ever. There's nothing too big or strong in this world or the next that can pull her from me. Our connection, our bond is stronger than anything we will have to face. The small part that worried and denied that it existed has just been washed away in this all-encompassing kiss. My fingers are stroking the back of her delicate neck. I tear my lips away from her and just hold her.

I hold her close and whisper, "Welcome back, my One Perfect Thing."

She doesn't smile but says earnestly, "Think the parents will wait a minute while we talk outside for a bit?"

I scoop her up and step down on a chair carefully. "Sure."

I nod to Sam across the room to take the helm of this group. Elle waves to Sam. She's so fucking cute. But I'm a bit worried despite her display of affection that she's gearing up to leave me. She's not a fan of lying, and I did a lot of it over the past couple weeks.

As we head for the door, my head floods with questions. How did Dasher know she'd be in her office? Does she blame me for him finding her or for not being there? I just need to see if I should be bracing for it now. Before we leave the room, I lean down and say, "Elle. Are you taking me out there to break up with me? I won't allow that."

Her grin goes positively mischievous. A sexy pout overtakes those pillow lips, and I don't know if I can handle this. She leans up to my ear, nipping and licking. Then she says the dirtiest thing and lets me know my Hellcat is all the way back.

"No. Not breaking up with you. But I don't know, it seems like someone deserves to be punished for such terrible behavior." She smacks my ass, and I laugh. "Or possibly you'd like me to get you to the brink and walk away. It's your choice. It's either start treating me like the love of your life or it's no orgasms for you, sir. What will it be? What do you want? Are you going to be a good boy or a bad boy?"

I drive my hands into her hair and pull her face to mine. I stop her just short of my lips. "I think you might just need a bad boy right now?" Her eyebrows raise.

"That's exactly what I need. But do you have time for that right now?" I hitch her back up and continue carrying her to the Jeep. Without another word, she reaches her arms around me.

"I always have time for that."

Elle

I'm possessed at the thought of him reclaiming me. Making me his again. I need him to know I'm his and he's mine. There is no other thought in my head than a desire to be filled with him. It's been four months since we've been together. Other than occasionally jacking him off, I couldn't get to a place of desire. And that was always for him, my love for him. Now, I flat out want him inside of me. I need his warmth. I need to come and release so much tension and apprehension. It's time to make up for the lost time. He's racing up to the Lookout, steering the Jeep with his left hand as his right settles on my breast. I'm undoing his pants.

"Why are we going up here?"

"Parents are home. That means Mrs. Dotson's at the Farmhouse."

He slams the car into park, puts on the emergency brake, and draws me towards him quickly. We take each other's mouths deeply and instantly. My body is searing for him. His tongue's darting and swirling inside my mouth. I nip his lower lip and try to catch my breath. Our white-hot electricity finally returns with a tidal wave of emotion and lust. His kiss is deeper and his tongue flicking my teeth, and I'm gasping at his lips.

"I need it, Elle. I need it. Remind me." He moans into my mouth, and I pull back and curl my lips into a sexy grin. He pulls my hair behind my ear. I move forward and lick his ear, my hands on his firm and unyielding pecs. He throws his head back and knows that I'm teasing him. His hands move up under my skirt as he pushes me to moan.

"Holy fuck, thigh highs. Jesus, I'm hard."

I continue biting and sucking his neck as his hand snakes higher. I inhale sharply as he begins to invade my thong. And then I am on his ear and release a long, stifled, and forgotten moan.

"Fucking finally. There's the sound of my love."

I'm panting now as I sit back into my seat. He's driving again with me leaning into him so he can feel my breasts bounce on the road against him. My nipples are taut and tight, aching to brush up against his naked body. I open his pants and begin to invade his shorts, and oddly he's wearing underwear. Makes it more compelling for me to have to work through another layer. They're black cotton, and I know they're probably hugging his rootstock tight. We make it around the switchback, and he slams the car into park again. He removes his hand from me and mine from him. Then he cranks the driver's seat all the way back. I get his drift, and I agree. I can't wait, either.

I stand in the passenger seat and shimmy my tight rosy skirt up, and it settles around my waist, revealing my cherry red thong and champagne-colored thigh highs. He swivels my hips and leans me over to see my ass.

"Fucking hell. Hellcat, that is the most achingly perfect backside. Juicy, taut, and fucking perfectly shaped." He squeezes, kisses it. Then he turns me back around and traces my seam with his finger. Then he pushes a finger into me. I'm so wet and ready for him. He curls gently inside of me, stroking that sacred spot.

I moan honestly. "Fuck, Josh."

He pulls out of me and flips me back around then nips at my ass "You're very good at picking out panties for me." I grin and look into his eyes.

I turn and lean down to kiss him. Deep and soulful. Then he smirks and reaches into the center console area and pulls out a wine opener. He flicks open the foil-cutting little knife and cuts my thong off me, tossing it onto the road. I smile as he stares at me, licking his lips.

"You just cut my panties off!"

"I did." He licks his lips.

"That was fucking hot."

"You're so beautiful. Look at that pretty little pussy just waiting for me. Months and months of wanting to see her again. Touch her. Taste her."

He reaches for me, but I'm already so wet. He slides his fingers along my lips below, and I throw my head back and moan. He teases me around my clit then quickly fills me with his fingers again. He pumps them into me as I stand there holding onto the roll bar of the Jeep. He leans over, pulling me to him and my clit lines up with his tongue. He spreads me with his fingers and tastes all that I have. He nips, and I scream. I just need for him to be in me.

"Enough teasing."

He jumps out of the Jeep and yanks his pants off. I get an excellent look at his amazingly hard, veiny, long and wide cock. He grins as he sees me staring. Stroking it, he says, "I promise to worship you properly later. But now I desperately need you to ride me."

He jumps back in the driver's seat, and I straddle him, bracing my knees on either side. His giant palms grip my hips and pull me down onto his cock. Both of us instantly moan loudly as he pushes in all at once. It pulls a bit. I'm so tight, but I quickly mold around him, driving past the pinch into pure pleasure. His hands are on my ass, squeezing and caressing. And my mind crashes open, letting all the emotion flood over me.

"Oh, god. You're so tight, my love."

"And I forgot how big you are." I buck into him again.

"Elle, I've missed you so much. I need you so much. I need this. I need us. You never leave me again."

"You sent me away."

"True. But I had a reason."

"Josh, can you just shut up and fuck me harder?"

"I'm going to make you come so hard, darling."

"Promises. Promises." I release with a moan, and we begin moving like wild animals. I grab onto the roll bar for support and bounce up and down on his dick as he thrusts wildly, both of us pounding and grinding into each other with equal power.

"Elle. Elle. You're so tight. Holy fuck. It's so good. Jesus, I missed you."

"Harder," is all I can utter as I come down to be fully seated on him and begin to roll my hips back and forth. Stretching backward, taking all of him inside of me.

"Oh, god! Oh. My. Fucking. God. I am not going to last long." His eyes look like they're going to roll back in his head. And I just keep moving. He puts his hands on my waist and helps me gyrate faster. The friction is so good, and he's so deep, and I'm coiling up, all my stress of the last four months mounting and begging to be let go. The taut-ness is getting too intense for me to take, and when he screams my name, I release into him. I fall onto his chest, convulsing as I throb around his dick, claiming him, milking every drop of his orgasm from him.

Both of us are breathing heavily as the low rumble of his laugh erupts and shakes my whole body that's tightly holding him. Then I begin to laugh too. The image of us in the woods, his shorts on the ground and my Chanel suit hiked up over my hips on a dirt road is inherently funny.

He tugs my face to him. "I'm so in love with you, Elle Parker. I've missed you every second you were gone. I missed you so damned much." We're so connected in this moment. I want him to just stay inside me. His deep aqua eyes are soft and loving. I feel whole again.

"I missed me too."

"But not me?"

"You and various parts of you."

He slips out of me, and I use an old t-shirt and a bottle of water in the back of the Jeep to clean up. He dresses and jumps back in the car as I fix my skirt.

I want him to know, "The part of me that Dasher shut off is also the part of me I took back from him today. I know why you sent me away, but don't ever do it again. We talk. We face these things together. Promise me."

"As long as I have breath in my body, he will never get close enough to do anything to you again. I will keep you safe. I promise my love. I'm so sorry I wasn't there today and that I sent you away."

"I love you so much, Josh." The broadest smile I've ever seen from him breaks over his face. "By sending me away, you brought me back. However, my love, you can't keep me safe. And you can't hide things from me. Like the Special Ops shit. But what I learned today is that I can keep me safe. I want you around me. But I think I'd like to hang on to Lou for a bit too."

"You're mine, and nobody fucks with what's mine. We have to go to this meeting. Our crew has been running the daily business while the moms and dads work on a solution. It's been a very frustrating process."

"Just let me fix my hair."

"It doesn't matter. You look perfect to me. Except for the Cosmo suit you've decided to wear to return to me. Where are the cutoffs?"

I hit him and then kiss him as I do my hair into a proper French twist. I may be back, but I forgot I can be both New York and Sonoma. And I won't make that mistake again.

"Get used to it. I forgot I like nice clothes. And I'm shipping all my pretty shoes out here, on your credit card. That's the price of sending me away and back to my closet. In fact, I want all my things here and only here." He kisses me roughly as if to seal the deal on forever.

Josh

We're seated around the Longhouse table. There's room for thirty-six people around this massive table, but we're only an uncorked army of twenty-seven. The Five Families, Mel, Sal, and our winemakers. It's eerie and kind of cool to see my whole childhood and current life come together in this historic room. Melissa rerouted the cameras from yesterday's feed to play while we're in here so that the lighting lines up. No one was in here, so it's good blank footage for that asshole to stare at when he reviews his tapes. When they let him out of jail. I take a seat midway down the table, Sam on my right and Elle on my left. She's seated next to Tabi who keeps making her laugh.

Adrian Schroeder, the patriarch of Schroeder Vineyards and my father's best friend, stands before the head of the table. Baxter, Tommi, and Ingrid's mom, Bellamy, passed from cancer years ago. Ingrid was little, and Bax was thirteen. She was the first person I knew who died. Unlike my grandfather, Adrian's a great single father. To our knowledge, he's never dated again; Bellamy was it. I respect that. I'd be the same way.

Whenever little Ingrid needed a mother, she'd seek out mine. She's sitting next to her now. I know she sneaks into town to see her sometimes. I haven't seen her in years. Except on like TMZ or that Fyre Festival promo video. She's a part-time model and an Instagram tastemaker. She's delicately beautiful with rich brown cascading hair, unlike Tommi and Bax's blonde. She looks exactly like Bellamy in my mind. Elle is staring at her, no doubt jealous of what she's wearing. She looks back at Tabi and continues talking. I'm not sure who Ingrid is wearing, but I'm sure it's expensive, designer, and someone probably paid her to wear it. But what Elle doesn't notice is Ingrid's jealous gaze towards her suit. And that Ingrid just snapped a picture of it. Elle's about to be IG infamous. Her thumbs fly on her phone. I pull up Ingrid's account. Sure enough, Elle looks gorgeous in the candid picture. As does Daphne, her Birkin bag. Ingrid hashtagged the hell out of it.

Even a boring meeting can surprise you. This one. High-light and highlights of the day. #gorgekickassstranger #chanel #isthatacrocbirkin #birkin #hermes #gottogetmeone #trea-surehunt #adultinggoals #perfecthoneyblondehighlights #blessedwithaperfectass #whodis

That's my Hellcat, *#goals*.

Adrian Schroeder is waving his arms up in the air and speaking loudly, "Alright, youngsters, have a seat. Grab a glass and settle in. While you idiots were taking selfies and bitching about Dasher, Ms. Rebecca Gelbert, clearly the smartest among you, found a small but doable loophole." His voice reverberates through the room. Bax has the same commanding and deep voice. We could be almost anywhere on their property growing up, and we could hear Mr.

Schroeder's voice reminding us of a blown-off winery task or to stop getting stoned in the back vineyards.

"Go ahead, Theresa."

Sam's mom steps to the edge of the table, and we all pay attention. She used to be a fifth-grade teacher and still has that air about her. To this day she claims the year she had Sam, David, Tabi, Baxter, and I was her worst year of teaching ever.

James Sr. and the rest of the old guard flank her. They look like a Sonoma Winery Justice League, and we're simply the Teen Titans.

David Gelbert yells from the back, "Can we screw him over now?"

"Yes, my dear, but it's a long con on a man who's spent his life conning us. Settle in while we explain a bit."

Adrian blurts out, "Alright hooligans, who's up for a little bootlegging?"

There is a rush of noise and my dad's eyebrows go up as I lock eyes with him, and he gets a mischievous smile and nods.

Theresa continues, "Legal, of course. No one outside of this room except Lou, Evan Bixby, who is my son's boyfriend and Elle's colleague, and of course Mrs. Dotson can know any of this. We're all on Mel's burner network now. You all know the rules of the burners. Now Mel wants to talk about our computers. And these include our work computers and the tasting room computers, the credit card machines, and any electronics."

Tabi pours more wine for her and Elle. I don't care how drunk she gets. I won't let her pass out. Tonight, I'm going to reacquaint her with all of her favorite things, and mine. My dick is twitching at the thought of fucking her, and we just did it. She opened a floodgate.

Artie Gelbert, David and Becca's dad and Poppy's uncle, takes over the explanation. "All of the wineries produce the same amount of juice, never appearing to be lacking in production. But once we all go to barrel and bottle, we skim. We skim the juice we already have in the barrels. We're going to bottle a collective second label called 'Prohibition' that will be a business created out of the Parker and Bixby LLC umbrella to keep it hidden."

Elle stands up. "I'm sorry, I've been in hiding for four months. What the hell is happening?" Everyone laughs loudly, and she smiles along with us.

Becca turns towards Elle. "Evan will explain, but remember that business license I took out for you to expand the company to California? Now it's a different business. But you'll still have to hang a shingle in SF and take on fake clients to throw him off. Sarah and Tina picked out a couple of spaces for you to lease."

"Okay, then. Bring it on."

Tina, Artie Gelbert's sister and Poppy's mom, steps up to speak. "If we shift our distributor's numbers to half from Prohibition and half from our regular labels, the wineries maintain the same profits from two different sources, and we can pay our bills, but it will appear that our namesake labels are failing. We won't be reporting Prohibition's profits to the Vino Groupies. Legally we don't have to because they have nothing to do with Prohibition. Our labels tank while Prohibition makes up the deficit and garners underground support."

Dad speaks up, "Prohibition will be blocked from Dasher on all social media platforms. Only print media will have any notice of it, but they won't be able to trace its origins. He literally can't google Prohibition wine." Mel smiles smugly. She really, really scares the shit out of me.

Melissa explains that all computers have been ghosted to our regular servers, but our actual cyber life will live in a different place: a massive server that has been built in Napa inside Schroeder's warehouse. This is where our real cyber lives will live. She and Tommi will be the gatekeepers for emails to get through the ghost wall, so Dasher thinks he's still monitoring our communications and transactions. They'll also filter our social media feeds. Lord knows how they can do that, but Mel is scary good. The room buzzes. Cameras and bugs need to remain in place. But we've all gotten used to censoring ourselves.

Dad continues by explaining, "Each winery will produce four flavors." We all laugh as he calls varietals, flavors. "Except for Schroeder. They'll do eight. They're approximately twice as large as the rest of us, so it's only fair they do more work. And that way we instantly produce a full slate of twenty-four wines. They can be single varietals or blends. Two whites. Two reds. All wine will be the Prohibition label with a secret coded logo indicating which winery it came from. And the names will be unique. All case orders will be red, white, or evenly mixed and be sold as a mystery."

"No one can take orders? Or buy what they want?" Tabi speaks loudly.

Elle turns to her, getting the gist. "No. We're not creating must-have wines to cellar; we're creating a must-have product that's cool and different. And there's no telling what product we'll have available so there can't be anything on demand. And it's what's around the bottle that matters to boost sales initially, not what's in it. You're suggesting we create exclusivity with everyday wine."

Mom addresses Elle, "Yup. Proud of us? We learned it from you." Elle beams from her seat.

Ingrid sits forward. "I know something about exclusivity, and if celebs can sell shit tequila and make a fortune, then we can certainly do this with a good product." Elle smiles at her and Ingrid grins back.

Dad continues, "The orders will be packed with whatever product we have on hand. The orders only indicate where to deliver. There's no way we can fill specific requests. It will be a subscription program, like a wine club with credit cards on hold for when it's available. When we have inventory, they order. When we don't, they don't. There will be a social media blast from Ingrid on that Instagram thing the day before the distribution. And the existing subscription numbers will be texted."

"From where? Who's texting?" Poppy asks for all of us.

"Mel and Tommi, basically. We fill orders until the supply runs out. No contact until there's product. We'll offer it to our respective wine clubs first and nationwide favorite vendors, but all contact will be in person or through the mail. We need to keep it out of the hands of locals, so it's not traced to us. Sorry Poppy, you can't carry your own wine. We old school this shit. No electronic orders. We fan out throughout the country to solicit bulk orders from wine stores."

Mel offers up, "Each subscriber gets a number. If they want the shipment, they text me on one of three dedicated burner phones with their subscriber number and number of bottles they want. If they post, tweet, or talk about the wine publicly, they're eliminated from the list."

"First rule of Fight Club..." David yells from the back, and we all laugh.

"Dad. That's brilliant." I exclaim.

He lifts his chin and indicates Mr. Aganos. "Subscriber numbers were all Costas' idea."

"Opa! Go Pops!" Tabi toasts him and pours herself another glass.

"Tabitha, agapité kóri, sit down and pay attention. This part is yours and Miss Poppy's."

My dad continues, "Ladies, you'll need to be point on distribution. We can't use our normal distributor routes, or even regular trucks, box delivery, label printers, etc.

We'll need to outsource everything and use Sal's people. Sal has a supplier in Illinois that we'll use for legal purposes for printing the labels. His trucks out of Texas will be used for shipping and he has a wholesale glass and box manufacturer we'll be using out of upstate New York. We're grateful for your partnership Sal."

My head snaps to him. He didn't tell me any of this and I have no idea how he got involved. Sal's lips move into a smirk and he slaps Mark on the back. Of course it was Mark who is saving our asses again. Seriously, thank god, he loves my parents so much.

I nod to my old college roommate and he places his hand over his heart and I know my parents must have shared all he Parkinson's information with him. I nod and turn my attention back to my dad.

"Tabi, you can command anyone, and no one will expect you to be handling teamsters."

Bax teases Tabi. "Actually, everyone would expect her to handle teamsters."

Everyone groans as my dad ignores us. "Gentlemen! The boys need to oversee our Estate vineyards, for appearances, and so that leaves you, Tabitha, with becoming the lead on Prohibition operations and production. You cool, Tab?"

Tabi raises her glass with the biggest smile. "Oh, I cool. So cool. Finally, fucking power. You bitches work for me."

"Tabitha!" Costas scolds her.

"Sorry, Pops." She sits back down and nods at her father.

Costas shakes his head at his daughter and turns back to the rest of us. "Sal, this man, he helps with delivery. The labels get designed under Evan. But they need liquor board approval. This is the hole. This is the way thatDasher can find us. Poppy, your ex-love was on the liquor board. He will help, yes?"

Poppy goes bright red, and Sal's attention shifts to her. She smiles meekly and says, "Yes. I can go directly to him and get him to fast track approval. But whose name appears on the license and application?"

Elle answers, catching on, "Anyone from my company except Evan or myself." She catches herself. "Whoops. Evan's company. I forgot I'm a vintner now."

Another giant laugh for my girl. Damn straight, she is. She's so fucking attractive. I just want to stare at her gorgeous eyes and the slight flushing of her beautiful skin. I tear away my gaze as Mom wraps up. Because otherwise, I'd fuck her right here without caring who watched.

"We still own all of our juice for this year and previous years. Everything we've barreled. As soon as we have wine ready for bottling, we open Prohibition. Our winery is the base of bottling because my packrat husband saved all the old bottling equipment. I guess, honey, there was a someday use for it all."

My dad looks like the cat who ate the canary. He's so proud we still have a shit ton of old equipment around.

Mom finishes up, "We'll open up the old routes at the back of the property that were used by our bootlegging ancestors to get your barrels here and the bottles out. If it lives in a tank, then we take the bottling equipment to the tank. But this will be base operations for the bulk of the bottling. Longhouse."

We all shift forward in our seats as my mom captivates us with how this is actually going to be done.

She continues, "Sal and Lou have people to excavate and build out more facilities. We'll use Schroeder's Napa warehouse for fulfillment. There are no cameras there. Schroeder is not on the lease. It's a share with a collective. This is all on us. Late nights ahead to save our asses from our own stupidity. Everyone get some fucking sleep. Tomorrow we bootleg."

I love when Mom swears.

Elle

James Sr. speaks very directly, "The Vino Groupies' ownership begins the last day of the last winery's harvest. We must make it appear we're working in good faith. It can't seem as if we're running two wineries. Will and Sarah are going to stay here through the harvest. Tina and Theresa will work on all paperwork and dual payrolls. They'll make it look as if we're personally paying our employees out of the sale money to make up for our lagging labels. We all stopped distributing our own labels a week ago. We need sales to appear to sag, so for now we hide our existing product. Our juice may look like it's the same or better than last year but it's the sales numbers they care about."

Josh adds, "There will be penalties on the equity if you're planning on returning the money to the Vino Groupies."

Goldie Aganos, Tabi's mom, speaks. "We are willing to lose that but will try and keep what monies we can. Why not get it all if we can?"

My heart leaps at the idea of the four of us at the Farmhouse again. But then quickly falls. I can't possibly have loud, dirty sex with their son in that house. We need a home. We need a place for us.

Costas' voice booms, "And when we tank our earnings, the contract says we forfeit the second payment. The money we decided doesn't matter so much. But most importantly, Mr. Asher, Darren remains on the hook for the bad deal and must make up the losses to these Vino Groupies. This is why he watches so closely. We're smarter, older, and have more resources. And we will remain in control of our labels and land. He will go to jail for money issues because we can prove that, and he does not have the millions to replace it. He will be a fraud. But most important he will not touch glykiá kai dynatí, Elle, again."

Tabi whispers loud enough for us to hear, "Sweet and strong." My heart swells, and my hand squeezes Tabi's.

David Gelbert speaks up, "But the assholes keep the profits."

James Sr. speaks up, "But young David, there will be none. Our labels have to tank. But each one of you, who doesn't currently own your namesake wineries will be named in the joint Prohibition label and company. When this is over, it will be yours to do with what you like. But for now, profits will be paid out to you through Bixby and Parker after Sal wipes the trail. Evan's working on the look and feel of the branding. Hell, if we can make money off merch, let's do that too. As long as a baseball hat can't be connected back to us. Fuck. Let's go viral as long as we're anonymous. It's vital we become popular quickly."

"I can make that happen. I can make all of this happen." Ingrid stands up and in a deep husky confident voice says, "How viral do you want to be?"

Jims yells, "Very." Ingrid nods to him and sits back down. Of all the kids' generation, Jims is closest in age to Ingrid. The he smiles at her it seems as if they're close.

"If all of this is legal profits, why do we need Mr. Pietro? No offense." Poppy asks politely.

Sal steps up. "No offense taken, Gingersnap. I wish I could have shared all of this earlier." Poppy smiles demurely. What the hell is going on there? I need to be more present in my life. Wow. I missed a lot.

Sal winks at her and turns towards everyone else. "Moving money is in my DNA. The bulk of my dealings don't do this anymore, but it's a skill I have not forgotten. I can make the income untraceable even though it's legal. It'll look like Bixby and Parker are making money and paying legit bills for their expansion to the West Coast. Everything gets taxed. The government gets its dirty cut. And it gets filtered back to you all for operations costs and profits. It's all on the up and up. We're hiding, not stealing."

I am three glasses in and eating this spy-and-hide shit up. I don't know how far we take him down, but I do know there will be enough comeuppance for me to be satisfied. Almost. I'd like him to be assaulted in jail. Is that too much?

Now that I got the gist, we need to leave. I move my hand up Josh's thigh, and he sits up straight. I lean over to see the bulge I know I've just sparked. I'm desperate for him. All the sweet nights he held me and evenings when I begged to sleep alone. I need to repay him. I'll say thank you for the rest of my life for him letting me work through this alone. But tonight, I want to thank him in the dirtiest way possible for pushing me away and over a cliff to find my way back to him.

Becca Gelbert stands up. "We're registered with the liquor board using Sam, Jims, David, Bax, and Tabi's new label. We transferred it to Prohibition and into Evan's assistant's name. We can start production immediately."

"You did?" says Tabi.

Mr. Schroeder, Adrian, stands up next to Jana Gelbert. The two of them hold up a graphic flag with a Five Families logo. "We're a real winery, together. The Five Families, as Mel calls us." Sal chuckles in the corner, and the irony is not lost on any of us.

"So, we're a gang now?" Poppy offers up.

"You're five gangs and one family, sweetheart," Sal answers her directly, winking at her. Poppy smiles at him and nervously moves one of her red curls behind her ear.

David pipes in, "To be fair, we kinda always were."

Adrian continues, "We're just hiding everything. We split the profits and costs into six equal shares. Schroeder gets two of the six shares because we're producing more wine. This is a done deal. You youngins have no say in this. The price point is flat, twenty-five dollars per bottle. Shipping is a flat rate per state. No exceptions. Let's save our high-end crap for the tasting room."

Bax asks, "Dad, what about Chapel and Bellamy's Ghost? Won't that be enough profit that Prohibition doesn't matter? That was their plan all along."

Becca raises her arms like she's going to preach. "Listen up, brothers and sisters. I found something so good. Will and Adrian are kind of geniuses at this spy shit. LC/W and Schroeder sold the Chapel and B's Ghost names and labels when the contract was signed. But as of today, those vines and land belong to LC/W's former vineyard managers, José and Manuel Apato. Purchased for a hundred dollars to start their new label *Para Mama*. Profit participation to be worked out after we regain ownership of our own vineyards."

There are some notable gasps, and Rebecca continues speaking.

"The sale of the Lodi vines went through yesterday. The original purchase of that land was a joint venture between the old guard, Lucien LaChappelle and Helmut Schroeder in 1992. The partnership was never dissolved. It was after Dasher's time, so he might not know this fact. No single winery owns the land, both of them do in a separate company." Will and Adrian each hold up a fifty-dollar bill and grin madly.

"But that's the Vino Groupies linchpin," I say as Josh puts his hand on my back.

David mocks his sister as she pops back up. "I do not think I have ever seen you this animated."

"Fuck off, David. I found the damn needle in their six reams of paper haystack contract. They bought *our* Estate lands, vines, names, and the Chapel and B's Ghost labels. All contracts specifically name the sale of Estate lands and vineyards. The Lodi vineyards are first off, not Estate and second are jointly owned by a different company, who was never named in any of the contracts. The deed and the Lodi vineyards were never named either. There are very specific legal words that identify an Estate winery. Two vineyards from different appellations, growing regions, even if owned by the same winery, cannot be legally called Estate. In short, they never bought the Lodi vineyards, just the labels. This ensures they won't be able to destroy and build on our land but to get our wineries back, they have to appear to fail. We have to have both pieces in place."

David stands up. "I'm an idiot."

We all laugh as Tabi says, "And what else is new?"

"Completely fucking confused." He shrugs and flips off Tabi.

Jana Gelbert steps forward again. "Here's the outline, dear David." She walks over to the white board that Theresa is holding and she it turns out the teachers in the room have written it all out clearly.

A. Our wineries need to appear to be failing.

B. We're going to fake failing. We hide our profits in Prohibition. If our Estate Wineries fail the contract is null and void and the wineries become ours again.

Jana speaks to David specifically, "You do remember what Estate means, darling?"

David looks frustrated, "Oh my god, Mom. Yes. The vineyard where the grapes are grown and the winery used to make the wine must be on the same property."

"Very good, David." We all laugh again while his mother continues the rundown.

C. By not turning a profit the deal becomes void. But we'll be fine because of the secret profits from the Prohibition label. We need to sell all the Prohibition wine we can produce.

D. Asher will be on the hook for the money lost by the Vino Groupies when the deal gets voided because he's the steward of the deal.

E. Without the Lodi juice they won't have enough wine profit to demolish our homes and develop the land. And we won't have any Lodi profit to bolster our sagging wineries' bottom lines. It all reverts back to us.

Goldie proudly steps up, adjusts her bright Greek blue-and-white caftan and beehive and announces, "Vino Groupies can have the Chapel label and the Bellamy Ghost, but they are just paper." She raises her face to the heavens and blows a kiss to her long-gone friend and label's name-sakes. "But they now have no juice to put in those little juice boxes they want to sell."

"HOLY FUCKING SHIT!" Josh slams his hand on the table as corks pop.

The room goes ape shit that Chapel and B's Ghost can't save anyone. Everyone hugs. Poppy rushes to me. She's a breath of fresh air. Tabi turns to me, and the girls form a tight circle. "This is so fucking cool."

Becca toasts the three of us. "If we can pull it off. We still need to sell a shit ton of Prohibition for this to work."

I smile. "Leave that to me. That's my secret power. I can sell anything."

Costas climbs on top of a chair and screams at us to be quiet. "Raise all the glasses! We will bottle, we will box and tape, and all of us will be victorious. Our names and wineries will live on. Now that Joshie has come to his senses and found the woman and his roots. YAMAS!"

I'm surrounded by all the girls when Tabi looks me right in the eye and says, "And you're all fucking here, right? No more disappearing and leaving us. I don't like many people, so you can't fucking ditch me now."

Sammy pipes in, "It was awful. I fucking hated every second of his idea and his demanding me to text you lies."

I hug Sammy, and she tears up a bit. I hold my glass out, and the other six women meet my glass. "I promise you. I'll never leave again. I love you all, and I'm so grateful to have friends like you who would lie, push me away, and keep information from me. So very grateful."

Becca asks, "Rosé on Tuesday?"

"I'll be there. With Lou of course." All the women laugh, and it feeds my soul.

Tabi raises her glass and toasts back because it's bad luck if you don't. "Stin oikogéneiá mou." We all pause and wait for the translation.

Baxter leans into the circle from behind Tabi, "To family." Tabi winks at him and licks her lips. He raises his glass and walks away.

I tuck away my happy tears for later and repeat a phrase I thought I'd never get to say again. "To family."

Josh

She's in the crowd as our meeting becomes a party to celebrate our ingenious parents. I'm still reeling from this fucking day. My god. Could more shit happen? It's a lot. She's always in my sightline even though I can't touch her right now. I feel like a planet circling the sun. I'm done being around other people. I'm staring at her, willing her to give me her eyes, but she remains laughing and joking, now with David and Poppy.

Sam's speaking to me, and it's as if the entire room is on mute. It's like everyone speaking sounds like the adults in *A Charlie Brown Christmas*. All I hear is her. All I smell are lilacs and orange blossoms. All I see is our future. And then there's a tug at my shoulder, and I realize my mom's trying to get my attention. I hug her. "You guys are too fucking much."

Artie Gelbert slaps me on the back and says, "This is the last fucking time we dig your generation's legacy out of a mess. Thank god your tits and ass had that business license in San Fran. Ya hear me, boy? Last time."

I hate Artie Gelbert. Lucien liked to use that term.

When I turned fifteen, I stood up to him and told him to fuck off. Lucien was proud of me but still smacked me into the ground for mouthing off. Don't call me *boy*, you patronizing asshole. You can't put me on the ground.

When my friend David's a dick, he's acting like his dad. Most of the time, he acts like his mom, Jana. She's funny, warm, and wonderful. Never knew how she stands Artie.

But Artie, don't step to me. You don't know who I am outside of Sonoma, and I'd scare the shit out of you outside of our bubble. I eat shit like you for fucking breakfast. I see that Sal wants to knock his teeth out for fun after calling me boy and referring to Elle as tits and ass.

There's an odd hush as I pull myself up to my full height to look down on him a bit. Everyone is listening. "Our signatures aren't on the sales contracts. Yours are. We'll fucking save our own legacy with your Hail Mary plan. But don't ever fucking forget who's digging in the trenches and whose ass is saving whom. It's my fiancée's company, which she built all by herself. She didn't inherit the business like most of us in this room. Her tits and ass didn't build it. She hustled to succeed, learning her business from the bottom up. And she knows hard work and hard times better than your pampered misogynistic ass. It's her company as the shell organization and branding, it's her former employee handling our massive tech needs, my associate's network doing distribution, Ingrid's influencers, Sam and David's winery permits, licenses and tax ID numbers you'll be using, Tabi's vineyard skills, Poppy's connections, and your daughter's brilliant legal mind that ultimately saved your ass. So boy, this is the last time we're coming to *your* fucking rescue."

There are cheers from around the room. My mom

smirks, and my dad laughs. I made my point but might have overstepped.

"Got it, Artie?" I slap his back and give him the out to not be a dick, and he takes it.

"Joshie, you got me. We need to work together." Asshole.

I look at Elle, and she mouths a sentence to me, "That was hot." And my dick twitches. I need to be touching her very soon.

"Josh." I turn my attention to my mom. "Josh, are you sleeping at the Farmhouse tonight? We weren't supposed to be here. We can stay at Schroeder's guest house if it's easier."

"No. No. Mom. You and dad stay in your home. I'm happy you're back. You look excellent."

"I feel excellent. I will keep up with treatments in the city, but I've been really good, sweetheart. I really missed the winery. I'm so happy to see you. And it seems Elle's okay. It took all my power not to let your father come back here and kill him."

"It took every ounce of grace that the two of you ever bestowed on me not to go Lucien on his ass."

"We'll get him, sweetheart. Your dad is very protective of Elle, and we're not sure what you did to make her seem so secure and powerful again, but I'm glad she has you. You two are welcome to stay in the Farmhouse with us. You can sleep in the same room if that's the issue."

"Oh, Mom. That is so *not* the issue. I would never subject you to what's going to happen tonight. We can stay up at the Lookout for tonight and then figure out a workable solution."

She rolls her eyes and then nods her head behind me.

She walks away, and I can already feel the heat coming off my sunshine before I turn around.

"What we're doing tonight won't be parent-approved?"

As I take her in my arms, the room dulls in sound and sight. All I see is her face. I'm gone. I have no power. I'll still pretend I do, but she holds all the cards.

"You're lucky you still have clothes on."

"Why are we still here?" she says with a lilt in her voice.

"No fucking idea."

We don't say goodbye but begin to weave our way to the front of Longhouse. I grab her suitcase at the entrance and throw it into the Jeep.

"Are we going to make it to Lookout this time?" Elle says with a sly stare, and I realize she has an armful of wine in her hands.

"What are those for?"

"I was just wondering if the *Joshua* Merlot really does taste like you. Or if it tastes better off of you."

"No. There's no guarantee we'll make it ten minutes up the path without fucking."

She smirks and gets inside the Jeep, hiking up her skirt as she sits. I totally forgot she was commando. Fuck me, that's a gorgeous view.

Elle

He commands, "Hands to ourselves, young lady. This is a dangerous drive in the dark, and if you even breathe on me, I may come." I laugh a big throaty laugh and pull down my skirt. We ride along in such sexual tension that it's thrilling. I reach my hand out to touch his, and he pulls it away.

"No. No. No."

"Well, if I can't touch you, I may have to just tell you what I'm going to do."

"Sweet god, Elle, don't do that."

"First, I'm going to strip down to my very expensive bra so that you see my nipples straining in it, aching to be in your mouth. But there won't be anything on the bottom, because the matching thong is somewhere in the woods providing shelter for a small woodland creature."

"Not enough material to shelter anything."

"Then I will need your help. Can you maybe inspect my ass while I bend over to remove what remains of my thigh highs?"

"You are the devil."

215

I laugh again, "And then I'm going to peel off all of your clothes, licking and sucking each and every inch of you. As I round up to your lips, I'll start kissing you so intensely you won't remember your name. And then taste all of you again, this time putting your insanely beautiful, immense and hard cock between my pink lips and take you so deeply..."

"That's quite enough."

"What? You don't want to touch the back of my throat with your dick?"

"I will not object to that. But that's about the only part of this show, you're going to run."

My stomach flips, and the idea of someone taking control because he loves me, not because he needs to dominate me becomes an outstanding thought. I did the work. Bicoastal therapists. And I'm ready. More than prepared to move forward reclaiming all the parts of my life.

Josh

She leaps out of the Jeep before I can put it into park. I grab her bag and follow her inside where she's turning on a couple of lights. I drop her bag at the door and sweep her into my arms.

"As much as I want to throw you down and tell you what to do. As much as I've fantasized this moment for four freaking months and all the nasty ways I want to make you come. As desperately as I want to make you desperate, you're going to have to guide us through this. That's what the therapist said. It's your show, my love."

There are tears in her eyes, and I wipe the first one that falls with my thumb.

I whisper to her, "No. No. Cosmo. I'm sorry I didn't mean to make you sad."

She curls into me and squeaks out, "You didn't make me sad. I'm just leaking happy. You went to therapy for me."

"Mostly it was so I didn't commit murder. But I also asked questions about how to be there for you and how to process all of this. They were only half on board with my sending you away plan. But your therapist in New York said that you were engaged and open to talking about everything."

"You called him?"

"I did. He helped me understand a few things about myself, as well. I had a very hard time coming to terms with you being afraid of my temper. That you hid from me because you were afraid of what I would do to Asher or that I'd judge you in some way. I only pulled out the Lucien stuff to force you to look at the whole picture when you were in New York. I wanted you to see a sliding door of sorts. But he's gone, babe. Or at least I'm getting a handle on how to handle the Lucien side of me. We had a couple of phone sessions."

She laughs into my chest and pulls her head back and stares at me. Those gorgeous glowing green and gold eyes dancing in the warm light of the cottage. There's a veil of softness over them.

"I love you so much," she professes, and there's a richness to her voice. Like she means it more now than she ever has.

I let her know my heart. "I didn't know I could love or need something as much as I do you. You're my blood and my oxygen. I'm a shell without you."

She smiles and says, "And so, my love, there's nothing you could ask me to do that wouldn't come from that place. That's the difference. I don't need to guide you. You already know what to do."

She kisses me softly. We let our lips lightly reacquaint and then she nips at my lower lip and it's game on. I crush her to me, invading her mouth. My tongue darts and swirls at a furious pace, pushing her up against the wall. I unzip her jacket and cup her lace bra that shows through her thin white shirt. A hunger returns for both of us, and I'm already hard as a rock. I slip my hand down to her ass, and my lips find her ear. I nibble just underneath and then whisper, "How wet are you? Do you need help getting there for me?"

Her voice comes out throaty and raw. "Never when you're near me." I don't hesitate to unzip her skirt.

"Turn around."

She does as she's told and arches her back just slightly as if she's presenting her perfect nectarine ass to me. I drop her skirt off her hips, and there it is in all of its bare glory. She drops her jacket to the ground. I lean down and kiss her ass slowly while caressing the cheeks. I stand and walk her further into the cottage, backing her up while I kiss her completely. I lift her arms and remove her silk tank top and throw it to the ground.

"Hey. That's Chanel."

"Don't care."

I roughly take her lips and pull her body to mine. She reaches for my waistband. I yank her hand away and stare at her sharply.

"No, Hellcat, we're only touching you right now." She moans in approval.

"Ok, if that's the plan, sorry I didn't mean to get off the agenda. Touch me." She unhooks her bra and and let's the straps droop on her arms.

"Show me now. I need to see them." She teases with a quick peek at one of her nipples, and then I crook an eyebrow.

"Angling for a punishment?" Her eyes flash, but she drops the bra on command. I'm on her tits in a flash, sucking one as she throws her head back. My hand busies down below. I kneel, dragging my mouth down her body. And she gasps. I'm looking at the prettiest pussy there ever was.

"Do you have something to hold on to?"

"Yes."

I see her hands move to either side of the exposed beam door frame that leads to the little kitchen. I place one of her legs, still in its stocking, on my shoulder, and I dive in. She's instantly moaning. And I eat like I'm starving. Which, I have been. I lap up every drop of her I can find.

"You taste so fucking good." I swirl and tug. She's loud and frequent with the moaning. I feel it down to my balls. My cock aches more with each moan. I keep my mouth on her clit while I circle her and wait for the go-ahead.

"Yes. Yes. Josh. Please. Make me come. I want to come for you. It's been so long."

"I can do that. I will make you come harder than you can imagine. Come on my face, baby."

I suck harder at her clit and thrust two fingers into her, pulling in and out before I twist and curl them looking for that magical place inside of her that's all mine.

"Oh. My. God. Josh. Josh. Oh." And she lets loose with a massive groan as I feel her tension building. She needs an epic release, and I'm not done building this for her. I stand and circle around to the back of her.

"Fuck. No. Josh. You have to let me come."

"I will."

"When?"

I lick her neck, and she groans, every part of her more sensitive as she lives on the edge. I reach around to hold her breasts. I knead them, flicking the nipples to attention while I stay on her neck. Still standing behind her with the most perfect view of her body. My raging erection pressed up against her back.

"Play with yourself. Keep yourself on the edge for me. But don't come. Not yet. Do you hear me, Cosmo?

Her beautifully manicured red nailed hand reaches

down to her own clit. I stand behind her watching from above. Fuck me.

"Elle. That's the sexiest thing I've ever seen. Do it just like that. Oh fuck. Hellcat pull back if it's too intense. I get to give you your orgasm, not you. Me. You're mine. These breasts and long hard nipples, mine. All fucking mine. And this orgasm, that you're desperate to untwist and unleash. I feel it. It's mine, and I ache to give it to you."

She throws her head back and I see her reach lower. I interrupt her and move her to the side. Her hands go to her breasts, circling her nipples and moaning as she leans into me. I reach my long arms down and cup her. Three fingers plunge into her while the heel of my hand remains fixed on her clit. And as I curl them into her soft spongy center, she explodes sliding down the front of my body.

"Oh, my fucking god. Fuck. Josh. Josh. Yours." And then the most epic moan rumbles through the cottage as she falls back into me. I catch her as she goes boneless with convulsions and shivers that seem to keep rolling through her. My fingers, still inside, I feel her wrap around them as if she can't let them go. My dick is poking so hard into her back. As she catches her breath, I remove my fingers and wrap myself around her. I lick my fingers while she watches, eyes wide.

"Fucking delicious."

"That was insane."

"That was just the beginning. You up for it?"

"I don't think you can top that."

"Oh. Don't fucking play, woman. Challenge accepted." I scoop her up and carry her to the bed. I throw her down and strip the remainder of my clothes. She's staring at me with her legs spread wide and glistening with her own desire. I roll her trashed stockings off her perfect legs.

"Remind me to buy you these in every fucking color of the rainbow." I toss them to the side of the bed. And now it's just us, naked and vulnerable.

I pull her to the edge of the bed, her eyes flash wide. Her perfect hair is now disheveled and sexy. I feel undone. She wraps her legs around my waist instinctively, I pull one back and crook a leg over my arm, raising it up as I plunge into her in one long, hard thrust.

Elle

Holy god, that feels so good.

"So good. So good. I want to be so deep in you."

I didn't think I could come so fast, but I do. I shake and convulse, and his eyebrows go up. "Damn, Josh. That's two."

"I want you to lose count." He's kissing me deeply and then stands back up and plows into me again. I need. He needs, I feel it. I feel it in his kiss and thrust. He's moaning, panting and completing me. I twitch my hips towards him and clench my ass a bit.

"Fuck. How did you get tighter? Shit."

Then I roll my hips as he stands paralyzed. Then doubles down on his motions and I know he won't last long. He reaches down with his thumb without warning I come again. I pull tight around him, and he growls as his release possesses him. I feel him come so hard, and I let all my tension go again, pushing me past what I thought pleasure could do. I roar with him as it continues to ripple through both of us. I black out and live in this other plane of bliss for the briefest of moments. He flops on top of me. Both of us are sweaty and breathing heavily. In between trying to catch my breath, I say, "How many is that?"

He looks at me. "Not enough. But it's enough for now."

He leaves my body, and instantly I want him back even though I have no idea how I could do anything else. I'm suddenly ravenous and thrilled for my controlling side. I filled the cabinets in this kitchen with tiny yummy tins of things and boxes of crackers. I also know there are charcuterie items and cheese in the Lookout fridge. I had a standing order to keep it stocked, and I know Sammy won't let me down. I'm thrilled as I open the freezer. I've learned in Sonoma, that no matter what time of day, if someone stops by you better have a cheese plate ready to go and a bottle to uncork. There's Vella dry Jack, Cowgirl Creamery, Mt. Tam, and Cypress Grove Humboldt Fog cheese in the freezer. And I'm going to eat every bit of it, probably off him.

He returns from the bathroom with towels and cleans himself and me up. I kiss him soulfully, and then I pull on his t-shirt to go prepare our feast.

There are jarred olives, salami, and dried apricots in the cupboards. I'm impressed with myself. Had no idea I would be the one to eat this food. I garnish with some wildflowers from outside while Josh finishes rinsing off in the shower. I pour two glasses of the highly addictive mineral notes and strawberry essence Gelbert Family Vineyards Grenache Rosé. I also down two bottles of water.

He emerges from the shower, and I can't help but stare. It's just so fucking hot. His dick is a work of art. My work of art. I instinctively lick my lips.

"My eyes are up here, ma'am."

"My apologies, Mr. Whittier." He rushes to me and

224

pulls me into an embrace. His body is hard and rippling. Water beading on the ridges of his abs makes me want to lick it off. I should rest, but instead, I run my hands down his equally hard pecs and brush his erect nipples. He lets out a little moan.

"If that gorgeous pussy of yours doesn't want to get fucked right now, fast and hard, you need to step away."

I'm immediately damp for him from the dirty way he's talking to me and decide to overlook my soreness. I'm going to walk it off and continue playing the game. There's always Advil. And I know the pleasure will far outweigh the pain. I'm just shocked he can go again. I reach down, cupping his balls, and slowly slide my hand out to his member that's already growing in my hand. He drops his towel and drags two fingers through my intense wetness.

"Me. The thought of me did that?" I go up on my tiptoes and kiss his neck and moan in the affirmative. "You are the most perfect fucking woman."

"Prove it."

He flips me around and kisses a trail down my neck while his hand squeezes my tits. He steps away from me. "Stay here." He then picks up my platter from the table and takes it to the bedroom. The lights bounce off the white vaulted exposed beamed ceiling and down onto him, and the bed looks ethereal. Then he returns to the living room, grabbing the waters and the glasses of Rosé, and moves them into the bedroom as well. I assume he put them all in the cozy little sitting area by the small fireplace in the hidden corner. Then he comes back as I look bewildered.

His voice is gruff and raspy with desire. "Turn around. Put your hands flat on the table." My body is tingling with anticipation, and I do as he commands. He bends me slightly forward and places a hand on my ass, squeezing. I know he's stroking himself to the sight of my ass and I arch my back, raising it up just a little. He walks away from me. My ass is on display, so I move to stand up.

"No! Don't you dare move. You wait for me."

"I was just—"

He interrupts me, and it's hot as hell with a quick sharp smack on my ass. I yelp, and then he sucks on the place he just swatted. It's so hot. I revel in it. I catch the peripheral vision of him stroking himself and his tongue licking his lips.

"No one asked you a question. This is not a debate. Fucking bend over and stay right there with your delicious and tight pussy waiting just for me." I moan in approval.

He continues, "Fuck, you're so sexy. That ass of yours. We need to revisit the backdoor subject." My breath catches, and I tense up a bit. I'm not sold on that idea despite that crazy orgasm on the private plane. "Stop with the worry face. Not unless you want to, Hellcat. Just put it on our ideas board."

I relax again but keep my hands flat on the table. He walks over and drags his finger through my slickness then slowly traces up to my ass and brushes with the lightest of forbidden pressure. Sensation rockets through me. My breath is gone as he pushes on the entrance, not breaching anything. I react in shock. But I moan a deep guttural moan at the pressure. A groan that is entirely involuntary, unexpected, and warranted. Holy hell, it was like a bolt of bliss blasted through me.

He reiterates as he kisses my neck, "Agenda item number one, backdoor visit."

I don't even know what to do with that. My nerve endings are just calming down from the slight invasion.

Then he's spreading my legs wider. He places two very thick coffee table books on the ground.

"Step up, my petite." And it clicks. He needed better access because he's too tall, and we don't have the kitchen step stool. As I stand on the books, he's instantly circling my entrance with the crown of his cock. My whole body wants him to fill me again.

I look behind me. "You promised this was going to be fast and hard. This seems more like teasing, soft and slow."

And without warning, he smacks my ass while I gasp again. He does it a second time. "You should know better. I said, don't speak."

"Whoops. Totally forgot." And he delivers two more in rapid succession, and I shriek a bit and grin. I can be nowhere else but right here with him. Totally present.

"My handprint is blooming red on your ass. Your precious and gorgeous skin. Mine." And he leans down, licking, kissing, and caressing the heated spot he just marked. I welcome the heat. I'm so beyond myself right now. I'm only here with him. Then his cock is back, but there's no teasing. He pushes his rootstock inside of me all at once. I'm so ready to take all of him, and at this angle, I can in one push. I meet him thrust for thrust, both of us moving quickly towards release.

His cock is pushing the boundaries of my vagina walls as they adapt and encase him. It's building in my belly, in my blood, and in my pussy. His hands on my hips driving me over and over. Both of us gasping each other's names and expletives flying. Then like a glorious gift, he reaches around and thumbs my clit again. Sensitive and pulsing, begging to be touched. That's all I need to find that fringe of rippling pleasure. I groan loudly as I feel him growl and then let go of whatever he has left inside of me. Both of us still move in unison while the pleasure tears at the fabric of what we know to be true. We're made to do this for the rest of our lives. Our bodies are made to do this with each other as often as possible. How could I have forgotten?

He flops down on my back and holds me. My arms barely support me and are shaking. My thighs are still quivering with afterglow and lust. Both of us begin breathing together, trying to regulate. He slips out of me, and as always there's a tiny bit of sorrow that I'm empty again. He picks me up, wiping my thighs with his discarded towel. Then he spins me around. I'm still standing on the books, and we're more eye to eye than usual. A soft sensuous kiss joins our bodies once again.

"'I love you' seems trite to express what I'm feeling."

My eyes well up at his sentiment. "I know. It's endless."

"Bottomless pit of desire and love for you. I keep waiting for it to be just something we are, but every day is more spectacular than the last."

I finish the thought. "Every day is more."

"And yet, still not enough." He kisses me and pops a stray olive in my mouth.

"I'm too tired to eat. Can we sleep first then eat?"

"We can, my love. We can do anything you want, Hellcat."

We nestle into the bed naked, and he wraps his arms around me. I spoon into him as we both drift off in the harmony that everything at this exact moment is perfect. I fall asleep for the first time in four months in total peace and contentment. Not a cuticle nipper in sight.

Josh

No fucking clue what time it is, but I know I haven't slept this well in months. She's in the exact same position as she was when we fell asleep. Except at some point, she put on a t-shirt and little shorts. I throw my left arm over her perfect fucking body and hope my dick behaves. I'm not sure she can take another pounding. I may have to head to the shower to jack off and get rid of his morning wood. She snuggles back into me and pulls my hand up under her chin to tighten my grip on her. The alpha in me loves that, more possession. She's mine.

Her voice is coated in sleep, but she seems alarmed. "What the hell is this?" She rotates my left wrist as she turns on her back, resting her head in the crook of my arm. She sees that it reaches around the entire wrist.

"My tattoo."

"Since when are you a tattoo guy?"

"You've been a bit preoccupied lately, my love."

"But how long have you had this. It's like a little

stranger staring at me. And are those flowers? Not a vine or grapes. Flowers?"

"They're your flowers."

"What are you talking about?" She climbs on top of me, smashing my hard-on to my stomach, and I groan. She scoots up so we're eye to eye, and I can't help but moan again at the friction. She smiles slyly. "I'll take care of that in a minute. Start talking."

"I got it about a month or so ago."

"Way after Dasher but before you sent me away."

"Don't say his name when my dick is hard."

"Fair enough, but in my defense, it's hard all the time."

"It's all your fault."

"Continue." She grinds into me, and I groan.

"It was supposed to be a surprise, but the timing was never right to show you. My watch band usually covers it up. I scheduled it after you said yes. You get a ring to prove to the world that you're mine, but I thought you needed something to show the world that I'm yours. I wanted the world to know."

"But I don't get the flowers." She examines them closely. "Is that lilac? What's the other flower?"

"Orange blossom. Do you know that's what you smell like? All the time. Sometimes more intensely than others. But I can pick that smell out of a crowded room and find you."

"I smell like lilacs and orange blossoms?"

"And sometimes cinnamon, but I liked the flowers better."

"I like that there's no color. It's sexy." She sits up and pulls my arm to her and licks the tattoo.

Then pulls her knees up to her chest. "What's it like to be in love with me?"

I scrub my hand over my jaw and consider my answer. "I feel like my life had the mute button pushed. And you turned the volume up on everything. I muted my family, my heritage. I turned it all the way down to keep Lucien's expectations and judgment out. I did it because I couldn't face who I was. I muted everything about myself in the process. It was a survival instinct, and then this loud, blonde, ball-busting bombshell busted through all of my defenses and found all the cracks in my armor."

I weave my fingers through hers, and she relaxes her legs. The sun is streaming in through the skylights, and her impossible green eyes flash joy and love. She's in my old Stanford t-shirt that's almost threadbare. I wish it were just a little thinner around her magnificent nipples, which are pushing out just a little in the morning chill.

"And soon the volume was so loud that you and my life couldn't be ignored. All my emotions that I'd turned the volume down on got poured into you. All the good and bad rushed back into my life, opening everything to me."

She's letting silent tears fall down her face. She sniffles and says, "And that's okay? It's okay that I let Lucien's words and actions come back to you?"

I sit up to face her, she scoots with me, and I lean against the grey velvet padded headboard. "Oh, Cosmo. You reminded me that good comes with the bad. You're worth all the bad I was afraid of facing. You gave me back my family, my community, and my world. I left my home to rot like dropped fruit. But you are everything. The most good I could ever dream of having."

She smiles and kisses me gently, and I wipe away her tears. "I understand."

"What's it like to be in love with me?"

She grins and shrugs. "It's aiiight."

I tackle her and tickle her. She's laughing, and I push forward. "Tell me!"

"You're hot. Have you seen you? You're like a mythical monument to hotness. And your ass. I know you like mine, but I don't think we have spent nearly enough time talking about that perfect, hard, round piece of perfection. And then I fell in love." I tickle her more. Then I stop, flip her over, and pin her to the bed.

"Tell me, my love. Tell me what it's like for you to be in love with me."

"Chaos."

I flip her back over and let her continue. "The constant twirling of visions of things I want to do or have to do. There are all these things I want to tell you or things I've done and can't wait to share. And all the emotions swirling together at once. Nothing making sense."

"Chaos? That's not good." I stroke her face and sit back to let her adjust. She leans back up against the headboard. I shift my legs from her as I lay them by her side. She holds my feet.

"No, but it is. I closed off so many pieces of myself. Fragments of me that were unimaginable pain and loneliness buried deep. Every small piece that bubbled up, I would immediately shut behind a door, so I could maintain control."

She pauses, and I take the opportunity to kiss her deep and slow, our tongues sweeping into each other's mouths, drugging the other with the kiss. And then she continues.

"I kept all of me in the dark and shadows. Slowly but surely, you began to open those doors for me. You engulfed all the hallways and rooms with light. Then all my random wandering pieces snapped together the night you kissed me.

Not our one-night stand, but at the Member party as part of the cover for he-who-shall-not-be-named when he showed up with Natasha from *Rocky and Bullwinkle*. I didn't understand it at the time. But now I know you stand at the center of my soul, holding up a giant ball of sunlight, and I'm not afraid to be in it with you. All the damn doors are open, and everything is lit. Every memory and impulse running amok. It's chaos I don't want to control but celebrate. And you and I are the calm center of it all. We're dancing like crazy in the light. I don't ever remember being as present and awake in my life except with you."

"Woman." I whisper.

She smiles and then puts on a more serious face. She has more to say, and I'm always willing to listen. "Dasher tried to dim that light and shut my doors. I let him. And I know you were pushing me to reclaim myself in New York. Distancing yourself and trying to make me jealous. But it was when I saw his face that I realized all the shit I let him take from me. And all I felt was a burst of light as I reclaimed it and pushed the darkness away. I didn't hide or throw anything behind a metaphorical door. I just raged forth. How dare he try and take away my One Perfect Thing. And as I claimed myself, I re-claimed you as well."

Now I'm misty-eyed. She moves her hand to my cheek. And I say to her, "I love you. Always."

"Always. And this is touching, but if I don't eat soon, you're going to die. I will kill you." She says this in the same loving voice.

I laugh at her. "You feel a thirst for blood, rage, and chaos. That's what it's like being in love with me."

"Pretty much."

"Perfect."

She adds one more thought. "Also, you know my body better than anyone in the world. Making love to you is probably the most amazing thing I get to do in any part of my day."

"Well, in that case." I reach down, and instantly she's ready again.

Josh

After another rinse off, I'm stunned at how many times we've had sex in the last twenty-four hours. I grab the cheese plate she made last night and two mugs of coffee. I add one little item to the cheese plate. And deliver it to the bed, which we're going to have to buy from my parents. I can't imagine it belonging to anyone other than us.

She instantly grabs a slab of salami, and my palms are sweaty as she overlooks the surprise.

"I don't think I have ever been this hungry. Caffeine! Thank you." She's smiling at me while she takes the mug from me. "You give me the best things."

I chuckle a little bit as I look down pointedly to the platter of meats and olives on her lap.

She asks, "Aren't you hungry?"

"Starving."

"Then come here." She lifts a piece of salami and holds it out to my mouth as I join her on the bed. She shoves it in and, without looking, reaches for another piece of something but comes up with my small turquoise box instead. Her eyes get wide as she looks at the dainty white bow.

"What's this?!"

"Open it."

"Why?" she asks.

"Do you realize we've never been on a date? Consider this a place marker. Pencil me into that calendar of yours. And you don't let me give you enough gifts."

"Mercedes, Halston, Daphne, and this." She holds up her ring finger and points to it.

"Yes. I did give you that ring, but I didn't buy it for you. I didn't pick it out. I didn't think about you and plan the perfect thing for my One Perfect Thing. Daphne was a guess and the car, you picked out. *This* is from me."

"We are absolutely nauseating, aren't we? I mean if someone heard all of our intense love stuff, they would throw up."

"Just open the damn thing."

She does and instantly begins to cry. She pulls out a ruby necklace in the shape of a heart, just like Jackson Browne's song from the night I knew I was falling in love with Noelle Parker. I put it on her, and she clutches it while kissing me.

"Thank you. I adore it. It's perfect, and I'm never taking it off."

"Never?"

"Nope. You'll just have to get used to having sex with it on."

"I can get used to fucking you in anything, but a constant reminder of that night, I can do. You know what?" I pause.

"What?"

"I hear it now. We are nauseating. We're absolutely disgustingly sappy."

She grins and giggles. "Yeah but I think I'm okay with it." I kiss her softly, and she purrs. "I love you so much."

My Hellcat.

Elle

We haven't left the Longhouse in three days. Poppy delivered dinner and extra food to us the other night. She even included an extra big bag from the Basque Boulangerie Café for our breakfast the next day. We've been working side by side in bed on our laptops. Or we sit outside on the little patio that Josh built that overlooks the entire vineyard. He leveled out the area near the bell that's still jammed into the tree. The bell is original to this Lookout cottage. During prohibition, it was rung if there was a raid approaching. I snap a picture of the bell and send it to Evan along with its story. Maybe he could incorporate it into the design deck he's building for the Prohibition wine label. We talked yesterday. He's still a bit freaked by Asher and made Jims return to him immediately after the Longhouse meeting. He promised to send me his three best ideas for Prohibition today. Mel's working on an unhackable share site.

If we're not working or looking at the view, we are fucking, making love, boning, screwing, having sex, and any other way you want to describe it. And in a myriad of ways.

We're taking a break this morning. I am insanely sore. I'm walking with a permanent wince. But I can't help myself. We have most certainly made up for lost time. The coffee situation is running low and could be our undoing. It might be the one thing that makes me come down off this mountain and out of his arms.

Josh is in the shower alone so that we're not tempted to fuck again. I'm in the sitting area in the bedroom, that way I can't even sneak a peek at his delicious and overworked rootstock.

WILL: *Hate to interrupt, but could I possibly book some time with you?*

ELLE: *You're not interrupting. When were you thinking?*

WILL: *Well, now. And ditch your boyfriend.*

ELLE: *Yes, sir. Be right down.*

I pull on some jeans and a t-shirt and peek my head into the bathroom.

"No. No. No. Why are you dressed? That's not what we agreed upon. We were going to sit outside naked and have a picnic with the scraps we have left in the fridge. Remember? Naked foraging." I grin at him and his incredibly gorgeous wet rippled body. I reach out to those abs, all eight of them. I think it's all the running and sexual frustration that made the last two abs pop out in the previous couple of months.

"Oh, my love, how I want to lick every single muscle on your body. But your dad needs to talk to me."

"Mood killer. Let me get dressed. I'll go with you."

"Seems he just wants me all to himself." Josh looks confused and a little hurt. I lean into the shower to kiss him. "You know I'll tell you whatever it is. And I'll steal coffee and cream from the Farmhouse."

"I'm not comfortable with you out of my sight."

"I can't stay locked away in your prohibition Lookout tower forever."

"We do have to get to bootlegging." He laughs as he says it.

"Think of it this way. I can get supplies."

He raises his eyebrows. "Get stuff we can eat off each other."

"Eww."

"Just do it."

"We have cheese."

"No. Like chocolate sauce."

I shrug. "I mean, if you like chocolate."

"You don't like chocolate?" I shake my head. "What is wrong with you? And how did I not know this?"

"I'm a mystery. When you get back, we're going to have a serious sit down about dessert." He crooks his eyebrow and lets his towel drop.

I turn and leave just as he starts to get hard. Nope. I can't take that root today.

Will's at the kitchen island. There's four grocery bags sitting on the counter with a note from Sarah that simply says, "For the lovebirds." I grin at her thoughtfulness.

I breeze in and pour myself a cup of coffee. He gets up and comes over to me and instantly hugs me. That's usually nice, but he's not letting go. I put my cup on counter and we stay like that until I speak.

"Are you okay?"

There's a shake to his voice. "No."

"What's wrong? Is Sarah, okay?"

"She's fine. She's at yoga."

"You're freaking me out, Will."

He keeps me in his bear hug. "You're just going to have to stay here while I get this out."

"Okay. But you're acting really weird."

"I've never really wanted to harm another human being before. I've wanted to punch people, sure, but truly harm. I mean, I did nail Asher's jaw that once but to darkly want to kill someone without remorse. I don't know how you did it and came through this."

"Asher?"

"Yes, my darling girl. I love you so much more than I ever thought I would. Your adoration of our son is one thing, but what you mean to Sarah and me is quite another. Usually, the in-laws get to meet the daughter-in-law and have to learn to love her. But we got to be there first. We got to know your heart and soul first. You were already a daughter to us. We're so lucky that Josh fell in love with you."

"It would have been strange if we ended up weird siblings."

"Stop. I'm serious. I've never been more distraught than when I heard Asher was in New York. Or felt more useless. When I heard how he undermined all of us and somehow got to that meeting, our hearts ached. But I've never been prouder of the clever and remarkable girl you are." He backs up, and I see him wipe his eyes.

"Hey. Will, I'm okay. I'm not permanently damaged. I don't have Parkinson's. She's the hero, not me. What brought this on?"

"The Sonoma County Sheriff was here this morning. You need to press charges regarding the restraining order. New York needs an on-tape deposition to continue. You might have to appear in court here and eventually you'll probably have to appear in court in New York. But more importantly, he was released last night and is headed back to California."

"Okay. I can deal with this. Francesca filed this morning. And it all gets added to my case against him. We serve him and arrest him once all the evidence is secured but only after we get the wineries back. I can figure this out too." Will's expression doesn't change. "There's more, isn't there?"

"Yes. There's a gag order issued for this particular problem. Somehow Asher seems to be protected up high. He is required to tour the property with the Vino Groupies to make sure we're upholding our part of the contract. Racking juice and barreling, etc. Our underground operations will go to Schroeder's Napa warehouse, the one with the server. The bottles we've already begun doing for Gelberts' first white will go, but we need to get all the juice bottled and ready for shipping by next week before they visit. You two need to come down from your ivory tower and help. Then we'll need to disinfect Lookout."

I smile at the joke, but I know what's coming. Will's hands are tied.

He continues, "When they come to inspect, you can't be here. Because of your restraining order, the Sheriff has asked that you not be here because Asher must be."

"Hold up. You better chain Josh down."

He doesn't laugh at my joke. "The Sheriff also gave me this."

"It's my file, isn't it?"

Will pushes a manila folder across the island and breaks down. He never saw the pictures after he beat me. Will and Sarah knew I was attacked, but I stayed away from them when the bruises were at their worst. They only saw pieces of what he did.

I rush over to him and hold him from behind as he speaks through his tears, "How can I be that trusting to not see what a monster he was? Oh, god. It breaks my heart. I want to protect you like your father would have. I'm so sorry I couldn't stop this. Your father would be so proud of your strength and resilience and your beautiful soul." I'm sobbing as Will talks about me like I'm his daughter. And I'm the luckiest woman in the world that I get to be that legally someday.

He continues, "I've broken bread with him, toasted with him, invited him into our home, and he did all of that to you. To another human being."

Our relationship has always been based in humor, and I need it to be that again. I need it normal. Will caring for me in this capacity is overwhelming and lovely. He is my family.

"At least you didn't sleep with him."

Will chuckles through his tears and turns to me and holds me again.

"It's only Asher's fault," I say. "No one else's. No one gets to take credit for that bastard except himself. He can't touch me now."

"He can. He can get to you."

I place my hand on his heart and look him in his copper penny eyes. "No. He can't touch me ever again. I will never crumble. I will never let him affect my life again. And god help him if he physically comes near me again or anyone I love."

"I love you, baby girl."

"I love you too, Will."

"Is there a reason we didn't vote him off the island when we had a chance?"

I smile. "He always had a delicious bottle with him. And he kept winning challenges." He pulls me into an embrace again.

"I couldn't handle if anything happened to you, so just be safe. Like forever. Just be safe. That should be easy enough. And your bubble wrap and gilded cage arrive tomorrow. You'll like it. It sleeps two comfortably. Sarah is the best roommate you could ask for."

My body floods with warmth. The last bits of any reserve I felt about being in a family and loved burst apart at the seams. I never thought ahead for myself. Even as Josh asked me to marry him, I could never contextualize my future. I couldn't see it. But safe in the arms of the only father I have left, I see it. And I can't wait to make him a grandfather.

* * *

I know why she wanted to hike. I understand why she's trying to keep my mind safe. It's twenty-four hours since Will told me that I have to leave so Asher can invade my home. We all agreed not to mention any of it to Josh until the day of the event, so he doesn't worry or plot Asher's demise.

Sarah is smoking me on this hike, but I am glad for the fresh air. And I'm not sure I can have sex again ever. Or at least being on this hike will stop me from jumping him for a couple of hours.

"Sarah, how are you doing this? I'm exhausted."

"Well, Will and I only did it once last night. I'm going to say your number was higher."

"OH MY GOD." My face goes bright red.

"Kidding. Yoga and determination. And we did it twice."

I'm huffing and puffing. She's leaving me behind in the woods, and she has Parkinson's. I'm not so outdoorsy. But I'm trying. "Is it hot today? It's hot."

"You're kind of a whiner today," Sarah scolds me.

"I hate nature."

"I know, but it's only a little further."

"Finnnnnnnnnnnnnnnnnne." I whine as she laughs.

We break through a line of trees and get an unbelievable view of the backside of the property. It's a large flat clearing.

"Damn. This is gorgeous." I hand her a water bottle as she sits down on a stump. "You okay?"

"I am. Stop fussing. What do you think?" She smiles at me.

"A view to die for. I've never seen the valley from the back side of your property. It's amazing." There are Cabernet and Merlot vines terraced up this high on the hill, but the only trails up here are for harvest vehicles.

"But is it a view you want to wake up to?"

"What do you mean?"

"I know the Farmhouse will never feel like yours." She shifts her weight and takes my hand.

"No. It will always be yours in my mind. And I want it to be. I know you guys are traveling in the future, but we're not taking your home."

"To be frank, we don't want roommates."

I giggle. I don't either. I also don't want to censor our activities because his parents might hear us. But I understand what she's saying. The Lookout is like living in a hotel suite, without real closet space. Josh and I are already fighting for dresser space. There are four little drawers, and we're each supposed to have two. But I have more stuff for drawers. He didn't like my logic, or maybe he just won the argument because he held me down, licking me until I submitted.

"You don't want to hear us."

"Or be heard."

"Eww."

"You think I want to hear this about my son?"

"Point taken."

"Build here. The Lookout is too small for the long term. I don't want you to go back to Santa Barbara." Sarah's never really asked Josh for much. Always given him latitude to figure out where and what he wants. Maybe it's the disease or the change in her son, but she's asking for what she wants. She wants us here. I do too.

"What if we fail to get the wineries back?"

"What if we don't fail? Don't ever wait for someday. Do things now. Build now. While I can help. Build big enough for your future. All the rooms you think you'll ever need."

"Sarah. What are you asking me?"

"Look. I don't give a shit about your wedding. I really don't. I'll try and care if it's important to you. I'm a simple person. I don't understand the flowers and frills."

"I know this. I just want you with me in the process. Poppy, Evan, and Jims can take care of the frills and flowers. What is it that you do want?"

"Babies." Her eyes sparkle, and she leaps up to get right in my face.

"Holy shit. We've never discussed it."

"Well, get to it. I want to run around with toddlers while I can. I want lots and lots of babies so get to birthing."

"Oh, my god. Okay. Noted."

"I love Josh with all my heart, but my biggest regret in life is that there aren't more of him."

My heart breaks for her. I wonder if my parents felt that way. We've never discussed anything other than neither of us have cousins. I hope Josh wants kids. I hug her fiercely. "I'll make sure there's more of him. I promise."

"I love you, sweet girl. Let me help you build your life here. And I'm not wearing pink at your wedding."

"Noted. No pink."

Josh

David, Poppy, Tabi, and Jims flew all over the country securing minor distribution for the label. Some were interested but most passed because they couldn't quite get behind the concept. They didn't think people would buy wine based on mystery. And then Elle came up with a hell of an idea to create an air of exclusivity but maintain our anonymity.

She found this fantastic anti-establishment but highly regarded sommelier. Rick Franzetti, with his 69k IG followers and more than that on Twitter. He's exactly who we need to light this up. He lives up in Anderson Valley. He's a badass and doesn't give a shit about what people think. She hand-delivered him six bottles of Prohibition last week. She left them on his doorstep with a note.

We'll be in touch.

-Prohibition Wines

She gave him some from each winery, and he went ape shit over the idea behind it and the wine itself. The next day, he tweeted a picture of the wine that simply said:

. . .

248

*Holy Shit. Who dis? Who The Fuck made this? COME TO
ME. Bring it all to me. I want to drink all of this wine. #pro-
hibitionwines #ineedallthewine #contactme #whoispro-
hibition*

Mel somehow gets his private phone number and Elle texts
him from her burner.

UNLISTED: *I can get you all the wine.*

RICK: *Seriously. Who is this?*

UNLISTED: *A friend with a Prohibition hookup. We
need your help. Total anonymity. Super secretive stuff. Keep
this like national security quiet.*

RICK: *This is some cool shit. But I need to tell you that I
figured out where "Namaste here for a minute and finish this
bottle" came from. I am very good at my job.*

He references the bottle that Sarah named. I panic a bit.
Are we that obvious?

UNLISTED: *Who do you think we are? Are we that
obvious?*

RICK: *First off, I won't tell a soul. Second off, it is
obvious to me, but no one else will get it unless they've
logged serious time at that Farmhouse kitchen island. Rhone
blend. Rich and jammy. Yoga. Ridic puns. That smacks of
my girl Sarah and her old man Will.*

ELLE: *My name is Elle Parker.*

RICK: *Josh's girl.*

ELLE: *Yes. How do you know Josh?*

RICK: *Don't. Got trashed with Gelbert last month, and
he told me that Josh was tamed by his equal. What do you
need?*

ELLE: *Can we come to you and chat?*

RICK: *Hell yes. This is the most intriguing thing.*

ELLE: We can be there this afternoon. We're a collective.

RICK: I figured since they don't all taste like LC/W. Just Sarah's. See you at 2:00 p.m.

ELLE: Thank you.

★ ★ ★

Sam, Elle, Mel, and I show up at his house that afternoon.

"Fuck me. Sam Langerford!" The two embrace.

"Did you know they were reaching out? You could have called me."

"Nah, I couldn't. We're into some covert shit. Mel here will explain." He shakes everyone's hands, and we settle into his backyard. Elle brought him some of her Rosé, the one named for her.

"Settle in, we have a tale to tell you," Elle explains.

Elle

"Are you shitting me? Fuck me, this is cool." Rick apparently likes what we're doing.

"Thanks. But for us, it's survival. It's how we get the wineries back and take down Darren," Josh explains.

"Shit, man, that Barry Marcus story is a legend in the Valley."

Elle leans forward and touches his wrist. "You can't tell anyone any of this, but we need you to make us cool to the world."

"Hellz yeah. The wine is dope, and the fucking plan is solid."

Sam speaks, "But dude, nothing can come from us. Any of us. We've kept it out of the Valley so far, but we need to unload all our palates to make this work."

"How much product and who else is involved?"

Sam answers, "When all is said and done, we should be at around three thousand two hundred. We'll bottle close to one hundred and eighty-one thousand cases."

"Damn, you bitches are busy. It's why you look like shit Langerford. You're all exhausted."

"And we can't tell you who else is involved."

"You know I can look up the deal, right?"

"You can't. That's why there's been no press on the sale. There's a gag order until they take over."

Mel speaks, "And I need all your devices." Rick slaps Mel on the back.

We sip the afternoon away coming up with strategies and ideas. Mel explains all the tech works on his phone and computer. Dasher hasn't monitored him at all, but she wants to keep it like that.

"This is all cool with me as long as it doesn't interfere with my own shit," Rick says while he sniffs another glass of ruby red liquid.

"Of course. We need help, not another employee," I explain.

"Cool. I won't tell a soul, but let's come clean right now before we move forward. You should know, I think I know who's involved. Sam and Josh. You assholes are too tight with your friends. And I know wine. This right here, that's all Tommi Schroeder. And this one." He picks up a bottle of white. "This one. Well, is it going to be an issue that I was on the 'Fuck It List?'"

I laugh too hard, and Josh scrubs his jaw.

Sam bellows through his laughter, "Where?"

"Giants Stadium tasting room."

Josh rolls his eyes. "Good god, Tab. No, it's fine. She's fine. She's so fucking Tabi."

"That she is. And I love me some Stafýli."

Sam stands up. "Fuck it. They're all at Starling bar right now. Come with us, and we can all plan together."

Rick stands up and looks directly at me and says, "You. You're my contact, right?"

"Yes."

"Then we need to get drunk and figure out how to corner the market on intrigue."

He hugs me, and I'm thrilled this is going to work. "Can we pay you?"

"Um, yes. And I will need more product. That Rosé was dope. I'm guessing the old punster Will named that one as well."

"No. That was Josh. It's named after me." I smile at him.

"Hellcat, huh?" Josh stands up and glares at him. Rick puts his hand out to shake Josh's hand. "No offense, man. I'm all hung up over my own bae, no worries."

"Good. Let's work out the money after you sign some paperwork."

* * *

He was all-in on our idea and burying Asher, who he called a "fucking wanking poseur." He's agreed to be our face to the world. He happily signed Becca's NDA—non-disclosure agreement—and was rewarded with a burner of his very own.

Some of the parents were skeptical about bringing in someone else. Josh defended me they finally accepted the plan when I convinced Rick to tweet, and run our IG account. I'll feed him with additional content. That way, it can't be traced to any of us. Our burners didn't tweet well.

He came up with an idea to take us to Bottle Rock, a three-day rock, wine, and food festival held annually in Napa in May. I'm pulling strings behind the scenes but working through Rick. I keep telling people I'm his assistant. He secured a spot to host three stage shows of a food and wine pairing expo with chef Michael Voltaggio, a friend of his. I called in some favors and lined up Dave Grohl, Chrissy Teigen, and Anderson Cooper to join those boys on stage for the cooking demo and tasting. I sent them all the Prohibition merch and a mixed case as a thank you. Well, Rick sent them. I, of course, made sure I'm not directly involved in anything.

Evan has an event friend hiring people to sell wine onsite. They'll be paid through his company. Sales onsite will have no money exchanged. They can sample on-site and buy by-the-glass. But if they want to order, they do it on their phone. They'll be given a black card with a number on it to text an order. We ship nothing less than half a case and if they want merchandise, they merely text "Hat" or "Black Shirt XL." Shipping is included in the price. They add their credit card information and an address to their text and get a thumbs up when their order is processed. Again, no human contact and no idea where these things were being shipped from. I think the merch warehouse is in Miami.

The onsite people basically function to pour wine and act as IT for orders. Mel will be on-site in case they need hardcore IT, but she and Tommi are just processing orders while listening to music from the VIP tent.

Now to the task of producing the rest of the wine we need to sell. The rest of the juice is ready. The new batch of printed labels should be here any minute. Poppy got the label approval on the same day she showed up at her ex boyfriend's desk. She flirted and he got it all done immediately. She also brought him a pan of lasagna, that pushed him over the edge.

Evan sent the approved labels into production. Ingrid

Schroeder is poised with mockup bottles for the IG launch. And Mel and Tommi are busy taking subscriptions from all of our existing wine clubs.

The labeling machinery is portable but extremely heavy, and it's a slow process, but it's getting done. I shared the new Gelbert Chardonnay with Rick today, and it's delicious. It's a lovely steely chard with lemon and tartness to it. All our wines are so different. We're doing an oaky Stafýli Chard as well.

Tabi assured us there would be another shipment of glass today. We need it. We desperately need Burgundy bottles for Chardonnays and Pinots. Which need the fat wine bottles. We have a ton of the skinny tall kind called Bordeaux bottles. Those are for all the reds, red blends, and the Sauvignon Blanc. We're halfway done with our massive bottling effort. We need a total of one hundred and eighty-three thousand cases to make this work. And we have to sell them all in order to compensate for the money we're bleeding from all of the Estate wineries.

Schroeder came up with this genius strategy: they have been giving away extra bottles of Estate wine like a sales perk if you buy five you get the sixth free. Buy ten you get two free but only in the tasting room. The Estate product dwindles, but the bottom line doesn't swell. It's all been nerve-wracking and fun at times, but we sit on a house of cards with all of this. There are so many ways this can go sideways. I'm nervous all the time. But I also feel unbelievably charged by this entire endeavor.

Josh

It's Wednesday, and we moved guys night to the Longhouse tonight. The giant table has been put outside, and the equipment now fills the main room. Mel's going to update us while we work. We're also going to use our other equipment overnight to get the Langerford Merlot and our red blend done. Our winemaker, Alena, affectionately calls the blend, Survivor. The label actually says, *"The Tribe has spoken."* Our four labels represent the four of us. My dad penned three of them and I came up with Elle's.

Namaste here for a minute and finish this bottle. (20% Marsanne, 50% Viognier, and 30% Roussanne)

Hellcat hath no fury like a drunk kitty. (100% Pinot Noir Rosé)

The floor Suits me just fine. (94% Zinfandel, 6% Petite Sirah)

The Tribe has spoken. (40% Cabernet Sauvignon, 20% Merlot, 18% Cabernet Franc, 15% Petite Verdot, 7% Carignane)

Alena's going to bottle and label with Poppy, Becca,

Tommi, Lou and Sal in the main building. They already know Mel's updates. That's right, Sal's manning the labeler and hauling glass. I fucking love it so much. The rest of the crew is with me.

Mark texted he'll be by to pick up Sal on Friday. Apparently he got a break in his case against the mysterious money guy and had to follow it up. I think it's funny that I'm essentially babysitting the head of a crime syndicate for the FBI. I suspect Mark has Lou on the payroll as well. But we all know Sal's not going anywhere. He wouldn't run and he seems to like it here.

"Now, am I going to be compensated for all the sex I'm missing out on?" David yells to the rest of us as we pass a bottle of bourbon between us.

Sam answers him, "All the sex? Dude, you haven't been laid in ages. Your dick is drying up."

"Fuck you, man bun." Sam's hair has gotten ridiculous. He needs to cut that scraggly shit.

"That's sweet, Gelbert, but you wouldn't like sex with me," Sam smirks.

Tabi walks into the conversation. "And pretty much from what I know, there's like only two people in the world who like to have sex like you do, Langerford. I'd lock that shit down. Sammy's a rare bird."

Bax appears at the door behind Tabi. He wasn't supposed to be here. He teases her, "And that's coming from someone who's trying to break the world record for weird fucking." We laugh and greet Bax warmly. Except for Tabi. She glares at him.

"It's not a world record, just a few items on a list." Tabi's been working on her infamous "Fuck It List" for the last five years. No one's seen the whole list. The guys and I think of her as a little sister, so we don't ask about it.

Sam says, "Tabs, didn't you fuck the face of Prohibition?" Everyone looks at her. I just smile.

She puts her chin in the air and turns away from Sam while speaking. "I did not know you knew that."

I add the details. "Oracle Park, VIP lounge during a Giants' game."

David exclaims, "Damn, Tab. During a game?"

"They won. We both got home runs. Does that matter?"

We all groan.

She shrugs and heads over to a stack of labels. Bax pulls her wrist back to him and whispers something into Tabi's ear, and she laughs loudly and then throws a roll of labels at him. "Get to work, Senator." He salutes her. He's always been the most respectable of all of us. And the only one who can control or consistently take the piss out of Tabi.

I shout out to him from across the room, "Bax. Head to the Farmhouse and grab a t-shirt and jeans if you need."

"You do know that my dad's house is like five minutes away. I can be back in like thirty minutes if I shower."

Mel offers up as she enters the Longhouse, "We don't have that kind of time, dude. Every minute counts. Dasher will be here in like eighteen hours."

My body goes ice fucking cold, and I turn quickly to her. I roar, "What the hell did you just say?"

Everyone in the room looks at me. Apparently, everyone knew this information but me.

Mel mutters, "Shit. Shit. Sorry guys."

"No. NO." I bellow. "Tell me the details, you assholes." Sam steps to me and puts his hand on my back. "Holy shit. Does Elle know?" They all nod. "Really, muthafuckers? Now I'm the one left out of the loop?"

Sam explains, "It's his right as steward to make sure we're all doing what we agreed upon. And he's bringing some Vino Groupies as well. Elle knows because the Sheriff had to request she not be here because of the restraining order."

"Then that should keep him out, not her."

David offers up an explanation. "The law, as Becca explained to me, basically says we can't keep him from doing his job, but she has to clear out, so the order remains valid."

"Then we'll go to Santa Barbara right now."

Tabi speaks up, "You have to be here. Legally. You must be working the vineyard, just like Sarah and Will. Elle is excused."

Bax says, "She's going to hang at Poppy's and help out for the day while he's in town. He's on a short leash, just our five wineries. She'll be fine."

"FUCK!!!" I roar as a delicate porcelain skin hand is placed on my shoulder.

"Who fucking told him?" Elle yells, and Mel raises her hand. "You're a dumb ho, Mel. I mean, come on. The plan was to tell him tomorrow. And aren't you the best at keeping secrets? Damn."

I spin her around as everyone laughs at her joke. "Woman! You do not keep things from me." I dip her and kiss her deeply. She breathes heavily and fans her chest as everyone watches her skin blush under my command. "And you assholes, I think I've made it clear: I need ALL the information all the time. And you're not hanging with Poppy. The two of you are hanging with Sal and Lou, no protests. No choices here. But I need all the info going forward."

Mel puts her hands on her hips, "Fine. Here are the deets. We're sold out of subscriptions. Get back to bottling, bitches."

Sam asks, "What are you talking about?"

"The paper orders from your wine club peeps. They took all the subscriptions. We should sell any remaining wine and merch through Elle's marketing plan. We're holding back fifty cases of each mix and then offering an exclusive complete two full-case limited editions to our top one hundred buyers for fifteen hundred apiece."

"You are shitting me?" Gelbert looks at her, confused.

"David, I'd never shit you. We have fifteen thousand valid credit cards on file and input into our system with a two-case minimum commitment. And a waiting list with another six thousand three hundred and twenty people, who committed to two cases if there's any left. Teamsters will be here at the end of the week, and we all start boxing this shit up." We all scream and hug. "I'm out. Time to celebrate. Gonna go do that Langerford clit trick to Tommi."

"Come on. That's my sister." Bax looks disgusted.

Mel winks at him and gives him a finger gun. "Exactly."

Tabi narrows her eyes to Sam. "What trick?" We all laugh and then get back to the bottles.

"What are we bottling tonight?" Sam asks, ignoring Tabi.

"Schroeder Pinot." Elle offers up.

"Jesus, Bax, I feel like all we do is fucking bottle your shit. How big is your freaking property?" Gelbert says as he passes the bourbon to him.

Sam yells out, "It's not the size of the vineyard; it's the strength of your tannins."

I offer up, "Motion in the tank."

Elle laughs and says, "The acid in your juice."

"Width of the vine," Tabi adds.

Bax laughs a lot.

Sam says, "The stamina of your legs."

I add, "It's the length of the finish."

"Or the girth of the rootstock," Sammy yells as she enters the Longhouse, and Elle immediately laughs and flushes.

Bax looks at all of us, grabs his very respectable and ironed khakis in a crass area, and says, "Schroeder's do alright." And we all bend over, dying laughing.

Josh

Today is the worst fucking day. The worst. I went on an exhausting run to sap some of my rage. He'll be here in front of me in a matter of time. We'll be face-to-face for the first time since her restraining order hearing.

The Vino Groupies still know nothing of his arrest or his police questioning in what happened to Elle. Gag order from the judge. We can't damage his business. Rick trolls him all the time on social media. It's awesome to watch the little bitch squirm and take the bait. He's a little bitch and deserves to be taken down in every aspect of his pathetic life. Fuck, I just want to kill him.

Mel found two other women locally with similar stories to Elle's in the police database. One from Petaluma and one from Richmond. Elle is setting up lunches with both of them. She wants them to press charges as well. Mel is searching police records for anyone across the country with a similar story. Melissa is focusing her search on anywhere Dasher's been invited to judge or present over the past five years. She's been also monitoring all the Vino Groupies communications for keywords and the arrest has never come up.

I'm out of my fucking skin. I do not know how the fuck I am not going to kill that fucker. Sam is here to literally pull me back. He's the only one besides Lou big enough to do it. I need Lou with her not here. Sam and I are the same height, but he's a bigger dude than I am. More weight on him so he can stop me.

We moved all Prohibition stuff to the Napa warehouse. We scrubbed any trace of our DL winery. We're going to be way fucking behind because of all this shit.

The first of the orders should have gone out today, and now they'll be delayed days. We don't charge anyone until right before we ship, so that influx of cash is delayed as well. And that's the cash that pays our employees, our vendors, our distributors and literally keeps the fucking lights on.

We all had to dip into the equity sale holdings to satisfy our bills for the month. And it's not like we can put that money back once the Prohibition sales come through. So, we'll have to hold that cash off and pay a shit ton of early withdrawal penalties. I want to bury this fucker for that alone. I'm legally not allowed to cover the winery expenses with my own personal income. Because right now we don't legally own our vineyard.

I don't know where Elle is, but I know she's safe. We all thought it best if she were a ghost. That way no one could slip up and give information to the Special Ops guy by accident. She's with Lou and Sal somewhere. Sal insisted he is by her side all day. I'm grateful we have the mob on our side. I mean seriously, who has the mob on their side? Even though he's quickly divesting himself of that world, scorpion, and frog. I'll never cart him across the water again. But he loves my woman like a sister.

He loves her open heart and ability to forgive and trust. And the ballbusting. He'd die for her, and that's who I want to protect her. Someone who would die for her.

We got word from Becca that Asher's finishing up at Stafýli and apparently Tabi was removed from a confrontation. Bax was her guardian. He physically picked her up and dragged her into the house. We knew she couldn't keep her mouth shut. She was taunting him.

Goldie glossed it over and charmed everyone involved, and then when no one was looking, put an evil eye curse on Asher. Would be funny if that's the thing that finally got him. She's spent the last hour smudging all the areas he was in and de-cursing her space. Goldie's the best.

We're last on their tour. They have expressed that they're disappointed with all of our current Estate production sales, but they're grateful Lodi will cover the losses. They still don't know that they don't own the Lodi vineyards. Becca has been with them the entire time like a host almost.

They arrive in the parking lot, and I disappear as they head to a Pinot block with my father and mother. I can see him from a distance in his black suit. He's in a fucking suit, walking through vineyards. At least the Vino Groupies are in jeans. That giant tattooed guy is with them. I wonder if he knows what a punk ass bitch Dasher is. He looks like the protective type. Maybe we can somehow slip him the intel on Dasher and see what happens.

I walk away into the caves to cool off. Literally and figuratively. They're scheduled to head to the tank rooms, then the tasting room and a chat with Alena on production and how the current numbers look.

I'm pacing the cave tasting room. The room where I broke Elle down, and I finally trapped her and told her I never chose to leave her. I run my hands along the length of the table, and smile. I touch under my watch band where my tattoo resides, and I wish she were here. I need to feel secure. I want her to kiss me and taste my fear then take it away. I'm going to get lost in her the moment she steps back on the property. More. There's never enough.

My thoughts are interrupted by an obnoxious sweet cologne. You don't wear cologne if you're a fucking sommelier, asshole. It fucks with your nose and palate. I don't turn around but slyly pull out my burner and text "*911 cave*" to Sam. I promised Elle I would do that if I thought I couldn't handle being near him. His high-pitched girly voice pierces the air around us and reverberates off the cave ceiling.

"Well, it seems my angel did as I asked her to do. She left you."

I turn around, and in a measured voice, I say, "No. She just couldn't stand the thought of smelling that cologne."

He pulls his shirt cuffs down. Like he's a cartoon villain or something. I want to bash in his fucking head. He's baiting me. I will not bite.

"In the end, there will be me. Joshie, it's time to learn I will win. I've worked way too hard for too long. I'm untouchable. Noelle's little complaints will blow over. And I will have your winery. Your estate. Your legacy. And Noelle. All will be mine, and you and your family will finally be ruined."

"I keep asking myself how the hell you got so delusional. I mean you are truly a talented psychopath."

"That's funny. When the Army dismissed me, they said I was a sociopath with attachment issues and a penchant for revenge fantasies. The joke is, they're not fantasies any longer, now are they?"

"Can't wait to *not* tell Elle a thing about you. Because she's done. She never mentions you. You're not even a thought in her day." Being ignored should piss him off and shut him down. I need to get out of here. My heart is racing. I'm trapped as he's in the only door. I have to go through him to get the fuck out of here.

The blood is pounding in my ears. I want to hit him until he can't breathe. I won't. I think I can survive his taunts. I can do it. I can maintain. No temper. Even keel. If she can fight against him and win, so can I.

"That's a shame. I was hoping to taste my angel again, Joshie."

I step to him. "Funny. That's not what I heard. I heard you're afraid of pussy. Shame too."

"I meant her blood. You know, when it dripped from her lip." Before I know what's happening, my fist is in the air, but it connects with nothing. Sam pulls Asher out of the way just in time.

Sam spins him around. "Get the hell out of here, you sick fuck. Now."

"I'm not done with my inspection. And I'm hoping to get Josh on assault charges."

Sam shoves him backward slightly. "Oh, sorry man, didn't see you there." He falls over a barrel that was just behind him and slams his head on the floor. I have to be honest, I didn't hate the sound of the thud. Sam tugs on my shirt, so my rage gaze is broken. We turn our backs on him and walk out of the cave while he struggles to get up. His head is most likely dizzy, his legs are tangled around a barrel and his ego bruised just a bit more.

The Vino Groupies and my parents are at the entrance to the cave as we exit.

"He's in there. He fell." I walk past my parents as my father's lips curl up slightly at the corners.

"Follow me, gentlemen," my mother says as she leads them inward with a mad grin.

Elle

Prohibition is working. It wasn't my idea, I don't know how to make wine, and I don't understand the specifics of terroir or malolactic something, but I can sell anything. Between Rick, Ingrid, the wine, and our merchandise, we're a thing. There's a blurb about us in *Time Magazine* with only Rick's quotes. The *San Francisco Chronicle* did a mini-feature last Sunday as did the *Washington Post*. There have been countless online blurbs about us. It's working, and I'm so excited.

The hashtag #whoisprohibition trends on the reg. Pharrell wore one of our hats on stage the first night of Coachella. I sent six cases to him the next day, along with Ingrid. She had them delivered in secret. Then he held a private tasting and tweeted the hell out of it. Ingrid was invited to the tasting. She documented the entire thing in real-time on a live stream that was seen by an army of people. Like she was simply a guest at the party. I particularly enjoyed her tasting the Schroeder Cabernet that is simply called *The Dark Red One*. She came up with that name, it's her favorite.

Justin Timberlake wore our t-shirt on stage after that, and now we're sold out of merchandise. Evan is working on a whole new line to become even more exclusive than the last round of merch that simply said "Prohibition."

The wine is all bottled. We box and label nightly, but we have to wait before we can even think about shipping. The wine is tasting amazing, but it needs to settle a bit. It's still a bit in bottle shock. It needs to settle before it's drinkable. The trucks will take it to Michigan where we will pay to have it shipped from there. It needs to sit for another week or so in a Detroit warehouse. Our lack of available, viable product only makes us more desirable. It was unintentional. We had no idea it would take off this quickly. We're scrambling, but the winemakers and vintners refuse to send out a product that isn't ready. I suggested we include a note telling people they must wait to drink. Then I was informed that they do that anyway because of shipping. Again, I'm a marketing person.

I'm the point person for Rick, and he's been quite busy. He's hustled us at festivals, private tastings, and random wine dinners around the country. After Bottle Rock, his friend chef Michael Voltaggio began serving our wine exclusively. And we were asked to sponsor a *Top Chef* episode. We just don't have enough product for that. I never dreamed I'd say that. But we don't. So much is committed already, and there's high demand. We're not raising our prices though. We like that it's an even price.

RICK: Yo.

ELLE: You rang?

RICK: Your boy has contacted me four times. Wants a piece of Prohibition and to know how to get a hookup. Wants to know if it's Cali produced.

ELLE: My boy?

RICK: *Fucking douche canoe, Asher Bernard.*

ELLE: *NOT MY BOY. And for the record, he beat the shit out of me and tried to rape me.*

RICK: *Fuck.*

ELLE: *Exactly.*

RICK: *Why isn't he in jail?*

ELLE: *We need the wineries back first, then a lifetime of jail for him.*

RICK: *Sorry.*

ELLE: *Don't be. Just keep mocking him, damage him as much as you want. And his palate is such shit he can't recognize Sonoma wine? Come on. Jesus, he's from here.*

RICK: *HA! So true. I'll bury him further and keep him away from you guys best I can. But he's at a program I'm a part of next week. I won't bring Pro/Ho.*

ELLE: *That's what people call it?*

RICK: *Just me.*

ELLE: *Hashtag the shit out of that. It's going on our new merch.*

RICK: *Save me a shirt. And I need more of your Hellcat Rosé. That shit is lit.*

ELLE: *Done. And thank you.*

RICK: *You know, you're the one paying me.*

ELLE: *Still. Thank you.*

Asher's probably trying to figure out why he can't research our wine. Gotta love Mel. I text Evan before I forget Ricks' genius slang.

ELLE: *For the merch: #pro/ho*

EVAN: *Fucking brilliant. How did you do that? I'm the creative.*

ELLE: *Rick. Stay in shades of gray and black. Pop a blue or green on it.*

EVAN: *You just bottle the shit, and I'll worry about a pop of color. Stay in your lane, winemaker's wife.*

ELLE: *You know that's you too!*

EVAN: *Oooh, wouldn't that be dreamy? Alas, he's yet to ask.*

ELLE: *Ask him yourself, pussy.*

EVAN: *What a perfectly perfect idea.*

I need for him to be with me always. I may have to prompt Jims to propose at least living together. I'm not Evan would ever really do it. Perhaps I pay a visit to Langerford today.

Elle

W e've been working day and night. All the initial shipments are in Michigan, and I'm so relieved. I have lunch next week with three other women who Asher potentially abused. And Mel found one in Indianapolis and Denver. Both places that Asher was on a wine panel discussion. I want to bury him in litigation and jail for years.

I got a text today from Rick. He told me that he loves the girl's wine the most. But I think he just likes flirting with Sarah and me.

The last run of labels arrived today, and we'll have to slap them on the bottles tonight. The second run of bottling with the remainder of the juice and then Prohibition will be no more. It will have done its job. It's outselling the Estates, which I'm quite proud of. Ingrid and Rick have us on the lips of every idiot who follows them on social media. And through the subscriptions and some well-placed articles, we've become the sensation with the older established gossipy set as well. Long live word of mouth. I'm excited for the break in the fevered pace as we careen towards harvest. As Prohibition winds down, we all need to amp up work with our Estate wineries.

But first, it's 'Rosé Tuesday!' The boys are pissed off that all the girls are taking off the afternoon but fuck them. We deserve it.

* * *

Rosé Tuesday was born out of Poppy wanting to make it look like her restaurant was busier than it has been. Tuesday afternoons suck for restaurants in Sonoma, so she thought if there were a gaggle of ladies drinking, it would look like the cool and hip place to be. But mostly there's nothing cool or hip about Sonoma. It's all just lovely and beautiful. The result of this experiment is we gather twice a month to get day drunk without other customers. Josh loves and hates it. It means his early evening is spent either shoving food in my mouth or cramming his dick inside of super horny me until I sober up a bit.

I'm the first to arrive, and Poppy is trying out new apps and desserts on us today. Becca strolls up as I take a seat on Poppy's patio. She's got her law partner and my criminal lawyer, Francesca, with her and Meg, the former film festival director who's always with Wade.

They wave and make their way over to me and just as they're about to say hello, Meg's giant bag catches a chair, and it yanks her backwards. She falls flat on her ass on the ground with the chair clunking after her. She's laughing, and I look horrified. I forgot she's a klutz.

Francesca keeps on walking and looks at me and says, "Don't worry. Meg trips all the time. Seriously, you'll get used to it."

"I'm fine. No worries. Nice to see you again, Elle." Meg puts her hand out to shake mine.

"Yes. Are you sure you're okay?"

"Scattered and confused, but physically I'm fine. I've learned how to fall over the years."

Becca gives me a big hug while Tabi and Tommi arrive together.

Tabi screams from the sidewalk, "Is that fucking *Meg*?"

"Tabi!" Meg pops up, and Francesca, without blinking an eye, grabs her water glass to steady it before it tips over. She's apparently a hot mess, this one. Now I want to know why she's scattered and confused. Tabi attacks her with a hug. And then Poppy joins us with a large platter and several bottles of Rosé. The restaurant is empty, but we all dig in and start pouring.

* * *

Several bottles in and I lean over to Meg as she shoves her big loose sandy blonde wavy curls into a backward baseball hat.

"You never said why you're scattered?"

"Oh. I have to decide if I'm moving in with my boyfriend far away from here."

I quickly say, "I'm not trying to pry but aren't you kind of with Wade? I mean and..."

All the women laugh heartily at me. Francesca puts her delicate hand on my arm. "You know he's my husband and I don't share in that way." I am mortified that I didn't actually know that, I thought there was an arrangement of some sort. "We're sort of sister-wives, but her boyfriend has been in Africa for the past couple of years and is coming back to the states."

"There's a lot to unpack there." I grab more wine and wait for an explanation.

"Fuck yeah, there is." Tabi giggles.

Meg begins in a very matter-of-fact voice. "Allow me to explain. I must go to lots of events and dinners. I hate going to things alone. I know you know Wade is a novelist and works for the *SF Chronicle*. The paper forces him to go to lots of things. He hates going alone."

Francesca pipes in, "And I just hate going to things altogether, and most people, for that matter."

I'm starting to get it. "Oh. The two of you attend functions together so that—"

Francesca interrupts me. "With Meg's help, I can stay home in my pajamas or work. Trust me, neither of us wants to spend that much time together. Everyone should have a Meg. Meanwhile, as they go to parties, I work. Someone has to make real money."

I laugh, but as I do, I feel a little bit terrible for Wade. I really like him. We have a great working relationship, and he's always funny and impressive. He's the one who wrote feature on Pro/Ho, he didn't know it was us though. His novel was on lists, surely he's kind of successful. I'm grateful for Francesca, and we'll work together on the criminal case against Dasher but personally not so sure about this woman. She just bashed her husband to me.

Becca turns to Meg. "I think you should go. Doesn't Tribeca want you to do your kids documentary program there?"

"Yeah, and Scott has an apartment lined up."

"New York?" I perk up into their conversation.

"Yes. Have you been?"

"I live in New York! I mean, I have a place in New

York. I mean, well, it's still mine, but I live here now. I live with Josh Whittier. I am—"

Tommi corrects me. "Quite the babbler right now. You live here now, and you simply own a giant closet in New York and a couch you never see."

"That's true. I don't know you well, but sometimes if you leap without looking, it's better." I squeeze her arm.

Poppy blurts out, "You? Not looking? The planner? The obsessive scheduler? You probably custom ordered the pillow and the patch of grass you fell on before you leaped."

I take offense that my opinion is being overridden. "Not true. Meg, you should go. I mean, I showed up in Wine Country on a whim of an idea for the weekend. That was a year and four-and-a-half months ago. Damn, it seems so much longer than that. I mean, last August, just a year ago, Josh and I weren't even talking, and now we're engaged."

Meg looks at me. "I think I will. Oh. My. God. I kind of made a decision."

Becca looks at her. "No, girl, you *did* make one."

Meg sips her wine and looks at each one of us in the eye and says, "I do not trust women. No offense. I'm going to have run this by a whole slew of men before it's an official decision."

Tabi jokes, "Women are the worst, none taken. She does have a gaggle of men who are at her beck and call." We all giggle again.

Meg shakes us off. "Most of them are gay. It's not like I have a harem. It's more like—"

Francesca interrupts her. "A committee." Francesca looks sour. She's going to have to go to stuff now. She's losing her sister-wife. She turns to Meg. "Although Scott is one of our dearest friends, I'm not sure Wade will survive without you. I know I won't." We all laugh, and Poppy pops another cork.

* * *

Lots has been decided. Poppy is only going to open for lunch on Thursday through Sunday. Except for Rosé Tuesdays and just for us. Meg is moving in the next month or two. Becca is going to spice up her relationship. Tabi added two items to her "Fuck It List." I am in support of one: she wants to be spanked in a California Mission. Fortunately, there's one in town so she should be able to get it done. And the second one, fuck a Jonas Brother, I protested. They're all married now. And they're cute and sweet, and they don't need any part of Tabi. Maybe the floppy-haired one could handle her, but he's married to Sansa and she'll cut a bitch. I hope she edits the list later. It's time to text Josh. It's time for him to be our bus. I have had many glasses of rosé.

ELLE: *Can you grab the passenger vans and cme get this."*

JOSH: *Who dis?*

ELLE: *It's ME. The love.*

JOSH: *I'm sorry. I don't know anyone who would get so drunk they can't spell van.*

ELLE: *Do it. I'll be worth it.*

JOSH: *Fine. Don't drink anymore.*

ELLE: *But it's so snohot, and Rosé is so cold and yummy.*

JOSH: *There's work to be done. Tell the other women to stop drinking and get to the packing and labeling.*

ELLE: *Oh, no. There are others here. I will test hem and tell me. We cannot be workers.*

JOSH: *Did you eat?*

ELLE: *Poppy didn't want to cook.*

JOSH: *She's the chef at that restaurant!*

ELLE: *She closed it up lick a drum.*

JOSH: *Give me twenty minutes, and I'll grab some sandwiches and chips for everyone.*

ELLE: *Someone is going to get blown.*

JOSH: *Hold up there, sloppy girl. Let's start with a turkey sandwich.*

ELLE: *Broadway Markets not Basque. It's faster. Get to the go tos, grab em all, and get them hearing now.*

JOSH: *Yes, ma'am. I will get them as soon as possible.*

ELLE: *Love you.*

JOSH: *Show me later. After you sober up. Glad you had fun.*

ELLE: *We all wants lots of chips. Not pussy tny bangs of chips. Big bags.*

JOSH: *Got it. Big bangs, not pussy tny ones.*

ELLE: *And Tabi needs a pickle. Likke four pickels., „And she asys fuck off sh'e s not pregnagt.*

JOSH: *Put the phone down. Stop texting, drunk girl.*

ELLE: *Your thee drank gorilla.*

ELLE: *HAHAHAH girl not gorilla. Autocorrrrrrrrrrrrrrrrrr*

JOSH: *PUT THE PHONE DOWN.*

ELLE: *IMMA put you drown Xo*

ELLE: *LOL. Down. Go down. Not drown. Here comes the emojis!*

Elle

I'm tired and heading my ass down to the Farmhouse for a hot breakfast. I'm over living in our cute bungalow. My clothes are hung at the Farmhouse, our bathroom is barely big enough for my hair products. And so over the apartment sized refrigerator. The bedroom is perfect. The rest of the bungalow is so freaking tiny. We're currently living in six hundred and twenty square feet. The deck that Josh built has become our living room. Simply because there's more space to spread out. I furnished our deck with a loveseat and four chairs. We've actually entertained on the deck, but the deck cannot sustain us long term. I want a hot breakfast. No more overnight oats from the fridge. The microwave can only do so much. I want an omelet.

Sarah's getting another infusion treatment and Will is already at the crush pad. It's just me and the dogs hanging out. Crush is going really smoothly as opposed to last year when we lost all the staff the night before. It's bittersweet, though. We still need the final numbers from our previous quarter. If they match up to what we've all projected, then this nutty plan might just work.

The remaining special offer cases and anything not promised to the wait list of subscriptions has miraculously sold out. Prohibition is dry. Not a drop left. The boys are glad to have it off their plate for now. Mel looks a little bit sad that this is all coming to an end soon. I hope she and Tommi stay together, but Melissa's a bit of a lone wolf. I scroll my feeds while sipping fresh coffee. I don't hear him come in, but I sense him. I always do.

Josh is standing across the island from me, holding a large scroll of some sort. There's a red bow tied around it. I slurp my coffee and sit back.

"What?"

"Happy Anniversary!" My eyes open wide.

"What the hell? I did not know we had one of those." I have it marked for the day we got engaged, but apparently, he has a different thought. He pulls up his phone reminder from last year to get the sprayer fixed.

"Cave."

I grin. That's a sweet man who remembers. "Well, then, Happy Caveaversary."

He crosses to my side and pulls me up and into his arms. I wrap mine around his neck and kiss him lightly. He says, "What did you get me?"

"Sexual favors." I wink at him.

"Cheap, but effective."

"What is this? Paper?" I stare at his expectant and sweet face. "Is it because the first anniversary is the paper anniversary?"

"Yes."

"Really?"

"No. You think I knew that shit? I'll give you a ream of copier paper on our first wedding anniversary. Open it."

I giggle, and then I hear a rumble of trucks outside. I go

to the kitchen window over the sink and peek. They're rolling up to the path that leads up the back of the property. There's a crazy machine out front that's clearing the trail a bit.

"What is happening?"

"Open this." He hands me the roll, and I unfurl blueprints.

"A HOUSE?! YOU BOUGHT ME A HOUSE?" I scream at him.

"I bought us a home."

"You bought me a house." I can't believe it.

"And a road."

"And a freaking road."

"And a freaking road." He slants his mouth over mine, and I go weak in the knees. We had sex an hour ago and yet still not enough.

"I love you and this idea, but we can't break ground until we know."

"Bullshit. Dasher's taken enough from us. We build today. We pour a foundation in the coming weeks. We stake our claim and build our home."

I chew on my lip. I am going to choose to be optimistic about him. I do have an issue though.

"What? I see the lip thing." He scowls at me.

"What if I hate the plans?"

"Look at them." There are interior mockups as well as detailed blueprints for the house. He pulls up a 3D model on his laptop. The interiors look flawless. The house is remarkably ideal. I don't think anything is perfect except him, well, and the rootstock, but I can't find anything wrong with the house. I don't have a tweak and that makes me truly speechless.

"How are you in my brain? How would you know about

the shower bump out or the nooks in the two smaller bedrooms? How do you know about my Harry Potter style wine cellar built under the staircase?"

"Mel."

"What? She's a mess."

"She hacked your brain. She's that good."

I put my hands on my hips, trying to figure out how this was done.

Josh continues, "Your friend in San Francisco. Pinterest, HGTV bookmarks, search history, etc. You spend way too much time fawning over cabinet hardware."

"Holy shit. It is MY house. But do you like it?"

"I like your face right now and if you'll look like that for the next seventy years in our home, then yes."

I study the blueprints a bit more. "Is that guest house? And six bedrooms?"

"Two of them are offices that can be converted into guest rooms or whatever." I wrap my arms around his waist as his arms go to my shoulders.

"How many people will be living in this house?" I say, leading somewhere we've never been.

"Enough." That's all he says, and I leave it alone.

"I don't know enough sexual tricks to pay you back for this."

"Can I have a hot tub?"

"Yes."

"Can I fuck you in our hot tub?"

"Yes."

"Then that's my anniversary present. But next year I'm going to need a tie or a grilling gadget or something."

"I promise to buy you something useless from the Sharper Image."

"That's all I'm asking."

He scoops me up and places me on the island, and I move our blueprints aside before he can undress me on top of our plans. He's nipping and licking my neck. His hands are under my shirt, rolling my nipple between his fingers when we hear his dad greet the dogs outside the back door. Josh removes his hands from me, and I fix my clothes and hop off of the island.

"We cannot get our house done fast enough."

"Amen."

Josh

Our employee harvest celebration was last night. It was a subdued and nostalgic affair. We can't let anyone know that we have a shot at getting the wineries back. We have to make them believe this is it. It was beautiful, and it was tradition but today feels empty. The tasting room is open, but all the machines have stopped, and all the barrels are filled. I walked my favorite Zin block this morning after my run. Just me and vines. It's the block that's partially hidden from all the buildings around the corner of our hills. I used to come here to hide from Lucien before I went to school in the morning. I'd sit between the leafy vines eating a peanut butter and jelly sandwich and reading comic books. Both things were banned by my grandfather. He hated anything sticky, which is tough on a kid, and thought comic books were a waste of my time. Dad found me one morning and pretended not to see me. He walked right on by. But from then on, we were never out of peanut butter, and every Monday morning there were three new comic books on the end of my bed.

Tommi Schroeder let us know that they will pick and

crush their last grapes in the next couple of days. That will be the last of all of us. Becca Gelbert is going to set the meeting with the Vino Groupies, and we'll all be briefed. The final numbers all come in today. We should be on target, but the stress of it all is overwhelming. Then we need to decide what to do with Prohibition. The successful winery with no wine. The demand is out of control, and we haven't decided what to do with it. There's no juice for it. Nothing is prepared to selling past our initial run. And we certainly don't have the facilities. We can't sustain the current model on top of our own personal wineries productions for another year. Do we invest and expand, or do we let it go and let it be famous for that great wine that existed for a moment?

I know Elle wants to figure out how to sustain it. She feels like since she was there from the ground up that's it more hers than LC/W. She's right in some ways. Baxter is okay with letting it go. I think he's thinking about getting political. I won't have time once Dad and Mom take off for their travels. I don't know. I'm undecided. I need to talk to Sam and David and see if they're serious about it. If this winery scam doesn't work we all have to fall back on Pro/ho. We'd be a bunch of vitners with no winery, no juice and no land, just a really successful name.

David's dad and aunt are running Gelbert for the time being, and Jims has Langerford handled with Sam's dad. The two of them might be able to take it over. I can help them work out equity partnerships with the girls: Tabi, Tommi, Poppy, Becca, and Ingrid. Since we all own equal pieces.

We'll see. But all I really want is to sip this Syrah, watch the sunset on our makeshift patio up here at the Lookout, and wait for the love of my life to come home. I want to take in all the views before they might not be ours. Tomorrow we find out if we can pull this off. It's agonizing to know that Elle will be near him. I'm trying to convince her to stay with Sal in Sonoma while the parents go downtown for the meeting with the Vino Groupies. She told me to go to hell and find a venue for the victory/defeat party. I didn't think she'd listen to me, but still had to try.

There is no way I'm sleeping tonight. Depending on Elle, that might not be a bad thing. Maybe we can figure some way to release all this tension. I'm scared for her to be there, but I know that not only will my Hellcat be walking into that room but also as the shark she was born to be.

Elle

We're ready and assembled. The ones that signed the contracts want to handle their own mess. The kids were told to stay out of the room. They're all gathering in the city to await the news. I insisted on being at the meeting, much to Josh's protest. But everyone except him agreed I deserve closure. The only other person from his generation in the meeting will be Becca. After all, it's her legal expertise we need.

"Whether you like it or not Lou will be outside the building. He can't touch you."

"I know all of this. I am really okay."

He scoops me into his arms. "After this, you never have to see him again."

"I'm about to press charges for aggravated assault."

"After that then. Good lord, this piece of shit is stamped all over our world right now."

I smile. "No, he's not. He's just an annoying little fly, and I'm about to clip his wings."

"Go slay that dragon. I love you."

"I love you too. And I'll make sure to get back to the castle as soon as possible."

"The other ladies- in-waiting and I will be excited about the conquering heroes arrival back at the castle."

"We'll be expecting mead and a feast." He kisses me again.

* * *

They're only expecting Adrian Schroeder. It's his meeting time to sign the final piece of the contracts and theoretically collect the check. After we tell them our agenda, the rest of the scheduled meetings will be null and void. That's why we're all showing up together.

My heart is out of my chest, and I can feel my phone buzzing with texts from Josh. Sarah and Tina Gelbert are clutching hands, and Will is at my back as I enter. I walk in first. There are six men and one stout woman sitting on the far side of the conference table. I've interacted with four of the people in the room. He leaps up at that sight of me.

"Angel!" Everyone files in behind me. Schroeder, Aganos, Gelberts, Whittiers, and the Langerfords. He looks rocked, and his jaw is open. None of us sits; there's no reason. The Vino Groupies and lawyers stare at Asher for an explanation.

"Gentleman and lady," I roll my eyes at his patronizing tone. He continues, "No worries. This is just old friends simply saying goodbye to their properties forever, together."

I speak even though it's supposed to be Will. He puts his hand on my back and doesn't stop me. "Hello, all. I've enjoyed getting to know most of you over the past almost eighteen months or so. We go back a ways, now don't we?

We thank you so much for your interest in the vineyards, but we have some bad news."

Becca passes out an injunction to stop construction work and the original deal memo and contract. There's also a new contract for them to sign everything back over to us. It says they have no legal claim to our labels, our properties, our vines, and juice. That the original deal is null and void due to the substandard profit margins of wineries and the lack of revenue created that would have funded their initial construction plans. Our individual sales numbers are also in the portfolios that they're all flipping through rapidly.

Dasher remains fixed on me. "Noelle, angel. Unfortunately, I have bad news for all of you and your entourage. Construction begins—" He says it like he's dropping a bomb. Will interrupts him.

"Not to blow your big reveal, man, but we already know about the strip malls, McMansions, and the Country Club." His jaw goes slack as he struggles to regain composure. Crack, muthafucker, crack.

Asher's high-pitched voice squeaks forward, "Then, hopefully, you can come and visit us for the demolition. You can watch it all crumble. I'd like to see your faces..." He's interrupted by a small bespectacled man at the end of the table.

"Mr. Bernard. Have you been privy to the production numbers and the sales figures? They're all in default. They're well below where they were last year and the standard for going forward with this deal. There's no way we'll get our permits and zoning requirements. This is getting rather messy. And we don't do messy."

Asher straightens up and begins speaking in a higher pitched voice. "This is all a done deal. I saw their production. I saw the vines. There was plenty of juice to produce the numbers on par with previous years. There's no way they can keep their business at all with these kinds of numbers. These numbers are fraudulent. Where did all the juice go?"

Artie Gelbert puts on a Prohibition baseball hat. I didn't know he had it with him and it will mean nothing to the builders, but Dasher will sure as shit know he's been fooled. Good move, Mr. Gelbert.

The bespectacled man speaks, "The properties, the product, and the labels do indeed revert to the original owners, and this document makes you liable for the cash amounts that our group has already paid out."

"Asher, my boy. You done, been had." Will lets loose and half the men get up from the table to leave without uttering a word. In the back of my mind, I think they're people from Sal's world.

Dasher just smiles that sickening Cheshire cat grin and looks at me in the eyes.

"Chapel."

Theresa Langerford steps forward to address this statement. "I'm sorry, what about it?"

"My darling angel, where are the Lodi numbers?" He leans back in his chair. We all grin and wait. The Vino Groupies pause and turn with wide grins on their faces as well. They all sit back down. It was Asher's ace up his sleeve. He has no idea Becca bested him.

Adrian Schroeder steps forward and speaks. His voice is smooth and confidently deep. "Why on earth would we have numbers from Lodi?"

Dasher leans over the table and spits his next statement directly to Adrian, Will, and me. "Because the production of Chapel and Bellamy's Ghost will cover all of your pathetic losses. You didn't think I'd have a plan to bury you all for twenty years without a safety net. That I'd even begin to strip you of everything without a foolproof plan. Do you? This is karma."

Sarah steps forward to speak. She's so gentle and calm. "My dear. I'm so sorry for your pain. I'm sorry for your loss and what you've carried with you for so many years. You don't know the first thing about karma, but you're about to." She bows to him.

Will puts his arm around Sarah as Becca pulls out the original contracts with the highlighted clause about Chapel and B's Ghost. She passes out copies of the new sales contracts of the Lodi vineyards, as well as the initial articles of incorporation that Lucien and Helmut had created when they purchase the land.

"Fuck!" the lawyer exclaims. Asher doesn't look at the paper.

"What?"

Costas yells, "You're a moron, and I've been waiting for seven months to tell you this, Mr. Dasher. And you should know that my wife put a curse on you. Not that you needed it because you've kind of done the work for us already. Enjoy your cursed life." We all laugh, and Goldie spits on the floor.

I lean over the table and look him directly in the eye. "Check-fucking-mate, asshole." He looks stunned as I say the words I've longed to say for far too long. "You are done."

The formidable man in the gray suit with eyes to match speaks directly to Becca. This man, he's like a trading card for sex. I have to focus back to revenge. His voice is deep and dripping with molasses as his slight southern accent curls around his words. "Ms. Gelbert, would you be so kind as to explain what the hell is happening."

"My pleasure, Mister Dunne."

"Brick." Everyone remains eerily quiet as this man's rich voice rumbles through the room, silencing all fidgeting. Becca doesn't even look affected by him. She straightens her shoulders and addresses him directly.

"Well, Brick, I'm sorry to inform you that you purchased only the labels, the names if you will. Someone forgot to inform you that the land isn't owned by any of our individual wineries. It used to be owned by a secondary and independent company run by William Whittier and Adrian Schroeder together. They alone owned the Lodi vines, and they're not part of any of the Estates. They sold them seven months ago. I hear they're having a bumper crop of juice too. Pity."

Asher roars, "What the fuck are you talking about?"

The overly muscled head of the Vino Groupies stands up and walks over to me. I tremble just a little. As in love with Josh as I am, this man is a mountain of a man as well. He's tall and brawny as if he's no stranger to an offensive line in football. He has these direct and intoxicating grey eyes that seem laser-focused on Becca. He looks as if he's chiseled from marble. I'm kind of melting in his presence. I'm not interested, but I am enjoying the view. I've never met him before. This man has stayed mostly in the shadows during negotiations.

He leans down to Becca and me, and I quiver a bit. He says, "Ladies. We just wanted to build. Without the juice from Lodi, we can't get around the city of Sonoma's building ordinances. We don't want to be in the winery business. Not sure what all the emotions are and don't care. Don't care about Asher's motivation, but it seems you've bested us. Our ironclad deal seems to be full of holes. Holes that Mr. Bernard will be filling." He winks at us as if he knows the man is a weasel as well.

Then as he parts our group, he turns back to Becca. He scans her head to toe slowly. Then I see her eyes flash with heat. He reaches out his hand, and she goes to shake it, but he holds it instead. He places a business card in her hand and then covers it again. His rumbling gruff voice is directed entirely to Becca.

"Rebecca Gelbert, you're a hell of a lawyer. Call me if you ever need a job. You can call if you need anything, come to think of it."

She winks at him. She's so much cooler than me. I'd just be babbling. "I'd love to take all the credit for the coup d'état, but it takes a village. And if you ever need a lawyer, you know where to find me." She reaches into her briefcase and hands him a very large cashier's check. "Deal is a deal. We keep the land, here's the money you paid us." He nods to her. She needs to get on that Alpine Slide and ride it to the bottom. I hate her current annoying boyfriend.

They all begin to exit, and Asher yells at the Vino Groupies and us, "You'll be hearing from me." The squat woman roars back at him.

"No asshole, you'll be hearing from us. You're about to get a bill that all of your lying and hustling won't be able to pay. Mr. Bernard, you're on the hook for our time, effort, expenses, and your commission."

Costas' deep, happy voice erupts. "You all have much to discuss. And Mr. Asher has a jail to attend and several assault trials to prepare for. Whoops, did you not know that piece of it all?" The Groupies all stare back at us from the door. "He likes to hit women. But we must go and the police will take it from here. We have wineries to run and lives to celebrate. Opa!"

Goldie moves to the front. I know she's rehearsed her part with Tabi. It's adorable. "My mother taught me good manners and to never arrive at a gathering empty-handed, so I'll leave you all with this." She hands a bottle of Prohibition to each person, saving Asher for last. His jaw falls open as he looks at Tabi's label. "Nkotsa! It means Gotcha."

Will and Jim Langerford cheerlead everyone out of the room chanting, "Pro/Ho! Pro/Ho!" My body is more relaxed than it's been in a year. I just need to see Josh. He's waiting for us with everyone else. He rented out Pier 23 Cafe for a celebration. I feel like all we do is celebrate and commiserate and gather, but this time it's a good one.

Dasher lunges and grabs my arm as I turn to leave. There's so much pain and anger burning in his eyes. Brick Dunne pulls his hand off of my arm. I say to Dasher, "I hope you find peace." I nod to Brick and then Costas pulls me to his warm side. I'm taken care of because I'm safe with my family.

This monster will be dealt with right now. I'll see Dasher in court, but beyond that, I'm done. Francesca enters with officers into the conference room that now only contains Dasher. I stand there with Costas holding me up. They arrest him for aggravated assault and attempted rape. They inform him that there are two counts in California and outstanding warrants for his arrest in Indiana, Colorado, New York, and Michigan for aggravated assault, assault and battery, public exposure, rape, and attempted murder. Apparently, he choked a woman so hard in Michigan she almost died. He left her in an abandoned event tent, and if the cleaning crew hadn't found her, she probably wouldn't have survived. She never pressed charges because she didn't know who he was and they never found out who did it. Until I convinced her to come forward. Mel found her story in an old post from the local newspaper.

She had a branding scar with a small impression of a dragon.

Francesca and Costas usher me away from the scene. The one where Dasher learns he's being arrested not for white-collar crimes of fraud, illegal surveillance, invasion of privacy, etc. but for criminal charges that will take him to maximum security prison. And he'll owe the Vino Groupies, whoever they really were.

Josh

I t seems like this is the most important first date of my life. Which is the most bizarre thing. There really isn't a part of me that's not entirely in love with every single piece of her. I'm going to spend eternity with her and yet, I've never taken her out on a date.

I thought about flying her to Paris or the Lake Louise Ritz Carlton. Then I toyed with renting out the Top of The Marq in San Francisco just for us. I have come up with a million perfect romantic date scenarios. And then I settled on one that's uniquely us. I told her to dress up, and I'm in a suit. I've donned her favorite navy-blue pinstripe with one of my custom shirts underneath and a tie she once told me brought out my eyes, aqua and green striped.

With Dasher's world crumbling around felony and a shit ton of misdemeanor charges looming, he's tucked away out of our lives. He's out on an extraordinarily high bail and on house arrest until his first trial date. Francesca pushed for incarceration until the trial but was denied.

Elle brought charges and will testify, but she's found seven more women who will testify as well. Some of them weren't as lucky as Elle. They didn't get away from him in time.

Evan is moving to San Francisco and hanging a real shingle on the building that was the front for Prohibition. The two of them are in discussions about what will happen to her building in New York. She's pushing to create an upscale nonprofit shelter complete with counseling services for women who feel they can't say anything because they're mothers or still have a roof over their heads and a job to go to.

The place would be for women who live with the shame more often than not because they feel their story isn't tragic enough to be considered sexual assault. Elle remains my favorite person. My favorite person that's ever existed. I'm pathetic but sincerely happy.

I grab the keys to the Jeep and a ring box. I know she said she didn't want a different one, that Emma's ring was fine, but I wanted something worthy of her. Worthy of us.

Elle

I step downstairs, and Sarah grabs her cane and leaps up as much as possible. She's doing really well, and only carries the cane because she's afraid of falling, but I'm going to convince her she doesn't need it someday. She's stronger every day. The progression seems to have paused and some days feels like it's reversing.

"Oh, honey. I feel like this is your prom. That is the most stunning dress on you. You wore this to that client dinner, didn't you?" She envelopes me in a hug.

"It is. It was the first gift Josh ever gave me." I check myself in the mirror. He doesn't know I'm going to wear the emerald halter vintage Halston dress tonight. I don't plan to wear it long. He was very adorable today, insisting on calling me and asking me out. Then we spent the day apart like it's our wedding day. We haven't had sex since yesterday morning, and it feels bizarre. But it's merely our first date. We haven't gone that long since I came back from New York. I feel almost like a virgin.

"No daughter of mine is going out in something that revealing." I laugh as Will enters the room. "I want you home by ten, and I am going to need to have a chat with this fella about how to treat a lady." My heart swells.

"I promise to be in bed by ten." I flash my eyebrows at Will.

"Stop talking. You are chaste and pure in my mind." He walks away from me as Sarah laughs.

"Your Prince Charming is here. Where's the genius taking you?"

"No idea. But I was told to dress and pack a bag." I lift a medium-size Michael Kors purse that contains my Tom Ford *Fucking Fabulous* 01 lipstick, two pairs of panties, his Stanford t-shirt, and the olive green LaChappelle/Whittier yoga pants. They laugh at my luggage.

He sweeps into the kitchen through the backdoor and stops dead when he sees me. He falls to his knees and puts his hands up like he's praying.

"Thank. Fucking. God. The Halston." I curtsey to him, and then in a second, I'm in his arms. He kisses me deeply in front of his parents.

"Save it for the end of the date, buster." Will jokes awkwardly.

"Dad, you do see her, right?"

"Not really." He glances over at Sarah, and my heart swells again, but this time because he honestly doesn't see anyone past her. I feel the same about their son.

Sarah gestures for us to leave. "Okay kids, be good and have fun. And be careful."

He guides me with his hand on my back and opens the door of my Mercedes. Before I can get in, he drags me to him and holds me close. Then he tickles my lips with his. I open to him, and his tongue quickly finds mine.

"You're so gorgeous. I have no words."

"Thank you. So are you." I look down. Sometimes it's

hard to remember he's sincere. Like it's hard to believe someone feels that much for me.

"Here. I have something to complete this outfit." He takes my hands in his and strokes my right hand and slips an insanely stunning platinum diamond ring on to my finger. It's so vibrant and significant. It's so big. I feel like I just gained a couple of pounds. I look at him and take his face in my hand.

"I have a ring."

"And now you have two."

"I don't need two." I'm serious. I don't even need one. I love a bit of glamour and don't even get me started on Daphne, but that's fashion. That's fun. This is the gross national product of Somalia sitting on my hand. He hands me an envelope.

"Please tell me you didn't buy me a jet."

"Do you want one?"

"No! I and I don't need this."

"You must be the first woman in history to complain about being given a three karat platinum setting Tiffany diamond ring."

"It's just—" He cuts me off and flicks the envelope. I open it. It's the receipt for the ring. Holy shit. The second piece of paper is also a receipt. This one is for the same amount, one hundred and ten thousand dollars to www.nomore.org. No More Domestic Violence and Sexual Assault Organization. My knees buckle that this man knows me so well. That my ring will permanently be tied to love and kindness means I'll wear it. I'll proudly wear it.

"Thank you." He leans to me and kisses me gently. I feel every part of his soul and give him every part of mine in that kiss.

"You'll wear it then?"

"Yes. I'll wear it. And thank you."

"It's just a ring." He winks at me as he gestures for me to get into the car.

"You know that it's not."

"I do, my love, I do."

I watch him cross in front of the car, and I can't help but tear up a little bit at how happy I am.

"Ready for our advent... what's wrong? Are you okay?" He cradles my face in his hands. "Cosmo, what's wrong?"

Tears are now streaming and ruining my makeup. My shaky voice bursts out of me louder than I expect. "Nothing."

"This is not nothing."

"That's just it. There's nothing wrong. I didn't know it could feel like this. That there's not a damn thing wrong in my life. I'm just happy." He pulls me close to him and lets me ruin his suit jacket a bit. He smooths my hair down and kisses the top of my head. I regulate my breathing.

"You scared the crap out of me. Usually girls wait until the end of the date to cry."

I giggle at him.

"I believe I've told you that sometimes I'm just so happy that it leaks out."

"Hellcat, you make me happier than I deserve or ever thought possible. Now can we stop being mushy? I have a woman to woo for the night."

She checks her makeup in the mirror and fixes her face. "Ready to be wooed."

"I'm going to use the money to help all of his victims and their families and help where I can. But now it's time to get back to our date." He leans over to my ear and whispers, "I'm going to finger you under that Halston at the end of our new driveway right now unless you stop me."

301

"What happened to wooing?"

"You don't want to come?"

"I never said that. No self-respecting woman would ever turn down an orgasm. I just think a lady should wait until the end of the evening for a good finger fucking. And if memory serves, it is a very good finger fucking." He laughs at me and kisses my hand.

"How about after the end of the first course?"

"Deal." My eyes flash at him with the thought of a public/private moment.

Elle

I absolutely crack up as we drive approximately eight minutes and park at Poppy's place. "Really?"

"I've heard good things." He grins as he gets out of the car, and I wait for him to open the door. It's a date after all. As we approach, there are only a few people there. I feel bad for Poppy that her restaurant isn't busier. We're greeted by Poppy who's dressed in a tuxedo and an apron.

"Reservation for..." She looks down into an imaginary reservation book, and Josh's hand is on the small of my back. I lean back into it, and he doesn't miss a trick. He lets his thumb caress my back. I want to lick him right now. It's what I would do on a date if I liked the person. I'd lean into him. "I'm sorry. We have a buyout tonight, and I won't be able to accommodate you."

Josh smiles at her. "I know you have a buyout. I'm Joshua Lucien LaChappelle Whittier, and it's my buyout."

"My apologies, Mr. Joshua Lucien LaChappelle Whittier. I didn't recognize you without your grubby harvest Prohibition Winery baseball hat. Please follow me." I giggle

303

at Poppy's joke, and he narrows his eyes at me. He pinches my ass, and I instinctively smack his hand.

"What was that?" Josh protests.

"I do not indulge in ass play on the first date."

We're walking towards the center of her patio area and his breath hitches. With his hand on my waist, he drags me close to him. His low, raspy voice wanton in my ear, "How many dates does it take to get into the center of that tootsie pop?" My eyes go wide as goosebumps erupt all over my neck and arms. And I wish to god there wasn't a rush of heat and a flood inside my brand-new thong. Not sure why I even wear panties anymore. The idea of granting access is intriguing but not something I ever thought I'd entertain. But this man. Oh god, this man. I want anything he wants to give me. Or do to me. Off the top of my head, I come up with a number.

"Eight."

"Eight dates?"

"Maybe. Maybe eight years or eight months, who knows?" His lips are on my neck. He drags his teeth and tongue up my neck to my ear and nips.

"I intend to find out. And I can tell by the deep pink flush of your chest and cheeks that it's something you will enjoy."

I gasp. My stupid skin telegraphing my thoughts again.

He pulls my chair out for me as Poppy reappears with a plate of appetizers. All my favorites. I do love little bites. But she makes the best gougers in the world. I think it has something to do with the access to the delicious Vella Cheese factory in her backyard. She pours sparkling, and the label catches my eye. It's LC/W, but it says, "From Emma to Regina to Sarah to Elle."

I yank the bottle out of his hand. "What is this?"

Josh smiles and says, "The first vintage of the sparkling with the restored Pinot Meunier."

"Hold up! Is this me?"

"It's for all the women who've held up the winery over time."

Tears sting my eyes again. "STOP MAKING ME CRY."

"Noted. I'll try to make you less happy in the future."

Josh

My Hellcat jumps into my lap and is instantly kissing me. I'd be happy if the rest of this date were her on my lap. Her tongue licks deeply into my mouth, and I meet her stroke for stroke. It's getting heated as I tangle my fingers into her hair that she took forever to do tonight, but all she does is moan my sound. I pull back. "We're in public, Hellcat." She nips at my lips, and then I pick her up and set her on her feet.

"Look, if we're ever going to get to date eight, we're going to need to get through the first one."

She pouts and it's sexy as fuck. "Good note. Be more Cosmo and less Hellcat while on a first date." She sits down across from me and sips the sparkling. Which really is hella good. It was Mom's idea for the label, but I'll take the credit tonight. I think the way she wants to show her gratitude is probably more up my alley than my mom's.

I'm sitting at a mostly empty restaurant. I bought out the tables that weren't already reserved, but everyone will be done soon. Poppy drops off another tray of yummy things that Elle is fawning over. Poppy vowed not to make us anything special, but clearly, she felt motivated. That's what my woman does, inspires people to be their best. Poppy hugs both of us and disappears into the kitchen.

I stare at her blonde hair glowing in the last of the sunlight and playing off her green dress. That dress changed both her life and mine. I'd never bought something for a woman, aside from my mom, that was actually for the woman. I'd bought lots of presents before, but none of them were perfect for the person. The thought and care I took in picking out this one dress was the first moment in my life I thought beyond myself and what it could do for me. It was the first crack in Joshua.

* * *

We're finishing some endive salad thing, and we're already through the bottle. I head behind the bar. The rest of the patrons have left, and as I'm bending down, I hear a voice I didn't expect tonight.

"Barkeep, a bottle of your finest ale for me and my men." I pop my head up to see Tabi hugging Elle and Sam in my face.

"What the fuck are you doing here? All of you?" Milling about the restaurant is the bulk of The Five Families. No parents but basically all our friends.

David answers, "Poppy mentioned you bought the place out, and naturally, we thought it was for us."

"Hell no, it's not for you, Gelbert. You weren't part of it."

"We are now." David grins.

"Fuck me. Is that Sal?"

"Yeah, he was in town and wanted to see Poppy." Jims

offers up as he pours himself a tequila neat with a squeeze of lime.

"And that meant crashing my first date with Elle? With freaking Lou in tow no less."

Sal approaches me and steps behind the bar. "Josh, you wouldn't turn away family, now, would you?"

"What the fuck is happening? Where's Mark?" I'm flustered and a bit pissed that my perfectly laid out plans are in shambles.

Sal winks, "I got off on good behavior. He had a thing. He'll be up tomorrow." I roll my eyes at him.

Tommi slaps me on my back and then pulls me into a hug. "We're all in town, and it's Wednesday. That's what the fuck is happening."

Fuck me, I forgot it's Wednesday. I look over at Elle, and she's surrounded by Becca, Tabi, and Sammy. Not sure where Poppy is, but it is remarkable that every fucking person is here. Elle sees me and waves. She shrugs with a bit of resignation.

I yell over the top of our friends, "THIS COUNTS AS ONE OF THE EIGHT!"

She throws her head back in laughter, radiating joy and light. She's so fucking beautiful and sexy. I've fucked her like a hundred times over the past week and twice yesterday morning, and it's still not enough. The distance between us right now is unacceptable. I'm overwhelmed with love for her in the middle of our chaotic life. She is my calm and my excitement.

I leap over the bar and scoop her out of her chair. I pull her towards me in front of everyone and slant my mouth over hers. She responds wildly. Her lips hard against mine, but her tongue soft and inviting. Everyone hoots and hollers and I don't care. I tear myself away from her and join Sam at a table at the end of the patio.

"There has never been a bigger whipped pussy than you." David chides.

"The bigger they come, the harder they fall." Sam jabs at me.

"Around her, I'm always hard, and we're always coming." I wink at Sam.

Sam slams his beer and raises the empty bottle to me.

Elle

This is the best first date ever. I know I'm getting laid, I know the food is good, and I'm surrounded by friends. Melissa is the only one missing. All thirteen of us are here and toasting. Poppy's hiding in the kitchen, and hopefully Sal went to retrieve her. We can all help her cook. She shouldn't have to cater to us.

"Where's Pop?"

Tabi answers up, "Where's Sal?"

"Really?! I mean, I knew he had a little thing for her but wasn't sure if she reciprocated."

Tabi continues speculating. "I think she's thinking about it. But I mean that's a whole lot to take on, right? I mean, that girl can get cray-cray if she even goes two miles over the speed limit. Imagine taking on someone who's committed actual crimes."

"Allegedly committed," Becca corrects us.

We all laugh a little too hard. I'm pleasantly buzzed. I head to the kitchen to find Poppy. Sal is standing just inside the swinging service door, but he's not moving and blocking me out. I sneak in through the other door, and my blood goes ice cold at the sight of Poppy with a bloody lip being dragged across the kitchen floor by Dasher. I'm instantly sober.

Dasher screams at Poppy while tossing her to the ground. "Where the fuck is my gentle angel? I thought you texted her and told her to come back here?"

"I did. You watched me. I did." Poppy says weakly.

Without letting go of her hair, Dasher looks towards Sal and says in a slithery voice to Poppy. "Then why is this Capo fuck here? Don't you move, you greasy fucking piece of shit."

Sal's voice is smooth but crackling with anger and hatred. "I don't move as long as you don't move on Poppy again. I'll stay right where I am. Let go of Poppy. The gun is over there, and I didn't come riding in suited up for the O.K. Corral tonight. It was supposed to be dinner, and you're supposed to be under house arrest until trial."

He yanks her hair, and I step into the shadows. Sal's gun is out of his reach but could be in mine. Dasher has a chef's knife and smaller knife in his hand, and I can't let him do this to anyone. I can't.

"You think a house arrest could stop me? Fucking disabled the bracelet without even a hint of an alarm. I can't be fucking stopped. I'm too good."

Poppy screams. "Please. Please just stop. Let him go."

"No, Gingersnap. I stay. Let her go. I won't do a goddamn thing to this fucking asshole. Or is it that you only like smacking the shit out of women?"

In an instant, he throws the smaller knife with wild precision, and it lands in Sal's shoulder blade. He flinches, and I can see him gut out his reaction to stay standing.

"Fuck. Fuck. You will bleed for that, you fucker," Sal growls at him.

Sal's grey suit jacket turns dark crimson around the wound, but other than screaming at Dasher, he does nothing. He's sizing him up.

It's my turn to end this for good. "Asher. Darren."

His head turns immediately to me, and I sidestep towards the gun. It would be a clean shot, close enough that I wouldn't miss. Can I actually take a shot? All I know is that at this moment if I can't talk him into leaving, I have an option.

"Finally. Gentle angel. Let's go, Noelle." He slams Poppy to the floor, and she hits her head with a sickening thud. She stays down, and my heart is racing faster than it ever has. I see her chest rise slightly, and I'm calmed for a moment to know she's still breathing. I nod to Sal that's she's okay, and he exhales.

Dasher says, "Angel. What are you wearing? This is not the way I like to see you. Where are your frills? This is too bold. I will fix that. You will wear what I want from now on. I can smell that piece of shit on you. It's time for us to head off to Morocco. Come."

I look puzzled, and I realize that Special Ops Darren knows who has extradition and who doesn't. How is this my life? I mean, guns and mafia and non-extradition countries. Good lord. I'm a farm girl from Kansas. I just want to live happily ever after in my wine bubble with the world's most perfect man. The thing standing between happiness and nothing is him. When Dasher's gone, then maybe my life can be the bliss I envisioned. Dasher can never come back.

I don't break eye contact. "Sal. Are you alright?"

"I will be, Cosmo." Sal grunts.

Dasher roars, "Her name is fucking Noelle. Do not call her anything but that."

I can hear Sal wheezing behind me but standing firm.

The smell of bitter copper fills my nostrils as he bleeds. I grab a kitchen towel as part of an excuse to get closer to the gun. I toss it behind me to Sal. I never look away from the monster that has disturbed our lives for too long. This will be the last day he haunts us. This is it. He will know I am the one who stopped him.

"Sal?" I sound scared. I wanted to sound like a badass, but my voice breaks as I say his name. Sal can't protect me right now. I have to protect him. I don't know if I can do this.

"Got it." Sal grunts. "It's bleeding pretty good, though. But I'm here. I'd never leave you. I'm not going anywhere, and neither are you. Got me, Cosmo."

Dasher roars, "You Italian slimy piece of shit, her name is Noelle."

I need information. I need Sal to help me, so I can help him. I have to signal him and pray to fucking god he gets my point. "If you don't call me Cosmo, what do you call me?"

Sal doesn't hesitate. "Legally, I'd call you ballbuster. And girly, it's on." We call my gun the ballbuster and he's indicated that the safety is on. I also know it's the gun Lou trained me on and got a permit in my name. Lou calls me girly. I can legally shoot this motherfucker. I know this because Sal is my brother from another mother. He'd do anything for me including getting me a legal gun permit to carry and conceal. One that I've refused to take seriously. I thought he was overreacting. I've never told Josh that I can really shoot now. Instead of making me safe, it always made me feel as if something terrible was going to happen again. So I ignored it, but I guess something terrible is always going to happen with Dasher around anyway. But not anymore. I'm not ignoring anything.

Dasher's voice is bellowing, demeaning, and desperate.

He unleashes all that he's hidden from me in the past. The parts that are so dark and scary I can't imagine that they're even a part of my life in a small way. "She's not quite a ball-buster. More of a ball sucker in my experience. Now, Noelle, are you coming with me quietly, or do I need to kill these two? They won't be quite as lucky as Jims. We're leaving now."

"I'm not going anywhere, and you won't be either." I'm shaking so much. I breathe in and out and try not to hyper-ventilate. I can do this. I can do this. One step at a time.

"I don't see your cuticle nippers anywhere, you dumb bitch. So, what I say goes. Time to jet." Fire rises within me and instantly, my nerves calm. I'm a fucking phoenix rising from the ashes like I told him I was. No one calls me a bitch. And no one takes my family from me if I can help it. I reach down and pick up the gun. I point it at him.

I say pointedly, "I don't need them anymore." He laughs at me. I take the opportunity to flip the safety. I quickly lock and load the Glock. I point it back at him.

"Did you just put a bullet into the chamber of that Glock? That was rather sexy, but my angel, put it down before you get hurt. You shouldn't play with things you don't understand." My hand is shaking and I hear Sal in my ear in a low, raspy voice.

"You know this. You got this. You got this for us. For your mama and mine. You can just go old school on his ass. You know how to fucking do this. You know this."

"What the hell are you saying, Salvatore? Shut the fuck up, greasy Capo asshole, or I'll carve you up while my darling angel bitch watches. I'll make this cooking whore watch too, just before I gut her."

And just like that, the adrenaline and endorphins release through me, I take an easy breath in and squeeze ever so gently. Braced for the kickback and aware I can take his life. I am steel and rock. I am immovable. He crumples to the floor. The knife goes skittering across the tiles. Sal pushes past me. He kicks the blade across the room and rushes to Poppy. He's instantly on his phone as Lou rushes in, no doubt identifying the sound of a gunshot.

That's the thing you're unprepared for, a gun doesn't explode in a crash of sound, it pops. It's brutal and quick. It's terrifying, and I won't need to use that dark power again. I could have slipped out and gotten Josh. I could have called for help. I could let the men rush in, but they would have been hurt. I've trained for this moment, they haven't. Josh would have attempted to kill him with his bare hands. I needed to protect us. Sal and Lou gave me that power.

Lou rushes to me, my arms still braced, the gun still aimed, and my eyes unblinking on the scene. He flips the safety back on and peels my hands off the weapon. He's whispering things that are supposed to be comforting.

Lou is standing there, and I look at him as my own knees go out from under me, and my world closes into darkness.

Elle

I 'm in a hospital bed, and he's sitting on the edge holding my hand. My eyes flutter open. "Am I okay?" Josh covers me with his warm hard body.

"Yes. You're fine, Hellcat. You passed out. Lou caught you. And you're a fucking badass."

I smile at his gorgeous face, his hair flopping over his sapphire eyes. I love him with everything I am or ever will be. "I don't feel like that. I just wanted to protect Sal and Poppy and you. And everyone out there. I knew what I was doing—"

He puts his fingers to my lips as I get animated. "I know. Sal and Lou told the police and everyone what happened."

"Are they okay? Poppy?"

"She's fine. Other than a busted lip and a pretty nasty concussion, she's fine. Sal is now in surgery. The knife did a lot of damage to his shoulder. He lost a lot of blood, but he'll be fine too. According to Sal, he only hit Poppy once, and then you came in and saw the rest. Lou told me all about your dates to the gun range. You should have told me."

"Where is he? Did he bleed out? I can't be a killer."

"You didn't shoot anything vital. Lou said you're really accurate. Why?"

"I shot his knee cap out. I hit his left knee dead on. Sal once told me, sometimes the old school kneecap is enough. It hobbles them for life and instantly takes them to the ground. People expect you to go for the kill shot and are ready for it. But a good old kneecap, no one protects their knees."

He grins and kisses my hand. "Calm down, my love. Rest."

"Where is he?"

"He's also in surgery, surrounded by cops who are taking him away for a very long time. His bail has been revoked, and he will be immediately taken into custody and taken to jail as soon as he's able to leave the hospital. He'll await his trials behind bars, where he should have been all along. Francesca is waiting outside with the police for your statement. She wants to talk to you first."

"Am I being charged?"

"No, but this was a violent crime."

I whisper to him, my voice harsh and cold, "You bet your ass it was a violent crime." He kisses me softly as his thumbs rub over my knuckles.

"You will have the power to send him to jail. You'll have to face him in court, but that will be it. I will be right beside you. If you keep saving yourself, what is it I'm supposed to do?"

"Keep making me happy. That's all."

"Okay. I'll keep you floating in orgasms, and you handle the firearms." My smile is interrupted by his kiss. He kisses me on my nose and then makes his way to my mouth. His sense of humor over me being the manly one is genuinely how I know Joshua is gone. I sit up, and I'm sore all over.

My body racked from adrenaline and endorphin with-drawal. I kiss him, and he's instantly swirling his tongue inside of me. I have an immediate need for him to be inside of me. I pull back and look him straight in the eye.

"I need you. Inside of me as soon as possible. I need that to prove all of this is over."

Francesca peeks her head in. "Just an FYI, he's being transferred to a prison hospital ward after they remove the bullet from his knee. You acted in self-defense, and it will be ruled that way." She places her hand on my elbow. She's just fucking weird, but a good lawyer.

"Thanks, Frannie."

"I'm out of here. I need to go say goodbye to Meg. She moves to New York tomorrow."

"Tell her good luck. And if she needs anything in New York, I know some people. Hell, if she needs an apartment, mine's just sitting there."

"I'll tell her, but she's moving in with her boyfriend. Okay, bye." Francesca turns and exits.

Josh looks at me. "Odd duck, that one." I grin in agree-ment. "After you're discharged, I promise to ravage you. But first, let's face this. And I don't want to alarm you, but I've never been so fucking scared of anything in my entire life as when I saw Lou react to what I now know was you shooting Dasher. Watching him react and then sprint towards where I knew you to be. Don't ever make me feel that helpless again. You can't leave me, not like that. Not ever. Do you fucking understand me? You are my everything. I can't live without you." He kisses me deeply.

"I'm not going anywhere without you. I promise."

A nurse comes in and checks on me. "Take these. It's a bit of Advil, but you're fine. I promise. However, there are approximately thirty people in the waiting room downstairs wondering if they can come up and see you, Ms. Gelbert, and Mr. Pierto. Were you at a party? Or are you part of some cult?"

I laugh. We are a bit of a cult, but I answer as honestly and joyously as I can. "Don't worry about them. It's just our family."

* * *

As we pull into Emma Farm, I see a cavalcade of construction materials piled up at the base of the hill where our driveway ends.

"Did you flip the blueprint? Do they have the updated ones? There needs to be a third bathroom on the upper level."

He rolls his eyes at me, but this stuff matters. "Yes. They have it all, but I still don't know why we need yet another bathroom. And why on the upstairs level. That was only going to be a big room for random toys of mine."

"Let's just say you got the toy part right. Don't argue with me. I'm right about this."

"You always are, but I look forward to a lifetime of arguing with you."

The End

Epilogue
JOSH

O ur lives seem as if they've begun again. It's been almost six weeks into our new era. Our deeper phase of happy. Fucking Dasher is locked up forever. He still has two more trials pending but has already been sentenced to four consecutive twenty-year terms that he will not serve concurrently. Elle takes great pride in the fact that he'll limp for the rest of his life. He's appealing, but so far no one will take his case. He's in a maximum-security prison in Michigan.

The civil litigation is on hold until his criminal elements are dealt with, but we may never need to pull that card. We're all safe and to be honest, none of us ever want to utter the word Dasher again.

Our wineries are thriving. Prohibition is thriving. Although its production has slowed down a bit since the parents started using their own juice again. Sam and David are running the day-to-day of Prohibition, but we're all still involved. Tommi Schroeder and I sell a large portion of our Estate juice to Prohibition. They've also got some land now where they're planting and cultivating as well as buying regional juice. And the Apatos sell a good portion of the Lodi juice to Pro/Ho as well. Somehow, I ended up owning two wineries when I set out to own none.

The sun is intense today, but the water is sparkling. I love that you can literally smell flowers in the air. It's the last push for the house to be completed, and so she insisted we have a honeymoon before we even get married. She was right. But she's always right. Even though she tried to surprise me, I knew where we were going because I remember everything she's ever told me. But she did pay for everything. I haven't spent one penny since we've been here.

Bali is so much more beautiful with her in this lounge chair beside me than she described. On our second night here, she sobbed. She just kept saying how complete she felt. How no matter what happens in life, she knows she's not alone in the world anymore.

We're holding hands, and she's slightly purring. She's sleeping curled up in the sun but never losing grip on my hand. What I didn't know when we arrived at our rented house in Jimbaran Bay was that we were staying for a month. She explained that without that amount of time, I wouldn't get the full beauty of the island. She arranged everything, moved heaven and earth, and we've been on a media and contact blackout this entire time.

My parents are just off of a couple of weeks vacation and offered to come and spend time at the winery. Sam and Sammy are supervising the vineyards. There's really no need for us, was how it was explained to me.

It's week three, and the thought of returning to the winery is dreary. Hopefully I can get my fill of her in a series of insanely small fucking bikinis over the next week. She stands in front of me in all her spectacular glory, and I don't know how the hell I got this lucky. She's the strongest and loveliest human I've ever known. I am complete around her and she's complete with me.

We decided to wait a while to get married. Now that we all have our wineries back and we're through our first harvest as the owners, she's plunged headfirst into the marketing of Prohibition. And Evan has already set his wedding date. Elle decided she didn't want to steal his thunder. I'm pretty sure they want to take turns being a bridezilla. I'm well aware that I will have very little say in that event. I told her my only condition was that I pick the rings, and they remain secret until the wedding. I also get to choose what she wears underneath the dress. That's all I want from the day. And to make her officially mine in the eyes of everyone for eternity.

I took ownership of the winery, and there's so much more to it than I ever imagined. I still invest for Sal when he needs it, but without him, we wouldn't have our legacy and land back. He turned out to be the guy I thought he was. There's so much going on that we need time to acclimate to our new life. We'll get married eventually. No need to rush. We have forever.

"Did you want something, Miss?" She's smirking at me, silhouetted by the sun at the end of my lounge chair. I grab her. Pulling her down on top of me, her skin is warm and glistening from the sun. She kisses me deeply and moves her body into a very familiar position. "When will I ever get tired of kissing you?"

She states very plainly, "Most likely after we're an old married couple, and you forget who I am daily." I pull up her large pink floppy hat brim and kiss her again.

I grin at her and say, "I did tell you that I love you, today, right?"

"No. You neglected to mention that. I, on the other, have told *you*."

"If you're face down and I'm buried in your pussy and you scream it, it doesn't count."

"I love you. Ha! Said it before you today." She grins triumphantly.

I wrap my arms around her and remove her hat so she can snuggle on top of me. I'm playing with her hair for a couple of minutes, and I can feel her begin to fall asleep. She's purring again.

"Cosmo, am I keeping you up at night?"

She says dreamily, "No. It's something else."

"This is our honeymoon of sorts. We're having it before the wedding, but I mean we owe it to honeymoons to make sure we fuck as often as possible. And if that means late nights, then so be it. If I can pay tonight, we'll finally hit our eighth date. I mean we just need to dig deep and gut it out."

I reach down for my rum punch and offer her some. She shakes it off. "You okay?"

She sits up straddling me, and I like where this is going. I grip her hips and slip a finger under her bikini tie, just waiting for the moment to tear it off her.

"Have you ever thought of getting a pet?" Caught off-guard. She's my caught off-guard woman and always will be. She bites her lip the way she does when she has a secret. I threaten to tickle her.

"What are you talking about? Tell me, my little Hellcat. Don't make me force you." She pauses, biting her lip harder. And I tickle her. She shrieks, and then I stop. "Hellcat?"

"What are your thoughts on an, uh, a kitten?"

Her dreamy green eyes sparkle and soften as mine go wide. She nods at me while she beams and then her eyes fill with tears. My hands move from her hips to her belly, and she places her hands on top of mine. I lean up and kiss her hands. I kiss her belly. I feel tears lick at the back of my eyes. Then I slide my hand behind her neck and pull her down towards me and kiss her. There's nothing I want more in this world than her, and now there will be even more of her to love because there will be this person who is half her running around our vineyard.

"A kitten. That sounds just about the most perfect fucking thing I've ever heard in my life, my Hellcat."

"I peed on seven sticks today. Well, two yesterday and then seven today and I'm like two months late." I think back. We'd had a lot of sex. But two months ago, she was switching from the shot to an IUD. When I got back to the winery, I instantly went looking for her. Then we fucked in the exact spot I found her.

"Tasting room?"

She grins widely, "I think so. We need to never tell anyone where our child was conceived." Our child. Holy shit. Our child.

I sit up a bit, so she sees how important what I have to say is. We've never discussed it, but I need her to know this. "I love you so much. More than anything in the entire world. I know you've heard it, but I can't stop telling you. And you know I want a litter, right?"

"So, that they're never alone. And they all get to give their kids, aunts and uncles and cousins. Annoyingly large families."

"Yes. Let's create a dynasty of cousins for generations to come. And hope that at least one of them might want the damn winery. You know Grandmama cat is going to lose her ever-loving mind and spoil the shit out of that little kitty."

She smiles at me and says, "As is Mrs. Dotson. She'll be the best great grandma any kitty could ask for. Now if you'll excuse me, my love, my fucking sexual beast, my reason for being, my 'One Perfect Thing', I need to puke my guts up."

I laugh as she runs back towards our bungalow. And then I let the tears that were threatening to fall on my cheeks come out. She's often told me that sometimes her joy is so great it leaks out. I didn't honestly believe her until now. But I should have. She's always right.

The End. (for now)

Thanks so much for reading !

Josh & Elle are back in more Sonoma stories along with the rest of the 5 Families.*

You can ONE Click the next stories in the 5 Families Universe Here:

Stafýlia Cellars Duet
(Tabi & Bax)
OVER A BARREL
&
UNDER THE BUS

Gelbert Family Winery Standalones
MERITAGE: An Unexpected Blend
(David & Nat)

RESIDUAL SUGAR
(Becca & Brick)

Come find out why Josh almost kicks Bax's ass for what he did to Tabi. Or how David Gelbert learns condoms don't always work. Or who on earth would be able to handle Rebecca Gelbert.

Chapter One of Over A Barrel is a the end of this book!

* * *

Over A Barrel is a friends to lovers, opposites attract story about the steamy and stormy history between US Senate Candidate Baxter Schroeder, and bold, brash Tabitha Aganos. It takes place over the course of 30 years and the events of one night. It tells the story of two lifelong friends who can't stop crossing the line. But they have to learn or they could lose everything, including each other.

Tabitha

In 24 freaking hours, I ended up catfighting, arrested for peeing on a duck and my boob popped out à la Janet Jackson style during a formal event. All of this further proves to my father why he was right in denying me more responsibility. And then good ole, sexy as hell Bax, figures out a way for me to adult. My best friend once again catches me as I free-fall.

This friends to lovers story begins with Over A Barrel and concludes in Under The Bus.

*(Spoiler alert- Elle is not a happy pregnant person)

Hey Kel What Else Can I READ?!

BOSTON BROTHERS: A second chance series

Interconnected standalone stories featuring the lives and loves of six guys who are either brothers or brothers from another mother and the women they were lucky enough to find. And then find again.

Keep Paris

Enemies to lovers, workplace romance with a second chance twist.

Keep Philly - Newsletter exclusive novella

Hockey, second chance twist, instalust

Keep Vegas

Billionaire, soul mates from the opposite sides of everything

FIVE FAMILIES VINEYARD ROMANCES

Interconnected standalone small town series exploring the lives and loves of five winery families.

LaChappelle/Whittier Vineyard Trilogy

Hey Kel-What Else Can I READ?!

(Josh & Elle)
Enemies to Lovers
Crushing, Rootstock & Uncorked

Stafýlia Cellars Duet
(Tabi & Bax)
Friends to Lovers
Over A Barrel & Under The Bus

<u>Gelbert Family Winery</u>
Meritage: An Unexpected Blend (Nat & David)
Secret Baby, Reformed Player, Single Dad
Residual Sugar
(Becca & Brick)
Reverse Grumpy Sunshine, Forced Proximity

<u>STILL TO COME</u>
SLATED 2024 (might be sooner!)
Pietro Family: A different kind of family story
(Poppy & Sal)
Mafia, Opposites Attract, Secret Life
(Pre-Order is Live)

Langerford Cellars: An epic second chance, funny,
romantic suspense
(Sam & ____)

* * *

CHI TOWN STORIES
Rockstar Romance? I've got you covered.

328

A steamy and funny standalone rockstar love triangle with no crossover duet.

Shock Mount & Crossfade

Always random and off on a tangent, film festival director, Meg Hannah, moves from Sonoma to New York in this duet. It's a reverse age gap-rockstar-love triangle-HEA guaranteed extravaganza.

Meghan Hannah tripped into their lives, much as she trips into almost any room. But now each man wants to catch her. But Meg's not sure she'll be able to get back up if she falls too far.

Present Tense

A first kiss 20 years in the making. Liam and Jillien have known each other most of their lives. Expectations and family obligations weigh them down. But just maybe they can they stop living in the past, choose each other and find themselves in love in the Present Tense.

* * *

CARRIAGE HOUSE CHRONICLES

Funny, steamy, smart Chitown Romance spin off novellas for when you don't know what to read next. Released randomly throughout the year!

Follow Me - Now available

Sound Off

Something Good appears in Twisted Tropes anthology first released later this year

For the Rest of Us Holiday M/M

* * *

Side Piece, a workaholics standalone romance.

A hot, hilarious, angsty Instant Connection- A story about cheating on their jobs not each other.

Married to their work, Tess & Alex find that sex is the easy part. But can they actually stop working long enough to find love?

Side Piece is an instant connection sweeping romance where Tess and Alex simply don't have time for romance. Their work schedules dictate their worlds, and they like it that way. But their pull towards each other is undeniable. Perhaps there could be more, if only their schedules overlapped long enough to fall in love.

Join me at www.kellykayromance.com to make sure you're up to date on all the cheeky, daffy nonsense that flows out of my brain and onto the page.

Did I thank you for reading? Wait. Yup, I did. But it's worth saying again, thank you.

Feel free to drop a review or a rating. Thank you.

Talk soon,

xo

Kelly K

A quick hello

Hi. How's your day? Mine is fantastic. I was writing the next thing. And it's everything.

There are lots of stories still coming from the "5"!

I don't want you to miss anything I have coming up so please visit www.kellykayromance.com. My website has exclusive Spotify playlists created around the writing of each book.

Elle was lucky, but some aren't. Why not help when you can? We all want to do something for someone else, and you just did. Thank you. A portion of the profits from Uncorked will be donated to www.nomore.org . An organization dedicated to helping victims of domestic violence and sexual assault. If you feel compelled to check out their essential work, the link is live and you can donate on the spot.

Or you just take care of you and your family around you. All of it matters.

Thanks so much for reading and spending some time with Josh & Elle and myself. I'm insanely grateful you're here.

A quick hello

Talk Soon-
Kelly K

Acknowledgements

There's no Kelly Kay without readers. It's nice to not write in a vacuum. For so long Josh and Elle spoke only to me. And now, apparently, they speak to you as well. I'm so humbled and flattered by the reaction of the readers and people in my life. It fills my heart that you love them all as much as I do. I have big plans for "The Five" and I hope you join me on the journey.

Thank you. A million times thank you.

If you enjoyed the ride, please review the books on Amazon and Goodreads. In fact you should do that for all books you like, it helps out all the authors. Especially us Indie Authors.

Thank you friends and fam who have read and loved my words. Also, Helmke with the clutch save on proofreading. Thank you Emily!

There is most definitely not a Kelly Kay without DJ Ali Kreg. My wingwomen for life, thank you sista. Now go update the FB group please.

Eric, thank you once again for giving me the latitude to find my way through all of this. I love you.

Charlie, for the love of Pete, please, please, just finish your Mobi Max fractions unit.

The woods. I'm surrounded by peace and beauty in a very ugly and isolating time. I feel a little more connected to everything despite being away from the city, our family and our friends. I feel like Thoreau was onto something.

A tiny bit about Kelly Kay

I used to create "dreams" with my best friend growing up. We'd each pick a boy we liked, then we'd write down a meet-cute that always ended with a happily ever after.

Now I get to dream every day, although it's a little steamier these days. And I've discovered I can and will write anywhere I can. Keep tuned to Instagram to see all the times I fit in a sentence or two. Follow me @kellykaybooks

I'm a writer, married to a writer, mother of a creative dynamo of a nine-year-old boy and currently a little sleepy. I'm a klutz and goofball and love lipstick as much as my Chuck Taylors.

Here are some good things in the world: pepperoni pizza, flair pens*, wine, my son, coffee, my husband, laughing with my friends, matinee movies on a weekday, the Chicago Cubs, a fresh new notebook full of possibilities, bourbon on a cold night, my family, wine, witty men, Fantasy Football, walking through the local zoo in the rain and that moment when a character clicks in and begins to write their own adventure. I'm just the pen.

*purple is my favorite Flair pen
www.kellykayromance.com

OVER A BARREL
CHAPTER ONE

BAX
Present /7:16 PM

Shawna's diamond ring keeps catching the light and making little rainbows on the floor. I bought the ring I knew she wanted, instead of the one I should want to give her. She's everything I need in a partner—smart, attractive, and accomplished. As I shift into the next phase of my life, with Shawna at my side, there's no way I won't be successful. It's a daunting path, but it's one I'm well prepared to walk.

It's weird being home in Sonoma. My life is in DC now and standing here, I realize this is the most distanced from winemaking I've ever been in my life. I grew up living and working at my family winery, Schroeder Estate Winery & Vineyards. But these days, I have a stake in a boutique label, Prohibition Winery, with my friends, the kids of the five vineyard families who are like blood to me. My life isn't here anymore. Pro/Ho remains and keeps me connected to my four best friends, but I mostly just drink the wine my friends produce.

Lately, we're only together around a crisis, so tonight's fundraiser should be a hell of a lot more fun, despite the cause. I scan the room, and my dad is talking to his best friend. They met in their early twenties when they were figuring out how to run their respective wineries. They're the core of the five families. They pulled in the other families to share in their winery highs and woes. They built an infrastructure to raise a tribe.

My entire childhood was in and around these people. Josh Whittier, Sam Langerford, David Gelbert, and Tabi Aganos. I trust no one like I trust these assholes. I don't even trust my sisters as much. But there's one who knows me better than the rest.

I adjust my bow tie and pull my sleeves down through my jacket. I glance up and wince. I reflexively put my arm around my fiancée to brace her against my approaching best friend.

Tabitha Aganos. Her almost empty glass of ruby-colored wine dangles from her fingers. Her nails are pointed and red. Not sure why she opted for claws, but who knows why Tabi does anything.

Her ebony hair is less severe than the last time I saw her. It's falling in such a feminine way. It skims that spot on her neck between her ear and shoulder and ends just above her collarbone. Her pouty lips are as crimson as her claws. She's wearing a body-hugging black dress that plays off her Mediterranean skin tone. She always says her skin is yellow and sallow, but I've always found it sun-kissed, rich, and radiant.

The dress doesn't leave anything to the imagination, but Tabi rarely does. No one is blunter than Tabi. Her curves are on display like an all you can eat buffet. She sways over to us, her bourbon eyes alight with some inner fire I'm sure she'll let spill out.

Shawna settles into me, and I glance down. Her golden blonde hair is set off by the black of my tuxedo. I kiss the top of her head and her intricate and precise updo. Her golden floaty dress and peachy skin are in direct contrast to the girl approaching us.

Her gilded gown crinkles as she snuggles into my arm. She's not one for public affection. I'm sure it's a show for hurricane Tabitha. Tabi and I have always had something inexplicable between us. It's faded lately, but there's no woman on the planet I know better than Tabitha Aganos. Despite my efforts to alter that over the years, she's ingrained in my DNA. And unfortunately, I know that look in her eye. She's bored and looking to stir any pot she can find. Any peace we've found in the night will be destroyed the moment that woman opens her mouth.

It's like it's all happening in slow motion, my heart freezes, and despite our formal setting, I burst out laughing. The first beats of Janet Jackson's "It's All For You" starts playing. Tabi shoves her wine glass onto some stranger and throws her hands in the air staring directly at me.

"OH, MY DAMN. That's my jam. Oh, shit. Yeah. It's happening, Bax! This IS happening."

READ the rest of the book right here just click on this title ——> Over A Barrel

Made in the USA
Monee, IL
23 October 2024

68311752R00206